Bride Leads the Chalet School

The Chalet School series by Elinor M. Brent-Dyer

This is a complete list of Chalet School titles in chronological order. Those titles printed in bold type have been published in paperback in Armada but not all are currently available. Please send a sae to the Marketing Department, Collins Children's Division, for an up-to-date stocklist.

Elinor M. Brent-Dyer

Bride Leads the Chalet School

ARMADA

First published in Great Britain in 1953
by W & R Chambers Ltd, Edinburgh

First published in Armada in 1989

Armada is an imprint of the Children's Division,
part of the Collins Publishing Group,
8 Grafton Street, London W1X 3LA

Printed and bound in Great Britain by
William Collins Sons & Co. Ltd, Glasgow

To my darling mother

Contents

CHAPTER 1

News!

The two pieces of news arrived the same day.

The first, which was good, came with the morning post, which reached the Quadrant somewhere about nine o'clock. By that time, the family breakfast was over and all the family were scattered – Mr Bettany to his work in the estate office; the girls to make beds, do light dusting, and see to the meals for the rest of the day; the boys to such chores as bringing in coal, coke, and logs, cleaning shoes and knives, rigging up in the laundry the lines for the week's washing, since it would be impossible to hang it outside today. Peggy, the eldest of the three girls, had gone to take up her mother's breakfast and discuss the day's jobs with her.

Mrs Bettany was slowly recovering from a very serious operation and, by doctor's orders, did not come downstairs till the afternoon. She had been talking about putting a stop to this and coming down in time for lunch, at any rate; but her family was still too near to those awful days at the beginning of November when they had not known if she would live to come back to the Quadrant or not, and they had all stamped heavily on the idea.

Peggy and her father had had several long talks about what must happen next term. It was certain that Mrs Bettany would not be able to see to the housekeeping for many a long day to come and who so suitable to take her place as her eldest daughter?

"Only," Peggy had pointed out, "if we do decide that I must leave school, we'll have to have it all signed, sealed and delivered before we say anything to Mummy. She'd raise the roof otherwise. You know what she is!"

Dick Bettany nodded. "I ought to, after eighteen – no; *nineteen* years of married life! Good Heavens! We shall be celebrating our Silver Wedding before we can turn round!"

"That's six years ahead," Peggy said serenely. "I'll be a grown-up lady of twenty-four by that time, and Rix will be hard at his Medicals. Even Maeve and Maurice will be nearly eighteen! Oh my goodness! What *aged* parties we shall all be!"

Her father laughed and ruffled the silky, silvery-fair hair which Peggy had insisted on having bobbed again that Christmas. The only alternative had been to put it up and she objected to the idea. So here she was with a head of Bubbles rings and looking much younger than just on the verge of eighteen.

"Well, about this school business. I'll be awfully sorry if it has to come to that, Peg. We always meant you to have a year abroad before you finally left school. When the Chalet School actually opened a branch in Switzerland, it seemed too good to be true."

"Never mind," Peggy said sturdily. "I've had a term, at any rate, and lots of people, even at the Chalet School, won't have that much. Anyhow, I'm so thankful to have a mother at all, I'll do it with a heart and half! You know yourself that if she has to worry about the housekeeping and all that sort of thing she won't keep on going ahead as she has done. Doc said we must try to keep her free from worry, and if this is the only way to do it, then I can't possibly make a fuss about it. No one would!"

There, the talk had ended since they both knew that,

as things stood at present, there was no alternative. All the same, when she was alone and could think it over quietly, Peggy knew that she was going to regret those two missed terms very much indeed. She had loved her first term at the new branch of the Chalet School, and Switzerland had been a never-ending delight. However, if it couldn't be, it couldn't be and that was all about it!

All the time she was making toast, boiling an egg and seeing to the coffee, Peggy was reminding herself that there had been the awful possibility that she would have had no need to do these things.

"I can't be anything but grateful that I have it to do," she thought as she looked over her tray to make sure that she had forgotten nothing. "Don't you be a selfish pig, Margaret Josephine Bettany! There are lots worse things in life than having to give up part of a year in Switzerland. Now have I got everything? Toast, egg, tea, cream, sugar. That's all, I think, as the honey's upstairs. Off we go, then!" And she picked up her tray and went off up the wide, shallow stairs, carrying it carefully.

Mrs Bettany was sitting up in bed against a pile of pillows when Peggy entered the room. It was a grey, wet day at the beginning of January. The wide lattice windows looked out over a flat, leaden sea and the sky was heavy with clouds. The bedroom itself, however, was very bright and cheery with its big log fire filling the room with dancing light, its white walls and the yellow net curtains peeping behind the heavy orange brocade. The carpet was cream with a pattern of yellow and orange flowers scattered over it and the cushions on sofa and chairs were of the same bright hues. Cheeriest of all was the invalid against the great French pillows who dimpled at the girl as she entered.

"Well, Miss Nurse! That my breakfast? Not before time, either! It's famished I am!"

Peggy laughed. "That's good hearing! Then perhaps you'll condescend to eat *all* your toast this morning, just as a treat for me. Even with the Aga, making toast is what you might call a scorching job." She set the tray on the bedside table and then sat down at the foot of the bed and surveyed the patient with satisfaction. "Getting a little colour into your face, thank goodness! You've been a very washed-out specimen up to today."

"Oh, I'm making headway now." Mollie Bettany spoke with complacency. "It won't be long before I'm chivying the lot of you as usual. I don't propose to stay here any longer than I can help, and so I'm telling you. Dear me, I don't think I ever tasted a fresher egg or crisper toast!"

"Then just you see and eat the lot!" Peggy retorted.

Mrs Bettany twinkled at her. "Just you watch me! Post come yet?"

"Not yet. Dad sent Jackie – I mean John. Oh, isn't it *awful*! – down to the village for the post-bag but he hadn't got back when I came up. Are you expecting anything special?"

"I am so. It's high time we heard from Canada. Sure, it's not like Jo not to write every week as you know yourself."

Peggy laughed. "Auntie Jo must have her plate full with all the kids, not to speak of twin babies just on four months old. Heaven knows how she'll ever get any books written now!"

"She'll manage! Jo can no more keep from writing than she can keep from breathing. 'Tis the very breath of life to the creature! Besides, the girls and Steve and Charles will be back at school by this time. Didn't she say that school holidays in Canada aren't the same as the ones you have?"

"I'd forgotten that," Peggy admitted. Then she said in a different tone, "Here comes the rabble! Ja – John must have come back with the post-bag. All right, folks; you can come in, but don't all yell at once."

The family, headed by their father who had met his second son when he came back from the village with the post-bag, came crowding in. They had all been to see the invalid before breakfast, but the post-bag was an important daily event and during these holidays it had been opened and the letters distributed in the big white bedroom.

"Hurry up, Dad," observed Rix, the eldest of the family since he was Peggy's senior by half an hour. "Unlock the thing and dish the letters out."

"Hold your horses, young man!" his father retorted as he unlocked the bag and drew out the pile within. "Now let's see. Mollie – for you from Madge. A couple for Peggy. Another, Mollie – Ireland this time. Bridgie's writing by the look of it. Buck up and open it and let's hear what she's finally settled to do. Here, Bride; young Elfie's fist, isn't it? A couple for you, Rix, so now, perhaps, you're satisfied. One-two-three-four-five for me. Mainly business, judging by the envelopes. Maeve, card for you and another for Maurice. And that's the lot. Nothing today for you, Jackie, my lad."

"*John*!" said the owner of the name stolidly. "Honestly, Dad, I'm not a kid now."

His father chuckled. "You can't expect us to get into the way of it all at once. You've been Jackie for fourteen solid years and it's only nine days since your birthday. Give us a chance!"

"I don't see," said Bride, the second of the Bettany girls, "why if we *must* change his name, we don't do it altogether, use his second one and call him 'Noel'."

13

Jackie's face was a study. "You just let me catch you trying it on!" he spluttered. "Just you try it! That's all!"

"OK – OK!" Their father put in his oar. "No one is thinking of doing it, whatever Bride may say, so keep your wool on. No one ever wanted you to have the name, anyway. It was that idiot of a godmother of yours who stuck it in at the last moment – Hello, Moll! What's happened now?"

Mrs Bettany had given a squawk that startled them all and they turned from the question of names to see her with an open letter, eyes like blue stars and cheeks pink with excitement. "Oh, just listen to this, all of you!" she cried. "'Tis the solving of all our difficulties! And me worrying my head off about what's to happen next term!"

"What *do* you mean?" Peggy demanded. "And do for goodness' sake finish your egg before it's stone-cold! It'll be simply uneatable if you leave it!"

Her mother dropped the letter and picked up her spoon and hurriedly scooped out what was left of the egg. Then she pushed the tray along to Peggy. "Here – take it! I'll finish later. For now – just listen to this, all of you!"

They left their own correspondence and came crowding round the bed to listen while she read aloud: "And now, Mollie, I must get down to business. Pat and Roger won't want me for a year at least, though they've made me promise I'll go out to them then. But, as you'll be seeing for yourself, it really is best for them to make their start in a new country by their lones. And even if they weren't going to Africa I'd never agree to live with them from the first. Young marrieds ought to be able to get away by themselves and not have any in-laws parked on them. It's not fair to anyone and

14

doesn't give a couple a chance to settle down together.

"This being so, I've been wondering if you wouldn't like me to come and run the Quadrant for you until you're quite fit again? I put the greater part of our things into the sale and they went fairly well. The house, too, of course. I've kept the few articles that meant a lot to Patrick and me, and what I had from Father and Mother, and I'm asking you to take them. I don't suppose I'll ever have a house of my own again; but you can never be absolutely sure in this world, so I've kept enough to furnish three rooms and the pick of the kitchen stuff. You've rooms and rooms in that old barn of yours! Rent me three and I'll furnish them. Then I can feel that I have at least a pied-à-terre in England when I come back for holidays.

"It's no use giving the things to Pat. Taking them out to Kenya would cost the earth and then, who's to say they'd arrive safely? But you told me yourself that you'd shut up quite half the rooms because you had no use for them. You can easily let me have three and we'll be businesslike, even if we are sisters, and I'll pay you rent and feel they are my own. And let me come to you until next June – I mean June in next year, of course – and take over the housekeeping and so on. By that time Peggy will have finished school and will be at home to help you and see you don't overdo things. Anyway, you ought to be all right yourself long before that. So don't argue, Moll, but let me come. Goodness knows when we'll have a chance of seeing each other once I go to Kenya and we've always been chums as well as sisters, and so has Dick."

"I haven't read the rest," Mollie Bettany continued, dropping the sheets on the honey dish whence Bride rescued them. "But isn't that the very idea we need? It is so! Sure, Bridgie's a better housekeeper than I am myself. You'll agree, won't you, Dick?" She turned to her husband eagerly.

"Good old Bridgie! You bet I'll agree," he replied. "I'll write to her myself and tell her she's a gift from Heaven to us!"

"Knew you would. And oh, Peggy!" she turned to her eldest girl, "this will mean that you can have your full year in Switzerland after all! If Aunt Bridgie is here, I shan't need to worry about a thing. She'll see to everything."

Peggy flushed and her eyes glowed. She had been troubled about having to lose her Swiss year and yet, how could she possibly go back to school when her mother was still so frail? If Aunt Bridgie would come and see to things it would indeed solve all difficulties as her mother had said. Aunt Bridgie was a darling and they all knew how strong was the bond that existed between her and her younger sister. And Daddy was almost as fond of her. Nothing could possibly be better.

"It would be simply gorgeous," she said. "Are you sure though, you can do without me?"

"Will you hear the conceit of it?" Mollie Bettany cried, laughing. "So you think yourself indispensable to me, do you, Miss? Well, if Aunt Bridgie will come, you're *not*! I'll admit I don't see how I could have done without you otherwise. But now I shan't be alone and you can go and finish your year in peace and comfort. I'll be strong and well by the time that ends and then the three of us can have fun together, running the place. Blessings on Pat that she and Roger want to go to Kenya! 'Tis the best news I've heard for many a long day!"

"I'm glad too," Bride remarked thoughtfully. "I want a year in Switzerland myself before I'm through with school and start college. The thing was if Peggy couldn't have it, it didn't seem awfully fair to me that I should. I was

16

beginning to wonder if we hadn't better cut it out, leave me at St Briavel's for my last year and let the Oberland go until young Maeve was old enough for it."

"All this without any reference to *us*, I suppose?" her father said with a chuckle as he looked at the big, bonny schoolgirl. "Don't you make any mistake, young woman. You and Maeve will each have your year out there and now Peg can finish hers as we've always intended. Bridgie deserves a leather medal! You've a godmother in a thousand, young lady, and don't you forget it! By the way, Moll," he turned to his wife, "does she say when Pat's wedding comes off? I must send that cheque to the kid. No use giving her anything else and I daresay they'll be glad enough of a little extra when they get out to Kenya. Poor old Patrick hadn't a lot to leave them. They spent so much on the boys, poor lads!"

His wife's face clouded as she remembered her three nephews who had been drowned when a squall overturned their yacht four years before. She looked thankfully at her own big sons and then recalled herself to the present.

"I hadn't got that far, but in her last letter, Bridgie said before Lent, so it can't be far off now. Give me the letter, Bride – What on earth are you doing to it?" she added in some astonishment, for Bride was sponging the sheets with her face-cloth.

"You chucked it down on top of the honey and I'm cleaning it up. There you are!" And Bride brought the ill-treated letter back to her mother.

Mrs Bettany took it and scanned the pages thoughtfully. "Here it is." And she read out; "Pat's wedding is fixed for February 3rd so 'tis busy we are as you may imagine. It's a very quiet one as her father died only three months ago. I hope Dick can come, though I know you won't and the children will all be at school, so I'm not asking them. But

17

tell them we're saving the top bit of the cake for them. I'll be staying with Michael and Kathie for another week after that, but Kathie's sister will be coming then and they have only the one spare room. So if you and Dick agree to my suggestions, I'll becoming along to you then. I'll send off my furniture and traps when I hear from you about the rooms. Just tell the men to put them anywhere and I'll see to them when I come."

"I think it's rotten of Pat not to ask us to be her bridesmaids," Bride grumbled. "I was looking forward to that – the first wedding in our generation! She could have bridesmaids, even with a quiet wedding. Is she going the whole thing and wearing white and a veil, Mummy?"

"Aunt Bridgie would have liked it. She still has her veil – Don't I remember what a picture she looked in it at her own wedding? – but Pat is to be married in her going-away suit with only your Uncle Michael's Mary for bridesmaid." She looked at the letter again. "They leave for Dublin two hours after the wedding and then cross to Holyhead by the night boat. They'll have to go straight to Southampton, for their boat sails at six in the evening, so they won't be able to come here for even a few hours. Bridgie says Rodger wants to get back to his coffee plantation as soon as possible. He has it with a syndicate of three others, you know, and another of them wants to come home for *his* marriage. Pat won't lack for friends, I'm hoping. Poor little Pat! She's had plenty of tragedy in her twenty-three years! I hope it's to be happiness for her from now on."

Bride was silenced and her father stood up and stretched himself. "Well I don't know about the rest of you, but I've got to do a spot of work some time. This lot to look at," he waved his letters, "and a whole pile of papers to work through in the office. Coming, Rix?"

Rix nodded and got to his feet. "OK, Dad. I've finished my share of the chores. By the way, Peg, Mrs What's-her-name arrived just before I came upstairs and was shrieking for you and something she wants," he added to his twin sister.

"You brute! And you never told me! Now she'll be mad for the rest of the day," Peggy wailed. "Tell her I'm coming at once. Mummy, you finish your brekker. See that she does it, Bride. Maeve, be a gem and go and do the flowers in the drawing room, will you? They look like last Sunday's wreaths in the cemetery!"

With this macabre simile, Peggy fled to see to the needs of the washerwoman and Bride set the breakfast tray back on her mother's bedside table and sternly commanded her to eat her toast and honey.

"I'll go and heat this coffee again. It must be stone cold by this time. Shan't be a minute! Maeve, go and do the flowers like a lamb. If anyone comes that has to be taken to the drawing room, they'll have a fit!"

Jack and Maurice had gone off on their own pursuits. Maeve ran downstairs to attend to the pathetic vases and Bride produced dusters after she had run the Hoover over the carpet and proceeded to set her mother's room to rights. Even the latest news did not mean that there could be any let-up from the daily jobs, and school training had dinned it well into them all that the sooner the work was out of the way the more time they would have to amuse themselves.

CHAPTER 2

A Second Surprise

It was the afternoon of that eventful day. Lunch was over and Mr Bettany had carried his wife downstairs and deposited her on the big chesterfield before the fire in the inner drawing-room. The rain was falling heavily and a moaning wind came in from the sea. It was January at its wet worst as Peggy had remarked when her mother arrived.

"Never mind. It's bright enough in here," Mollie Bettany replied as her elder daughters packed her round with cushions and tucked a bright rug over her knees.

Peggy looked round the pretty room with satisfaction.

"There's nothing like a log fire for comfort, is there? And Maeve has done the flowers beautifully. You really have a gift that way, Maeve. There isn't one of us can touch you when it comes to handling flowers."

Maeve gave her an adoring look. "I love doing them," was all she said, however.

Peggy gave her a nod. "Well, you prove it," she replied. "Now, Mummy, is that all right? Another cushion behind your head?"

"Mercy, no! Let me alone, you two! You'll be smothering me with your cushions! Sure no one has ever said I'd to be *killed* with kindness!"

"There's gratitude for you!" Bride grinned as she tossed down the cushion she was holding and flung herself into a nearby armchair, spreading out her long legs luxuriously.

"Well, folk, I don't think we're likely to be bothered with visitors this afternoon – not in this downpour. What shall we do?"

"I vote we get our work and books and have a cosy afternoon," Peggy said. "I'll just run upstairs for my knitting. Shall I bring yours as well, Bride? Where is it?"

"In my top drawer. Bring another ounce of wool as well, will you? I've nearly finished the ball I'm busy with and I'd like to have that jumper finished to take back to school."

"What are you doing, Dad?" Peggy looked at her father. "Joining us?"

He shook his head with a rueful face. "No can do. I've got to go through those papers about the new road and that means a good two hours' work. Have tea ready at four and I'll try to finish by then. Coming, Rix?"

Rix, who had been sprawled on one of the wide window seats, looking out over the sea, got up lazily and stretched himself. "Guess so. You want me to check up on your figures."

"Brat!" his father said affectionately. "All right; come along."

They went out of the room laughing, and Jackie, or John as he insisted he must be nowadays, went with them. He had taken to fretwork these holidays, his uncles and aunts in Canada having clubbed together to give him a treadle fretsaw for Christmas, and every spare moment was given to his latest hobby. The younger twins had already departed on their own lawful occasions in what had been the nursery but was more commonly called the Glory Hole these days when there were no nursery children left.

Peggy ran upstairs to fetch the knitting and presently

she and Bride were both hard at work, Bride on a new jumper for herself and Peggy busy with a bedjacket for her mother who was running short of those useful articles. Mrs Bettany had produced a frock she was smocking for her youngest daughter and while their fingers flew, they chatted hard.

Mollie Bettany had been very young when she married – barely eighteen, and her first babies had arrived two days before her own nineteenth birthday. She had been a really young mother and now that Peggy and Bride were growing up, they found in her a delightful chum. In fact, as Bride had remarked to Peggy only the night before, there were times and seasons when they felt as if they were the parents and she the child! She was almost as keenly interested in school affairs as they and was ready to enter into all their fun. Her mercurial Irish nature had helped to keep her youthful, and even now, at almost thirty-seven, there were days when she looked hardly old enough to be mother to even Maeve and Maurice, the younger twins.

Bride entertained them with an account of the evil doings of a new Junior Middle who had arrived from Australia the previous term. Emerence was an enterprising young woman who had been brought up on the principle that you should never say "No" to a child. As a result, she had been a regular firebrand all the term, though its end found her slightly tamed. The prefects as a body had loathed and execrated her, but at this distance of the holidays, Bride found that some of Emerence's more surprising pranks were very funny.

After an hour's work, Mrs Bettany laid her smocking down. "'Tis tired of it I am," she said. "We've worked enough for one afternoon. Get the Ludo board and men,

22

Bride. I'll challenge you two to a game – and beat you into the bargain."

"Will you indeed?" Bride tossed her knitting on to a nearby table and jumped up. "Come on, Peg! We aren't going to let a challenge like that go past us! You haul up that table and I'll get the things."

"Put your work away properly!" her sister retorted. "You are an untidy brat! You'll have half the stitches down if you don't look out."

"Fussypat!" was Bride's reply. "Oh, well, perhaps I'd better. I loathe having to pick stitches up again."

She took up the knitting and rolled it up before putting it down by her sister's work on one of the window seats. Then she scurried to a bureau to hunt out the Ludo set while Peggy dragged a gate-legged table up to the chesterfield. They had settled down and Bride was rattling the dice-box violently when Peggy, who had ears fit to hear the grass growing as her youngest sister had complained more than once, suddenly lifted her head alertly.

"A car!" she exclaimed. "Who, under the sun, is brave enough to come to call in weather like *that*?" And she pointed to the streaming panes.

"Oh, fiddle! It's only the baker's van, I expect," her mother said.

"Not the right day. Pendry called yesterday. It's a car all right. There goes the front door bell!" as a great peal rang through the house.

Bride dropped the dice-box and jumped up. "OK, Peg. I'll go and see who it is. You aren't as hard-hearted as I am."

"I'm more polite, you mean," Peggy threw back at her.

Bride paused at the door to grimace violently at her sister. Then she vanished, followed by a cry from her mother of, "If it's anyone you think I'd like to see, show them in here. I'm convalescent now, and I *won't* be perpetually treated like a permanent invalid."

"Take whoever it is to the morning room and switch on the little bell-fire to take the first chill off them," Peggy shrieked as Bride's steps died away in the distance.

The Quadrant was built round a grassy quadrangle and, the drawing rooms being on the seaward side while the front door looked across the park to Exmoor, it was quite a journey between the two. Peggy had time to throw a couple of logs on the fire and push the knitting under a big cushion before her sister came flying back with a face full of excitement.

"Who d'you think it is? The very last person you'd have expected! Give you three guesses each!"

"*Not* anyone from Canada?" Peggy cried eagerly.

"Talk sense! Who's crossing from Canada in weather like this? If that's the best you can do you may as well give it up at once. It's Auntie Hilda!"

"Hilda Annersley?" Mrs Bettany sat up with as much excitement as her daughters had shown and there was an avalanche of cushions to the floor. "Where is she? What have you done with her? 'Tis the rude girl you are, Bride Bettany, to be leaving her standing on the doorstep. 'Tis ashamed of you I am! Go and bring her here at once!"

"Oh, I didn't!" Bride said in shocked tones. "She sent me to tell you while she got her damp things off and took the chill off her first. She said she wasn't going to risk giving you a cold."

"And here she is, anyway!" Peggy cried as the sound of light footsteps in the corridor reached them and the door opened to admit a tall, graceful woman, some years older than Mollie Bettany.

A chorus of welcome greeted her. Peggy raced across

24

the big room to fling her arms round the newcomer and reach up on tiptoe to kiss her while her mother created a second avalanche as she swung her feet to the floor and stood up exclaiming, "Hilda Annersley! Why didn't you tell us you were coming? Has a wire gone astray, now?"

"From me, do you mean?" Miss Annersley kissed Peggy and then freed herself firmly. "Certainly not; I never sent one. It was a sudden decision on my part. Stand still, Peggy, and let me look at you."

Peggy laughed. "You ought to know me after all these years," she said demurely. "I haven't grown at all, if that's what you mean."

"So I see, so far as height is concerned. You never will, short of a miracle; you're not built that way. But as to growth in other ways –" She stopped short and examined the charming, Saxon-fair faced lifted to hers with thoughtful grey eyes. "Yes; I certainly see growth here. You aren't a baby any more, Peggy. And that's as it should be at eighteen."

"Oh, I'm not – not yet!" Peggy protested. "Our birthday isn't till the end of the month. We've a good three weeks of being seventeen, yet."

Miss Annersley laughed. "You're as bad as ever Jo was. How she did hate having to grow up, to be sure!"

"Do you think she ever has – really, I mean?" Bride asked with a giggle as she recalled some of her beloved aunt's exploits as recently as the week before Christmas.

"Oh, I think she's completely grown up now, whatever she may do when she's in one of her madder moods. But now let me see your mother." She set them both aside and came to kiss the invalid and then scan her carefully. "This is an improvement, Mollie. The last time I saw you –"

"The last time you saw me, my dear, I was a poor, feeble thing that couldn't lift her head – couldn't move

25

it, anyway. D'you remember the sand-bags they had set all round it, Hilda? Sure, I couldn't have stirred it if I'd tried from now till next Christmas!"

"And with a face on you the size of a postage stamp," Peggy added.

"Well, you've improved on that," the visitor replied with a laugh as she sat down in the chair Bride pushed up. "Where is the rest of the family?"

"Dad and Rix in the estate office and the kids somewhere around – Glory Hole, probably," Peggy replied as she pressed her mother back on the sofa and rearranged the cushions. "It's wizard seeing you like this, Auntie Hilda. How long can you stay?"

For reply, her Head Mistress turned to Mrs Bettany. "Can you keep me for one night, Mollie? I had really meant to write, but then decided it would be easier if I came and we talked it over. I've been staying with Daisy Venables in her rooms and I was so near and there was so much to say, it really seemed to be better to have a personal interview. I only decided when I was on the platform at Exeter and there wasn't time to ring or wire you so I thought I'd risk my luck and just come."

"You'd have been sold if Maeve and Maurice had been indulging in measles or mumps," Bride told her with a chuckle.

"They weren't very likely to have mumps, seeing they spoilt everyone's Christmas holidays last year with it," Miss Annersley retorted. "As for measles, they've had that, too, haven't they? Yes; I thought so. Well, then, Bride!"

Bride grinned. "You win!"

"And anyway, aren't there four sides to the house?" her mother protested. "Sure the lot of you could be having chickenpox, mumps, whooping –"

"Hi! Stop!" Bride cried. "We'll be having the wretched things next if you go on like this. All right, Auntie Hilda. Your luck's in and we're thrilled to see you. Why have you come, by the way?"

"Bride – Bettany! Hilda, you don't smack her enough at school. It doesn't do to be too kind with imps like Bride," her mother protested. "You're as welcome as April showers and May flowers put together, Hilda, whyever you decided to come, and well do you know it!"

Miss Annersley nodded. "Oh, I wasn't afraid of that, my dear. Bride, it was really you I came to see."

"*Me*?" Bride looked stunned. "But why me?"

"To ask if you will be our Head Girl for the rest of the year." And having flung her bomb, Miss Annersley sat back and watched the effect with interest.

Bride stared at her in blank amazement. "Will I be *what*?"

"Will you be our Head Girl for the rest of the year?"

"But – but – what's become of Loveday? *She's* Head Girl this year."

"She *was*. Come and sit down, Bride, and let me try to take that thunderstruck look from your face. Loveday has left for the present. When she returns, it will be to Switzerland. So, you see, we can't count on her for St Briavel's any longer. We must have a Head Girl and you are the obvious choice. What have you to say about it, Bride?"

Bride gasped and fell into the nearest chair. "But I don't understand! *Why* has Loveday left? I'm sure she had no idea of it when we broke up. Why, only the last night she kept us talking till all hours about some new ideas she had suddenly evolved for the Sale. And she had thought out one or two other things and we spent

27

literally *hours* discussing them and thinking out how we could fit them in. Some of them were jolly good, I may say," Bride added. "Auntie Hilda, for pity's sake tell us what on earth has happened!"

Miss Annersley broke into peals of laughter. "My poor Bride! Don't look so desperately tragic about it! There's nothing wrong with Loveday – rather the reverse! An uncle of her father's was part owner of a big cattle ranch near Rosario in the Argentine. He died in the autumn and left his share and all else he possessed to Loveday who was his god-daughter and bore his wife's name. Someone must go out to see to all the business. That someone has to be Mr Perowne who is Loveday's trustee until she comes of age. They will probably want Loveday herself; so Mr Perowne has put in a manager on his own Cornish estate and he and Mrs Perowne and Loveday all flew to Rosario a week ago. It will mean at least six months there and Loveday certainly won't come back to school until September. It was understood that she was to have her final year in Switzerland, so she won't return to St Briavel's – or not as a schoolgirl."

"Good gracious!" Peggy and Bride were round-eyed at this news. "Then Loveday is an heiress?"

The Head nodded. "She certainly is. The trouble is that no one seems to know how long it will take them to settle things up. I don't know what the laws of inheritance may be in the Argentine. Here, it is a year and a day at longest; but other countries do things differently. However, even so, as Mrs Perowne told me, it will make a big difference for them all."

Bride grinned. "I should say it would! Loveday always had to be careful over her pocket money and she once told me that she wanted to go to Cirencester to have a proper farming training, but she didn't know if they'd be

28

able to manage it, things were so tight at home. Well, she can have it all right now – if she wants to go on, that is. She might just decide to – to rest on her oars, so to speak. You never know!"

"Rubbish!" Peggy spoke with decision. "Whatever else she may do, lazing about just being an heiress is the last thing Loveday is likely to want! Her idea is much more sure to be to carry on her share of the ranch. Or if she doesn't do that, she'll go in with her father. The Perownes have heaps of land, I know, and she always was crazy on open-air jobs."

Bride nodded. "Lots of land and precious little else! Loveday would be awfully bucked to be able to help her dad."

"Well, there it is," the Head said, quietly ignoring this passage between the girls. "Whatever may happen when Loveday reaches her majority, it is quite certain that she won't come back to the Island; and as it's equally certain that we can't carry on for two terms without a Head Girl, what about taking it on, Bride?"

Bride sat up, looking serious. "I'd love it from one point of view. I know it's a fearful honour and all that, and I *would* like to be able to say I'd been Head Girl as well as Peg, but there are things against it as well, you know."

"Such as –?" Miss Annersley looked inquiringly at the girl.

"Well, what about Bank? I was Bank Prefect last term and it takes up a certain amount of time. It isn't just handing out the cash. With some of those young demons of Middles, it means finding out exactly why they want extra money. And then there's balancing up. And you know what the end of term is like for it, as well, and the Head Girl is generally up to the eyes, anyhow, at

29

the end of term – beginning, too, if you come to that."

"Miss O'Ryan will take over. She's been spending a week with me since the news about Loveday came and we discussed the matter. She said if you would take over the post of Head Girl, she would fit Bank in somehow."

"How exactly like her!" Peggy said warmly. "Biddy always did pitch in and help when it was necessary. I remember that from Tirol days."

"Yes; it's very decent of her," Bride agreed. "Do you want an answer d'reckly this minute, Auntie Hilda? I mean I'd like to think it over a bit. It – it's come rather as a bolt from the blue, you know."

"I realize that. But the whole thing came rather as a bolt from the blue to *me* as well. Suppose you go off with Peggy and talk it over together while I have a chat with your mother? I must go back tomorrow at latest and I want your reply then, but we can leave it till tomorrow morning."

Bride looked relieved. "I'd really like to think about it first. Oh, I expect I'll say I will. But it does need thinking over. It's rather a big thing, isn't it?"

The Head laughed. "Not too big for you, Bride. You might quite well have had it for a term already. It was only the fact that Loveday was six months the elder and quite as capable as yourself that decided us – that, and one other point."

"Oh? What was that?" Bride looked interested.

"We'll go into that later. Now run along and have your chat with Peggy."

Peggy stood up. "Come along, Bride. We can see to Auntie Hilda's room and then we'll do tea. We can talk while we work."

Mrs Bettany gave Bride no chance to refuse. "Off you go! Auntie Hilda and I want a good old gossip and your

30

presence is not required. Be off with you both! Oh, Peg, tell Daddy that Auntie Hilda is here, will you?"

Peggy nodded, tucked her arm in Bride's and they left the room to go and see to a bedroom for Miss Annersley before they raced down to the kitchen where Peggy slipped on an apron, turned up her sleeves and set to work to mix the dough for splits while Bride piled china on the trolley and cut the great plates of bread and butter that the appetites of three schoolboys demanded. Not one of them, so far as that went, had any use for drawing room tea, unless it was Peggy. The rest brought healthy appetites to every meal.

While they worked, the sisters discussed the latest news from every point of view. Peggy was urgent that Bride should take on the job.

"I did it, and I'd like you to do it; and Maeve, when her turn comes," she said eagerly. "It would be such fun if we could say we'd all been Head Girl at school!"

Bride made a face at her. "It's a fearful shock, let me tell you. I was nicely settled with the Bank and, though I made a fuss about it to Auntie Hilda, it isn't *all* that much work."

"You can't plead that as an excuse. Biddy O'Ryan has cut the ground under your feet by offering to do it for you."

"I know." Bride gave a groan. "Most officious of her, I call it! She might have waited to see if I wanted to be Head Girl before she said anything. I'm not so sure that I do."

"Rot! Of course you do!" Peggy turned out her dough on the board and began to roll it out. "Look here! Auntie said there was another reason than age why you weren't chosen and she'd tell you later. The trolley's ready. Take it into the drawing room and see to the tables and ask

31

her about it. It might help you to decide as they want and, honestly, Bride, as you *ought*!"

Seeing no help for it, Bride put her plates of bread and butter on the under-shelf of the trolley and trundled it out of the kitchen while Peggy proceeded to finish her splits and pop them into the oven.

She found that Miss Annersley had produced some crochet work and her hook flashed in the dancing firelight as she chatted with their mother. Bride came to admire the beautiful work and demand to be told what it was for when it was finished.

"Part of Daisy's wedding present," the Head said, smoothing it out complacently on her knee. "I've promised her half a dozen afternoon tea-cloths and this is the second. I have some lovely Irish linen and I'm sending them away to Belfast to be made up when they are finished. Mdlle de Lachennais will embroider her initials on each. She does that sort of thing so much better than I can."

"Daisy will be fearfully bucked," Bride said pensively. She turned to set out the small tables absolutely needful when the younger ones had tea in the drawing room. When she had finished, she pushed the trolley into the corridor and came back to pull up a pouffe beside the sofa.

Her mother nodded to her. "That's right. Come and sit down a minute. Auntie Hilda has been talking to me and now she'll tell you."

Bride curled her long legs under her and looked at the Head. "I'm all ears," she said. "Go on, Auntie Hilda. What's the other reason? *I* wasn't sorry, you know," she added. "I like a quiet life!"

Miss Annersley went straight to the point. "It's this. We did think of you for Head Girl. You were the first mentioned. But – and it was rather a big but – Peggy had just held the post. We didn't want you to have any trouble with people saying that *of course* you were the one to be chosen! You were Peggy's sister and Lady Russell's niece. I know what girls can be like – some of them, and we have our share of silly girls like any other school – and it might have made things difficult for you. Loveday *was* the elder and she has made a good Head Girl as we knew she would. Now, however, she has left so far as St Briavel's is concerned and you are the obvious choice."

"There's Primrose – and Nancy – and Tom, too," Bride said.

"I know; but we want Bride Bettany, my child. You are older than any of them and you have been brought up in the school and are soaked in our traditions – or if you're not, you ought to be." The Head spoke decidedly.

Bride laughed. "That's true, of course. Well, as I said, I didn't mind in the least last term. And anyway, with all the trouble about Elfie, it really was just as well that I was free to carry on for her for the first half of the term." She stopped and thought hard, the other two watching her bright face keenly. Suddenly she looked up. "Very well. I'll carry on – though what sort of a mess I'll make of it, I just wouldn't know," she added laughingly.

"Why should you make a mess of it?" Miss Annersley asked serenely. "You've plenty of sense and tact and the girls as a whole like you. I don't think you will either be so strict that you'll drive them into wild rebellion nor yet so flabby that things will go to pieces. Use your wits and there's no need for you to be anything but successful."

"I know Peg was, but I'm not Peg nor anything like her," Bride murmured.

"No one wants you to be anyone but yourself. Don't be silly, Bride!"

Bride chuckled. "Consider me a squashed beetle at your feet! Well, I'll do my best and saints can't do more."

"No one wants you to do more," the Head retorted briskly. "Be yourself. Put the school before Bride Bettany and her likes and dislikes and I know that this will be as good a year as any we have had."

CHAPTER 3

The School is Started

"Tom – Tom Gay! Hi, there! Stop a minute!"

Tom Gay, who had been hurrying along the corridor leading to the Prefects' room, paused and looked round. "Hello, Annis! Had decent hols?"

"Yes, awfully, thanks. Dad was home for Christmas. But that wasn't what I wanted to ask you about."

Tom raised quizzical eyebrows, and the gipsy-faced girl of sixteen who had stopped her went faintly pink. "Not? Then what was it? Hurry up, Annis: I've tons to do and no time to do it in."

"It was just to ask you if you'd heard this yarn that's going round about Loveday Perowne and if you know whether there's any truth in it."

"Yarn? What yarn?" Tom spoke sharply. "*I've* heard nothing."

"Well, it started with Valerie Arnott. She says that she heard during the hols that Loveday had left all of a sudden and I wondered if *you'd* heard anything."

Tom gave a long low whistle. Annis stood watching her eagerly. She herself was a sturdily-built girl of sixteen; very attractive with her bright, gipsy face, curly black hair and very dark brown eyes. Tom, standing five foot eleven, towered over her. Her wavy brown hair was cropped in boyish fashion and her fresh-coloured face was characterised by a square jaw and a pair of honest grey eyes with a very direct look. She was plain, but her friends always declared that there was something especially nice about her face.

Now, she turned her straight gaze on Annis and said, "Whatever next? So far as *I* know she hasn't left. Where did Valerie get hold of this yarn?"

"She said it was an aunt of the friend she's been staying with since New Year's Day. The aunt lives not far from Newquay and the friend hangs out somewhere near St Austell. The Perownes' place *is* somewhere near Newquay, isn't it?"

Tom nodded. "Quite right: it is. I've stayed there with Loveday – last summer hols, to be exact. It's a gorgeous old house, but needs piles doing to it. The Perownes are jolly poor for their position – like most of us these days," she added with a grin. "They've just had to let the house go. Mr Perowne prefers to spend what cash he has on the land which he farms. I believe he's quite a big pot in the farming world," she added.

"Well, according to Val, her friend's aunt said that Loveday's folk had come into a fortune and they've all gone off to South America somewhere to claim it."

"Not really? Well," Tom said consideringly, "that's a jolly good thing for them if it's really true. But I know nothing about it, so I can't help you, I'm afraid."

"Oh, it's a good thing for them, I know. But if it *is* true, and I don't think Val would have been broadcasting it if she wasn't awfully sure, what about the school? Loveday's Head Girl. What's going to happen if she's left in a hurry like that? It isn't exactly a job just anyone can fall into."

"Oh, gosh! I hadn't thought of that – no time, of course. The first I heard of it was just now from you." Tom's brows creased in a frown. "I wonder how much truth there's in it?"

36

"Val seemed to think it was true enough," Annis said as she gazed up at Tom with wide dark eyes. "I thought *you'd* have heard something. You and Loveday seemed fairly chummy this last two terms or so."

"I haven't heard a word." Tom passed over the hint that she and Loveday had been on extra close terms of friendship. "As a matter of fact, beyond cards at Christmas, neither of us has written. At least, I certainly didn't and I don't suppose she did either. Life's too full for letter-writing and especially at Christmas when your pater's a Vicar. All the Christmas treats for the kids and the old women and the choirboys and so on to see to, as well as the decorations and extra visits to the sick and things like that."

"Do you do all that?" Annis asked in awed tones. "And how can you *bear* to visit sick people? I'd never know what to say to them."

"No; I suppose not. But don't forget, my good kid, that I've grown up amongst it all. Anyway, it has to be done and I've got to take my share. About Loveday, I'm afraid I can't help you at all. You'll have to hold your horses till Abendessen when the Abbess'll have something to say if it's true. You needn't worry about *us*. Someone will be appointed in Loveday's place, you know. Now I must get cracking. See you later!" And, with a nod, Tom sped on her way, leaving Annis looking dissatisfied.

The big prefect – Tom could overlook everyone else in the school – turned into the prefects' room where she found five of the elect sitting round the fireplace in which burned a bright wood fire. Like everywhere else in the school, the room had its radiator which was working overtime, but a fire was a cheery thing on a wet, dismal day like this. The girls had permission to light one when they wanted it, provided they attended to it themselves, and Nancy Chester, coming shiveringly into the room after finishing her unpacking, had proceeded to set it going. The rest drifting in, one after another, had thankfully pulled up chairs round it and now they were all talking hard. As the Head of the Hobbies Club entered, they all stopped and looked round.

"So here you are!" Nancy exclaimed as she made a long arm and yanked a chair round from the table. "Come into Neighbour Row and see if you can help us to solve the latest problem."

Tom sat down with an air of acknowledgement. "What's up?" she demanded.

"The strangest tales are going round," Nancy said. "We wondered if *you'd* heard anything. You're by way of being fairly chummy with Loveday, aren't you?"

Tom stretched her long legs before her and shoved her hands well down in her blazer pockets. "I've just had young Annis at me with a yarn about Loveday leaving, if that's what you mean. I haven't heard a thing about it myself. We don't go in for writing billets-doux to each other. Both miles too busy; and anyway, letter-writing never was much in my line."

"Don't I know it!" Fair-haired Primrose Day spoke with emphasis. "When I wrote hectically at the beginning of the summer hols to ask if you'd any of my hankies mixed up with yours, did you bother to reply? Not you! You left it till the beginning of the term. Of course," she added fairly, "you hadn't, as it happened; but you might at least have sent me a card with 'yes' or 'no' to let me know what to do. As it was, I was completely stuck to know whether to buy more or struggle along with what I had and what I could – er – snaffle from the family stock. In the end, I bought some and mine were here in the laundry all the time."

"I heard all about that last term," Tom told her with an infectious chuckle. "Give it a rest now, for pity's sake!"

"Yes, do!" Bess Herbert, the school's librarian chimed in. "At any rate, it was only hankies and one can always do with a few extra. Likewise, it's four months ago. Don't rake up past things like that, Nancy, life's too short! Look here, Tom," she turned to the impenitent Tom, "what exactly did Annis tell you?"

"Just that Val Arnott had heard from the aunt of the pal she stayed with after Christmas that the Perownes had come into money in South America somewhere and had had to go off to see about it, taking their One and Only with them. Didn't like to leave her behind for so long, I suppose. Annis seemed to think it was true. She said young Val wouldn't have been broadcasting it all over the school if it wasn't. And she's right there, of course."

Lesley Pitt, editress of the school magazine, nodded agreement with this. "She'd be an awful little flat if it was just hearsay. The Abbess would have something to say to her in that event. Val's got her head screwed on the right way and she'd never risk a fuss just for the sake of making a sensation."

There was a minute's silence after this. Then Bess said, "That's all very well, and I don't doubt for a moment that you're right about Valerie. But have you thought what happens to the school in that case? We can't go on without a Head Girl and who is there to take it? We're all of us pretty well tied up with our own jobs."

"Nancy, perhaps," Primrose suggested. "She only sees to the outside rooms and that doesn't include the Art room, even. Rosalind has *that* on her plate. The rest is a mere trifle, really."

Nancy turned pale at the idea. "Primrose! What a

39

simply ghastly idea! I hope to goodness it's only your own imagination and that *that* isn't proposed! I couldn't possibly take it on, and if anyone suggests it I shall turn it down flat and so I warn you!"

"Why on earth?" Primrose asked. "Not that I really think it *will* be you. Much more likely to be Tom or – or Bride, for instance. But if they did think of you, I should have thought you'd have been overwhelmed with pride at the honour."

"'Overwhelmed' is the word for it," Nancy retorted. "Not with pride, though. Don't you think that for a moment. But it's exactly what I should be. Oh, no; Head Girl definitely isn't my cup of tea! You have to be very up and coming and sure of yourself to be a Head Girl. I mayn't be exactly diffident, but I haven't the self-assurance for that job. If I had to take it, I'd be asking advice all round and never knowing whose to take and that wouldn't be good enough."

This was so true that no one even tried to contradict her and the meeting was interrupted by the arrival of two more of their crowd – Madge Dawson, the school's most musical member, and Julie Lucy, who was Nancy's cousin and great friend, as well as being Head of Netball.

"Hello!" she said as she came in. "How's everyone? Had good hols?"

A chorus informed her that they had enjoyed life during the Christmas holidays and the pair pulled up more chairs and joined the ring round the fire. Before anyone could say anything about the latest sensation to them, the door opened once more and Bride Bettany walked in. She shut the door behind her and then stood looking at them all with an expectant expression though only Tom noted it for the moment.

"Bride Bettany! What happened to you and Elfie?"

40

Primrose demanded as she made room for her. "Why didn't you join us at Cardiff as usual? And where *is* Elfie, by the way?"

Bride strolled over and sat down. "Dad had to go to Cardiff on business so he said Maeve and I might as well go with him and he'd bring us as far as Carnbach and see us on to the ferry. We picked up Elf at Clifton and she's with Matey at the moment, explaining why she brought her trunk with her instead of sending it." A slow, broad grin curled Bride's lips as she added, "Matey doesn't seem to be her sweetest self. However, Elf's got a good excuse for once. Her kid brothers have spent the hols having chickenpox and she's been staying with friends because of infection. I don't suppose Matey will say much to her, but she does like things to go according to Cocker – Matey, I mean. The Woodwards' place wasn't free from infection till yesterday so Elf couldn't see to her packing before and Dad said we'd bring her trunk along with her to save any trouble. You know what it *can* be when you send things by road or rail." She stopped and looked round the circle.

Tom sat up and drew in her legs. "What's up with you, Bride? You look exactly like a cat that's eaten the canary and is watching the family hunt for it."

Bride protested. "I'm sure I don't! What a disgusting simile. Really, Tom!"

"Then why are you looking like that? Something's up. Look here; do *you* know anything about this business of Loveday's?"

Bride nodded slowly. "I do so. You might say I knew everything."

This caused a slight sensation.

"Go on and tell us then, can't you?" Primrose said impatiently. "Or have you been told to say nothing for the present? In that case, of course –"

41

"Oh, I'm going to," Bride interrupted. "The Abbess said I must – thought it would be best if you all knew before she said anything to the school at large. But I'm waiting for the rest to turn up first. No sense in having to repeat a thing if you needn't! Elf knows, so she does't matter. Who else is missing? Let's see; Audrey and Rosalind – oh, and Anne! Where are they?"

"Rosalind won't be here till Monday at soonest," Julie said. "She caught a fearful cold last week and Mrs Yolland wrote to ask if I would mind taking on the Art rooms for her until she's back again. That was Tuesday and she said that Rosalind was still streaming and needing a dozen hankies a day! The Abbess knows, of course. As for Anne, they found a couple of Junior Middles in trouble over something and Miss Dene got hold of her and asked her to see what was wrong. I don't know anything about Audrey's whereabouts –"

"I'm here," said a fresh voice at the door as Audrey Simpson, the Stationery prefect, walked in. "Sorry, everyone, but Miss Dene called me into the office to say that they'd been late sending the new stationery and it only arrived this morning so she wants me to give her a hand with unpacking it and putting it away. Hello, Bride! How's your mother now?"

"Much better, thanks. She's been coming down before lunch for the last ten days or so. Doc called yesterday and he said she was making strides so long as she didn't try to do too much. Luckily," Bride went on, thankfully postponing her announcement as long as she could, "my Aunt Bridgie from Ireland is coming to live with us for a year until my cousin Pat and her husband are settled properly on their farm in Kenya, so she's going to run the house until they send for her to join them. It's a blessing," she added. "If Aunt Bridgie hadn't been able

42

to take over, it would have meant Peg having to give up Switzerland and none of us wanted that."

"No; that would have been rotten luck for Peg," Nancy agreed. "I'm awfully glad Aunt Mollie's coming along so well, Bride. Give her my love when you write and tell her I said so."

Bride nodded; but before she could speak, Tom had butted in.

"Well, now that we know that it's all OK about Mrs Bettany – though I'd no idea it might have meant messing up Peggy's last year – you get busy and tell us about Loveday. Is that yarn of young Valerie Arnott's true?"

"I don't know what sort of a yarn Val may have been spreading about," Bride retorted. "I've only just arrived – more or less, that is. Matter of fact, Elf and I were here an hour ago, but Matey got her claws into us and told us to unpack and be done with it before we did anything else. Then she told Elf to go and see her in her room when she'd finishd, as I told you before. But I've seen no one to tell me what sort of yarns are going the rounds."

"Then never mind that, but get cracking and give us the real story."

Bride gave herself a little shake. "Oh, bother you, Tom Gay! Can't you wait two minutes?"

"Not half a minute! So get on with it!"

Seeing no help for it, Bride gave way. "Oh well, I suppose I'll get no peace till you do know and if Anne's got a couple of kids in trouble in tow, goodness knows when she'll be free! OK; I'll tell you, but don't interrupt until I've finished, anyone. Your comments will keep for the present."

They all looked at her and realized that she meant what she said. It was so unlike sunny-tempered Bride

43

to talk like this that they knew that something serious had happened. Tom made a pretty good guess at what was coming, but she had the wisdom and tact to hold her tongue.

"Loveday has had to go to Argentina with her folks," Bride began. "An old uncle or someone has left her half a cattle ranch and a young fortune into the bargain. Mr Perowne went to see that no one tried to diddle her and Loveday had to go herself because it's hers. It meant being there as soon as possible as no one seems to know much about the laws out there. They'll probably be away six months which would bring it to June and, as she's going to Switzerland for her last year, anyhow, Mr Perowne said it wasn't worth while to let her come back here for just a month or so, so as far as we're concerned, she's left."

There was a moment's silence as they digested this. It came as a real shock to most of them, and if anyone else had told them they would have been inclined to regard it as what Primrose Day had once termed "one of the more brilliant efforts at leg-pulling". But it was quite clear that Bride was in deadly earnest and, in any case, leg-pulling was not one of her usual amusements.

Nancy spoke first. "How – what a very extraordinary thing! Especially as I'll swear Loveday had no idea of this when we broke up last term."

"She hadn't," Bride confirmed her. "The news came a week later, just before Christmas. I believe it was the biggest shock of their lives – especially when they found it meant dropping everything and making for Rosario, almost on the spot."

"Well, then, she really won't be coming back?" Primrose said rather dazedly.

"That's what I said. Or not until she goes to the Oberland in September."

"But then – well, who's to take her place?" Nancy demanded. "Can you tell us *that*?"

Bride went darkly red. Before she could speak, however, Tom had helped her out. "Can't you guess, you – you mooks? Bride, of course! That's right, isn't it, Bride?"

Bride nodded speechlessly.

"Well," Tom spoke slowly as she rose to her feet and rested her broad shoulders against the mantelpiece, "I guess it's the best thing the Abbess could have done in the circs. Matter of fact, I'd made sure you'd be it last term. Loveday came as a complete shock to me. She always seemed one of those quiet, mousey folk who never shine particularly. Not that she didn't make a jolly good fist at it," she added generously. "She wasn't anything wildly brilliant, but she did quite a good job. All the same, Bride, I'd always thought you were the obvious one to follow your sister. Of course, as the Abbess told us last term, Loveday *was* the oldest; but apart from that, which didn't occur to me, I'd have pitched on *you* myself."

Bride had recovered her self-possession by this time. "Thanks for the flowers! I certainly didn't expect it myself. I don't see any reason why you should have been so sure I'd be the one to follow Peggy. In fact," she added with a chuckle, "if you want to know, I rather thought it might be *you*."

"Me? Oh, what utter rot!" Tom flushed to the roots of her cropped hair. "Oh no, my dear! I'm not the kind to be Head of the school and an example for all the kids to follow. Not after all that's been said about my language! Goodness knows I've tried to reform slightly, but it never gets very far. My pater says it's bred into me now and can't be got out. Anyhow, I never even dreamt of it. Don't think I'd have liked it either," she wound up.

Before anyone could reply to this, a bell rang and the party had to break up at once. Abendessen, as they called supper in imitation of the days when the school had been in the Tirol, was ready, and as prefects they were expected to see to it that the rest of the school took their places in the dining room decently and in good order. Three of them ran down to the dining room itself to await the coming of the rest of the Seniors and the Middles.

The rest took up their posts at the head and foot of the stairs and in the corridors. Rules never really began until the first full day of term, but it was expected that the prefects would see that the younger girls were not too uproarious, especially in the corridors and on the stairs.

As usual, it was just as well that this understanding was obtained. Bride, at the head of the stairs, had to call to order the Dawbarn twins and their fellow criminal, Norah O'Connor. Not that that was anything surprising! Only the term before, Tom had vowed that those three were all born to be hanged. Mary-Lou Trelawney and her own special gang had also to be reminded that, even on the first night of term, you didn't talk at the top of your voice all the time, and certainly not in the corridors. Apart from little contretemps like these, however, there was no trouble. Valerie Arnott's startling story had not reached the younger girls and Dora Robson, her chum, had suggested that it might be wiser to wait a little before saying anything more about it in case it was a mistake and she got into trouble for wild gossip.

When the meal ended, Miss Annersley stood up and rang her bell. The hum of chatter that had filled the room ceased at once. All eyes were turned to the Staff table and the girls waited for what they supposed would be her usual beginning-of-term welcome. The prefects, of course, knew better. All the same, they were keen to know just how the Head would break the news to the rest, so they listened with all their ears.

Miss Annersley told them the story briefly, merely saying that as private affairs had taken the Perowne family to South America for the next six months – whereat Valerie gave Dora a triumphant look – and as Loveday was going on to the Oberland branch of the school for her final year, she would not be returning to the St Briavel's division, for it would not be worthwhile for her to come back for the three or four weeks which would be the most left of the term by the time she came back to England.

"That, of course, means that we must have a new Head Girl," the Head continued. "Bride Bettany is next in age to Loveday and would have been chosen last term if Loveday had not been the elder. She is appointed now for the rest of the year and I am sure you all wish her a happy two terms."

Here she had to pause, for a storm of clapping broke out. Bride was popular in the best sense with most of the girls and, like Tom Gay, a good many of the elder ones had been surprised when she had been passed over in favour of Loveday the previous term.

The Head gave them full rein for two minutes. Then she rang her bell again for silence. When she got it, she turned with a smile to the crimson Bride.

"I am very glad to see that you all approve of our choice," she said. "I expect Bride herself will have something to say to you later; but now I want to finish what I have to say myself. You all know what a busy person the Head Girl is, so this means that Bride must give up the Bank. In future, Miss O'Ryan will take charge of it.

The other arrangements are unchanged, of course; but if you need extra money for anything, you must give in your name to Miss O'Ryan on Friday night and go to draw from your Bank on Saturday morning. Do you all understand? You do? Very well, then. That is all. Stand for Grace and then clear the tables as quickly as you can or Prayers will be late. I shall have more to say to you as a school tomorrow night when the new girls will have arrived. Stand!"

They rose to their feet, and when they were standing behind their chairs she repeated the brief Latin grace they always used. Then, while the Staff filed out, the girls hurried to clear the tables before they lined up and marched quietly along for Prayers.

Having been begun in a Catholic country, the Chalet School had always numbered a goodly proportion of Catholic girls and Staff among its inhabitants, so they always divided for Prayers. The Head took the Protestant girls and now that Miss Wilson, once the co-Head, had gone to the Oberland to take charge of the branch out there, Mlle de Lachennais, the much-loved Languages mistress who had been with them since the school's early days, performed the duty for the Catholics. In England, the Protestants were naturally in the majority, so they went to Hall while the rest passed on to the big drawing room; but when Prayers were ended, they always joined up to hear anything the Head might have to say. Next day, the new girls would have arrived and she would give them her real beginning-of-term speech.

This practice was new, having been begun only the previous term. For the two terms before that, there had been trouble with the new girls. Carola Johnston, now a shining light of Lower VB, had literally gate-crashed the school last January; and Katharine Gordon had come by mistake altogether the following term, her real destination having been a Chalet School at Tanswick, a watering-place further east along the coast. Thanks to a whole series of misunderstandings, as well as the fact that her parents had been prisoners in Communist China at the time, there had been quite a good deal of worry for all concerned. However, that had been straightened out and Katharine had remained at her first school where she had made good her footing during the term. All the same, the two events had been thoroughly annoying and it had been decided that, in future, former pupils would return the day before the new ones to prevent any more happenings of the kind.

Miss Annersley knew that the girls were aching to discuss the latest turn in the affairs of the Chalet School, so she was merciful enough to keep them a bare five minutes. She welcomed them back to another term; reminded them that the school's annual Sale of Work in aid of the big Sanatorium up in the Welsh Mountains would take place at the end of the term; told them that though rules were more or less in abeyance that night, they would come into force next day and she hoped there would be many fewer conduct marks this term. Then she dismissed them, well aware that their tongues would never rest until they were all safely in bed and the bell had rung for Lights Out.

CHAPTER 4

'The One and Only Beauty!'

Clang-clang-clang! The rising-bell tolled pitilessly and Mary-Lou Trelawney, who had been dreaming of home, sat up and cleared her eyes of sleep-mists by the simple method of rubbing her clenched fists well into them. On one side of her, Gwen Jones, prefect of Leafy Dormitory, followed her example, but most people either lay buried happily under the bedclothes or else groaned loudly.

"That awful bell!" Doris Hill grumbled. "*I* don't see why we should have to get up so early. At home, I'm never called till eight o'clock. I'm sure growing girls like us need lots more sleep than we get here."

Mary-Lou heaved up her pillow and flung it at her friend with a sure aim which caused her to subside with a muffled yell.

"Don't be a lazy little lunkhead!" Miss Trelawney advised. "You don't yatter about growing girls needing sleep when it comes to bedtime, I notice."

Doris shoved the pillow off her on to the floor and sat up. "It was early morning sleep I meant," she said with dignity. "And *what* was that you called me just now, Mary-Lou?"

Mary-Lou emitted a gurgle. "'Lunkhead'," she repeated with a grin. "It's Auntie Jo's latest. I heard her use it when she came to see us for a day before she went back to Canada at Christmas. I thought it rather neat myself."

"Well, you be careful how you use it," Doris advised.

"If the prees hear it, they're safe to drop on it as slang."

"I'll risk it!" Mary-Lou retorted as she scrabbled under the bed for her slippers.

"Well, I've warned you," was Doris's response to this.

At this point Gwen, who had tumbled out and pulled on dressing gown and bedroom slippers, caught up her towels and sponge bag and made for the door, pausing to remark as she opened it. "I shan't be three minutes and you've got to strip your beds as well as dress and say your prayers, so I'd advise the lot of you to show a leg!" Then she shot off down the corridor.

Mary-Lou pattered down the dormitory to study the bath list at the far end. Then she called to the occupant of the cubicle opposite hers, "I say, Verity-Anne! Come out of it pronto! You're a first-bather this morning."

The clothes were flung back with a squeal of horror as a small girl sat up in a flurry of flaxen curls flying in wild tangles about her. "Oh, Mary-Lou, *no*! Why didn't you tell me sooner?"

"'Cos I didn't know till this minute. Why didn't you look for yourself last night?" Mary-Lou demanded severely. She and Verity-Anne were dearest of friends, but that did not mean that she was going to play Verity-Anne's Nanny.

"Who's next on the list?" that young woman demanded as she struggled frantically into her blue gown, grabbed up her towels and sponge bag and made a wild rush for the door where she tripped over her trailing waist-cord and would have fallen headlong if Doris, whose cubicle was next door, had not jumped forward and caught her.

Mary-Lou glanced at the list again. "Catt Watson, so you'd best scram. You know how she hates being kept waiting."

Verity-Anne did. She delayed no further, but scuttled

off at top speed leaving Mary-Lou to go and strip her bed for her before attending to her own.

"Matey or someone'll catch you doing that some day," Doris Hill observed. "You know we're supposed to do our own."

"Of course I do. But can you think what time the kid would get down to brekker – I mean Frühstück – if I left it to her?" Mary-Lou demanded as she tossed the underblanket over the rest of the bedclothes and then humped up the mattress so that the air could pass under it. "She'd be late every morning in life, she's so slow. Mother says she can't help it. She's naturally slow and the way she was brought up before she came here made her worse."

Doris gave it up and attended to her own bed while Mary-Lou, having seen to Verity-Anne's, raced back to her own and performed the same tasks there. That done, she was ready when the first-bath girls came back to the dormitory to take her turn. With her went Doris, Penelope Drury, who was a thorough little tomboy, and a mop-headed, wide-eyed innocent known as Christine Vincent, who took everything literally and, not unnaturally, frequently found herself in a scrape as a result. Even a year and a term of school had not yet cured her and her friends had stopped pulling her leg out of sheer boredom, for she fell for it every time.

Mary-Lou was needle-sharp in everything she did. She was back in the dormitory, pulling on her stockings before the rest returned and was calling across to Verity-Anne to ask if she had been in time, leaving the bathroom.

"Yes, thank goodness!" Verity-Anne replied in her tiny, silvery voice which nevertheless carried quite as well as her chum's more clarion notes. "I never saw her. She was late for once."

52

Mary-Lou fastened her house-slippers and proceeded to attend to the rest of her under-garments before she said, "That's not like Catt Watson. She's always on time for everything, and you were latish and take donkeys' years to do a thing – unless you didn't bath properly," she added as she slipped her arms into the sleeves of her blouse and began to button it up.

"Of course I bathed properly," Verity-Anne returned with dignity. "I always do."

. Mary-Lou chuckled. "I know it. I just wanted to see if you'd rise – and you did! I wonder what's happened to Catt, though?" she added.

"Overslept, I expect," remarked Lesley Malcolm, another of their gang.

"Coo! Won't she be mad if that's happened!" By this time Mary-Lou was fully dressed and engaged in plaiting her long, fair hair. "I say! I can't get over Loveday's leaving like that! But isn't she lucky to have gone to South America?" she added. Mary-Lou was the child of an explorer and had fully made up her mind to follow in the footsteps of her father when she was grown up.

Verity-Anne, who was struggling with a wild raffle of curls said, "I don't think so. I should hate to go to South America after what happened to Daddy. And I should have thought you would have, too, Mary-Lou."

Mary-Lou looked suddenly grave. "I know what you mean. Father was killed there. But you know what Gran says – that she always knew he'd never die in his bed. Anyway, it's a lot better for him than having to be horridly ill and suffer a lot of pain and *then* die," she added as she put away her brush and comb.

"You folk can stop yattering now," Gwen interrupted. "I'm just going to say my prayers, so shut up, all of you!"

53

And, judging by the sound, she flopped down on her knees at the same moment.

Quite half the rest followed her example and there was silence in the dormitory for the next five minutes or so. After that, it was a regular scrimmage to finish off beds, hang up pyjamas to air and leave their cubicles tidy enough to pass muster with Matron. No one had any time to worry as to why Catriona Watson (shortened unofficially by her peers to "Catt" Watson) should have been late for her bath. The subject was forgotten for the time being.

Downstairs, they went to their common room since lessons had not yet begun. Ordinarily, they would have hurried to take out books and pencil cases in readiness for work. Only those unfortunates who had early practice did anything else, once the term was fairly begun. Mary-Lou, who did not learn music, always saw to Verity-Anne's possessions, and Lesley, who also escaped, did the same by Doris. The fifth of their gang, Viola Lucy, younger sister of Julie, had begun the violin last term and so far, did only half-an-hour's practice a day, so she escaped early work at present. Verity-Anne and Doris had gone to the pianos assigned to them, but the other three congregated near the radiator in their common room and discussed Loveday's departure with eagerness. Mary-Lou had some news to impart to her chums, but as it was also Verity-Anne's news, she kept quiet about it at present.

The bell rang for Frühstück twenty minutes later and they lined up and marched smartly along to the dining room where, once she was seated before her bowl of steaming porridge, Mary-Lou glanced across at Verity-Anne who sat opposite. Verity-Anne shook her head gravely, and helped herself to milk. Frühstück was *not* the time for such news as they had to impart. Mary-Lou made a face at her – and then glanced apprehensively at Primrose Day who sat at the head of the table. Primrose, however, had noticed nothing. She was involved in an argument with Emerence Hope over the porridge. Emerence said she hated it and Primrose informed her that, hate it or not, she was to eat it and no more nonsense, either!

"But I don't *like* porridge," Emerence whined. "Why must I eat it if I don't like it?"

"You liked it well enough last term," Primrose told her calmly. "Anyhow, you either eat it or go to Matron, so take your choice."

This settled the matter, as Primrose had guessed it would. Emerence held Matron and all her works in holy horror and in any case had only objected from a wish to make a nuisance of herself as the prefect had more than half suspected. If ever a school harboured a stormy petrel, the Chalet School had one in Emerence Hope. If she could have given rein to her feelings, Primrose would cheerfully have shaken the young woman; but she was not in the habit of letting naughty Junior Middles guess that they had upset her, so Emerence knew nothing about it. Seeing that the Senior meant what she said, she picked up her spoon and, after the first two or three reluctant mouthfuls, forgot that she had said she disliked it and shovelled it in until her bowl was scraped clean. Primrose chuckled inwardly but, being a tactful creature, she said nothing. The kippers and fried bread arrived and everyone liked kippers. Primrose drew a breath of relief at having disposed of Emerence so easily and paid a little more attention to her own meal.

When breakfast was over, they had first to make their beds and then get ready for the daily walk which was only omitted when the weather was quite impossible.

This was a fine morning, with pale January sunshine and a fresh breeze. Everyone hurried as much as possible, for the quicker they were, the longer time they had for their walk. By twenty past eight, they were streaming off in long lines that seemed to take every direction. The three Third Forms and the two Seconds departed with their form mistresses on a march down the one road the Island boasted, to the most western point where they could hang over the wall at the top of the cliff and watch the waves break over the Merry Maidens, a long, knife-edged reef that ran far out to sea under the water.

The Junior Middles, escorted by the Head's secretary, Miss Dene, herself an Old Girl of the school, and Miss Lawrence, the Head of Music, went to the tiny fishing village opposite the mainland. The elder Middles set off with Miss O'Ryan, another Old Girl, and Miss Stephenson, who was resident art mistress, for Kittiwake Cove which was the school's bathing-place and camping ground in summer. The Seniors and prefects, as became such elderly folk, were left to themselves and while the Seniors decided on a walk right round the park, the prefects, with one accord, decided for the playing fields.

It was Elfie Woodward's suggestion. "Let's take a dekko at the pitches," she proposed. "If only this weather keeps up, we can have some jolly good practices this afternoon."

"And we can also see what's happened to our brook and its pond," Nancy added. "Come on, people."

They strolled away through the shrubbery, that being the nearest route to the playing fields and also giving them the chance to see their water attractions which were still very popular with them, having come into being only halfway through the previous term.

"This is my last year here," Elfie said with a sigh,

"and I'd like to make this term's matches successful.''

"It's mine, too," Madge Dawson chimed in. "I go to the Royal College in the autumn. That's why I'm not having a year at Welsen as I thought at first."

"Oh, Madge!" Bride cried. "What on earth d'you want to do that for? I thought our crowd would all be there. Do change your mind and come."

Madge shook her head. "Nothing doing! I shall be seventeen and it's time I was working really seriously at my music."

"You do three hours a day now, as well as harmony and all that rot," Bride responded. "I should call *that* taking it really seriously. What more d'you want?"

Made laughed. "How little you know, my lamb! It ought to be five or six hours now and all the rest you so rudely call 'rot' for the working hours of the day. I've only just begun on counterpoint and thorough bass. No, Bride! I'd love Switzerland, but I'm really dying to get properly to work and I'm looking forward to the College, I promise you!"

"Well, I think it's ghastly of you! I thought we'd all be going in a body and it would be so wizard being all together out there."

Tom, who had been eyeing her doubtfully, now spoke up. "Well, you wouldn't get it in any case. I'm not going myself."

"Not going? *Tom*!" It came as a chorus.

"Don't deafen me," Tom said mildly. "It won't get you any further."

"But, Tom," Nancy protested, "why aren't you coming?"

"No cash – and it's not exactly necessary, either, for the job I'm taking on."

"What do you mean? *What* job are you taking on?"

Audrey Simpson demanded severely. "I thought you really had made up your mind and were going in for teaching classics."

"Well, I'm not – or not very likely; though it might include that later on. I really couldn't say about that."

"What exactly *are* you going to do then?" Nancy queried.

Tom grinned broadly, comfortably certain that she was about to create a minor sensation. "I've fixed for keeps, you know, this time. I'm going to be a missionary."

"A *what*?" Again it came as a chorus.

"Missionary. Are you all deaf? Or don't you know what that means?"

They were silent from sheer amazement. Whatever Tom Gay had intended to do, mission work was the last thing any of them would have thought of. While most of them had made up their minds about their futures by the time they were sixteen, Tom had "swithered", to quote Primrose, choosing first one thing and then another. Bride had long made up her mind to teach. Modern languages were her delight and when her year in Switzerland was over, she meant to go to Oxford and read for her degree. Then she wanted a sojourn at the Sorbonne in Paris to gain her Bachelières-Lettres and after that, she hoped to teach in one branch or the other of the Chalet School. Elfie's idea from the time she was ten had been to be a Games and Drill mistress; and Julie Lucy was to follow in the steps of her father who was an advocate of the Guernsey Court. One or two of them would be needed at home and the rest were certain of their own minds. Only Tom had remained an enigma.

Finally, Bride spoke. "I see," she said very seriously. "It's a tremendous thing, Tom. I do hope you'll be happy in it and – and so on."

"Where do you hope to go to work?" Primrose asked.

"London," Tom replied gravely, now that the telling was off her mind.

"*London*! But – well – well I mean – why *London*?" Nancy stammered.

"You think missionaries aren't needed there?" Tom gave her a straight look. "You think again, my child. What about all this juvenile delinquency we hear so much about these days? It strikes me that we ought to look at home a bit more than we do. Oh, I know we're getting rid of all the awful slums that were a hotbed of crime; but people don't seem to be so much better for it. I've gone into it with my pater and he says he'll back me right through – university – theological college – training place. Mater doesn't much like it, but she says it's my life so I must do as I like about it. And that's what I like. I shan't change again – not now. My mind's made up."

"And not before time, either!" Bess told her severely.

"But why not have your year at Welsen with the rest of us, anyhow?" Nancy urged. "Can't you possibly?"

"As I told you, we can't afford it." Tom was always honest and saw no reason to hide the facts. "Besides, it isn't really necessary."

"Oh, but it is!" Bride cried. "If London's what you're aiming at, it's a port and look at all the foreigners who swarm there! I'm sure it would give you a bigger pull with them if you could talk French and German, at least, fluently. As for the cash part, what price the school's own scholarships? – I mean the ones the two aunts offer. I can quite well imagine you being chosen for one of them."

Tom went darkly red. "Well, I can't. And look here, Bride, you're not to say a word to either of 'em about all this. D'ye hear?"

It was Bride's turn to redden. She had been intending

59

to do that very thing. "Why on earth not?" she demanded.

"Because I say so. I *can* speak French and German after a fashion – this place has seen to *that*! – and I mean to dig in at them all this year. I can see what a big help it might be just as well as you. But Switzerland is OFF! Now that's enough about it. Come on! If we don't get cracking, we'll end up by being late for Prayers and that'd be a nice thing for the kids to chat about, wouldn't it?"

Seeing that she meant what she said, Bride gave up the argument for the moment and they went on. Presently, they were standing beside the little brook that rippled along to a wide, shallow pond whence it escaped by means of a brick-lined tunnel to the sea so that there was no danger of stagnant water. It was a very recent feature of the landscape, having happened – quite literally – when Miss Burnett, the games mistress, had leaped on to a flowerbed where she had gone to disentangle Mary-Lou from the rosebush with which she had become entangled. What no one had known was that there was a very deep well just at that spot. Heavy rains and the lapse of nearly two centuries had caused the rubble with which it had been filled up to wear loose and the rains had set going again the spring which had filled it. The old overflow had also been freed and the water had found its ancient pathway.

The first any of them had known of it – the brook, that is, had been when the present party, with the addition of Loveday Perowne, had been out for an after-tea walk about a week later. Some evil imp had put it into their heads to have a race and, in trying to leap what had hitherto been a grassy path, four of them had landed into a morass from which Julie, at any rate, had been rescued with some difficulty.

Julie herself stood gazing at the brook thoughtfully. "A pair of my shoes is down there somewhere," she remarked. "What a ghastly fright I had that night. I made sure I was done for! It was a horrid shock – such a messy way to conk out!"

"We had just as ghastly a fright," Lesley retorted with a grin. "As you say, I began to think we'd have to set up a tombstone round here for you!"

"And that, I suppose, is why you had to write a ballad about it for the mag! Heaven deliver me from my so-called friends!" Julie replied with some bitterness.

"Oh, I didn't – I promise you I didn't!" Lesley protested. "I haven't a notion where *that* came from. It arrived one morning, quite anonymously, and it was too jolly good to miss out. But I certainly didn't write it and I don't know who did."

"I could make a good guess at the culprit," Bride said with a chuckle as they moved on and crossed the plank bridge at the pond end of the brook.

"Who, then?" Julie demanded.

"Auntie Jo, of course. Oh, *I* said nothing to her about it – not with you begging and praying us all to keep it dark from everyone and then the Abbess saying we weren't to let the others know. But we weren't the only ones, you know. I'll bet most of the Staff knew the whole story. I imagine one of them told her and she promptly produced that – er – effusion. There's one comfort, Julie. I don't see how any of the kids could guess who was meant. The names were all altered, you know."

Julie, who was a sweet-tempered creature as a rule, let herself be pacified by this. "OK, then. We'll let it go at that. It would be awfully like Auntie Jo! I'll ask her about it if ever I get the chance."

"You do. You have my full permission to slay her," Bride replied.

"Yes – if she doesn't get in first. You know what she

61

is!" Julie sounded rueful. Bride's Aunt Jo was adopted aunt to all the Lucys as well as Mary-Lou, the Chesters, and the cousins of the last-named families, the Ozannes. They had all known her from babyhood and they all knew her for an incorrigible tease with her wits well about her.

"Well, you can't do anything about it at present," Primrose said. "Here we are at the playing fields. The hockey pitch looks in pretty good shape, doesn't it? I should think we could manage a practice this afternoon, Elf."

Elfie cast a knowledgeable eye over the pitch and nodded. "Yes; that'll be right enough. And the netball courts are En-Tout-Cas, so we needn't worry about them. Let's take a dekko at the lacrosse field."

They had just time to decide that a lacrosse practice would also be possible before Bess glanced at her watch and gave an exclamation. "I say! We must fly or we'll be frantically late for Prayers and wouldn't the kids crow! All the prefects, including the Head Girl late! Come on!"

They set off at a rapid pace which quickened to a run when they heard voices which warned them that their juniors were returning. However, they just arrived before the rest came streaming along, by which time the prefects were tidy and their usual dignified selves, even if they were rather more flushed than usual.

The morning was spent in settling back to work and seeing that they had all the stationery they needed. The authorities were merciful, seeing what a fine day it was, and lessons ended half an hour earlier than usual to give them time for a run in the garden before Mittagessen. As Miss Annersley said in the Staff room, "We may expect plenty of bad weather this term, so let them get all the fresh air they can now. They've had very wet holidays."

After Mittagessen, the various games practices were

duly held and they all came back to the school for four o'clock tea, healthily tired and with enormous appetites. Preparation for an hour followed and then they went upstairs to change into evening frocks. Abendessen would be earlier tonight in consideration of the new girls. Even the prefects were anxious to know about them. During a period with them that morning, the Head had hinted at a rather surprising turn of affairs and they were curious to know what it was. As for the Juniors and the Middles, they always regarded the advent of fresh people with deep interest.

"I wonder how many there are and what they're like?" Mary-Lou said as she wriggled into her regulation brown velvet with its muslin collar and cuffs. She yanked free her fair plaits which dangled nearly to her waist and fastened the dress up before she continued. "Let's hope we haven't anything more like Emerence last term. Wasn't she the absolute *edge*?"

"Doesn't look as if she'll be a lot better this term," Doris Hill remarked, wandering along to have her dress fastened. "Do me up, Mary-Lou, and I'll do your Kenwigses for you again. They're squint as usual!"

A chuckle went round Leafy at this. Last term the girls of Upper IVA had read an abridged version of *Nicholas Nickleby* for prose literature and, with one accord, her chums had christened Mary-Lou's plaits "Kenwigses" when they saw the picture of that immortal family.

"Thanks a million," that young lady said as she kindly buttoned up her friend's back. "I knew they were. I simply can't get them straight by myself."

"How do you manage at home?" someone asked.

"Oh, Clem does them then." Mary-Lou pulled her towel round her shoulders and sat down to let Doris

63

brush out the long fair hair, part it neatly and begin to plait it up again.

"Aren't you Leafyites ready *yet*?" came Bride's voice from the doorway. "You'll be jolly late if you don't hurry up."

"We're all ready but Mary-Lou, and Doris is doing her hair again for her," Gwen explained.

Bride came striding to the cubicle. "All right, Doris. Run along and I'll see to it." She set to work on the shining locks. "Can't you plait your own hair *yet*, Mary-Lou?"

"Only if I have the pigtails down my front – and then they get into everything," Mary-Lou explained, handing over her ribbon.

Bride took it and tied up the plaits across the back of her head. "That will be better for you than having them dangling all over the place now they've grown such a length." She turned Mary-Lou round and inspected the result. "Yes; it looks all right that way."

"It'll be wizard having them tied up like this," Mary-Lou replied. "They're a sickening nuisance, but Gran won't let me have it bobbed though I did ask."

Bride laughed. "They look very nice. If you'll only take enough trouble with it to keep it decently brushed and combed, you'll have lovely hair, Mary-Lou. Put your brush and comb away now – hi! Into the bag, first, you careless monkey! Do you want Matey after you?"

Mary-Lou grinned. "Matey'll be up to the eyes with new girls tonight." She pushed brush and comb into their bag and laid it in its proper drawer.

"I shouldn't rely too much on that," Bride told her from a long experience of Matron. "She's never too busy to spot untidiness as you ought to know."

"Oh, well, you've got to take a chance, sometimes,"

Mary-Lou retorted before she went scuttering off, leaving the Head Girl to follow at her leisure.

Bride laughed to herself as she switched off the light and sauntered downstairs. "It isn't cheek – it's just Mary-Lou," she murmured to herself. At the foot of the stairs, she was met by two excited people who had plainly been waiting for her and stopped to demand what had happened.

"Oh, Bride! You wait till you see our very latest in the way of girls!" giggled Betsy Lucy, sister of Julie. "We really have got *it* this time."

"What on earth are you talking about?" Bride demanded. "No; don't tell me here. Come into this room first. Rules are rules, even if we've acquired the Spotted Wonder from Barnum and Bailey's for a pupil. Now then; why all the excitement? And do try to stop giggling!"

She had ushered them into a small form room and switched on the light. Now she sat down on one of the desks and looked at them. "Well? What have we got?"

"A BEAUTY!" Betsy told her, all in capital letters.

Bride opened her eyes. "A *what*? Do talk sense, Betsy."

"But I am!" Betsy protested. "That's exactly what she is. What's more, she means us all to know it as well as she does."

Bride turned to her companion with an air of resigned patience. "What is all this in aid of, Katharine? See if *you* can give me a saner answer."

Katharine Gordon giggled again. "But it's just as Betsy says," she protested in her turn. "That's exactly what she is and from the way she talks and behaves, Betsy's right in saying that she means us to be sure of it."

"She's pretty enough." Betsy had got over her giggles now and spoke with a certain judicial weightiness. "In fact, she is *very* pretty – all fairy-tale golden curls and big blue

65

eyes and pink-and-white face. But Blossom Willoughby is every bit as pretty, if not more so, and if Sybil Russell were here, this new kid couldn't touch her."

"If you come to that, if your own Peggy was here, *she* could give her spades and aces and beat her hands down," Katharine chimed in. "But she *is* rather a picture. Only Peggy is rather special. I never saw Sybil you know."

"You will next term. They're coming back after Easter," Bride said.

"Thank goodness for that!" Betsy exclaimed. "But honestly, Bride, I never in all my life saw anyone so stuck on herself as this new girl is! She can't pass a mirror without admiring herself in it! In fact," she wound up, "she quite obviously thinks that she's the one and only BEAUTY in the world!"

CHAPTER 5

"This is Diana!"

As soon as she decently could, Bride stared round the dining room when they had all sat down after grace. She had to admit that Betsy and Katharine had roused her curiosity and she was only sorry that Lesley Pitt was seated at the other end of the table and much too far away for any confidences. There had been no time before Abendessen, either.

She knew where the new girl was likely to be sitting and glanced across at the two tables beyond where most of the Lower VA sat. She caught a glimpse of Betsy between Elinor Pennell and Marjorie Jenkyns. On the opposite side was Katharine with Hilary Wilson and Madge Watson, her own particular friends on either side of her, while three seats further on was the Blossom Willoughby that Betsy had mentioned. Then she caught sight of a head of golden curls gleaming under the electric light and decided that this must be The Beauty of the Senior Middles' chatter.

"She *would* be sitting with her back to me!" Bride thought disgustedly.

"*Bride*!" It was Lesley's voice. "Do wake up! What on earth are you dreaming about? I've spoken to you *five* times!"

Bride started and came back to her own table, turning red as she saw that the others were all looking at her in rather startled fashion. "Sorry! I'm afraid I wasn't thinking," she apologized. "What is it?"

"I only suggested that it might be as well to go on with your soup. It'll be stone cold if you leave it much longer, and however nice cold soup may be in summer, I can't think of anything much more revolting at this time of year!"

Bride laughed. "How right you are! Many thanks!" and she began on her soup without more ado.

Julie Lucy, who sat at the Head Girl's right hand, gave her a smile. "If you're feeling stunned by the number of new girls this term," she murmured, "I can't say I blame you. We seem to have collected a regular mob! It might be last!"

Bride nodded, finished her soup and laid down her spoon just as the maids began to clear the plates away. "Have *we* been honoured with any, do you know?" she asked, looking swiftly round the table.

"Hardly likely. You know they don't like new girls beyond the Upper Fourth," Julie replied. "Oh, I know we often get folk for Lower Fifth, but never at this time of year; and no one appreciates them at any time."

"No," Bride agreed. "A new girl in our part of the school is a distinct rara avis."

"*Must* you use Latin while we're eating?" complained Rosalie Browne who possessed the distinction of being the prettiest girl in the Sixths.

Bride, while laughingly disclaiming any intention of using Latin, thought to herself that if Miss Golden Head in the Fifth could beat Rosalie, she must be something out of the common, for the latter, with her cloudy fair hair, perfectly featured face and deep blue eyes was a lovely creature. Bride herself had few claims to beauty, and Tom, sitting at the other side of Rosalie, was downright plain, "But if this new kid can beat our form lag for looks

– or Julie, either – she must be a complete howler!" Bride thought slangily as she attended to a plate of scrambled eggs.

After that, she put the question out of her mind and joined in the talk about what matches they had in the near future.

When the egg plates had been collected and they were all busy with stewed gooseberries and custard, Valerie Arnott, who was seated halfway down the table, suddenly remarked, "I say! Julie's right about the new girls. I've been counting all I can see and, believe it or not, there are *eleven*!"

"Aren't there some at the other tables, Bride? I can't see behind me."

Bride nodded. "About a dozen at least, I should think. It's on the odd side, isn't it? I wonder what's happened? Three or four is our Easter term limit as a general rule. And that's not to say that there aren't a few at the lower tables, either," she added.

Elfie Woodward – the Sixth Forms all sat together for Abendessen – laughed. "I imagine some school or other has conked out and we've got a backwash as a result. I wonder if any of them are any good at lacrosse?" Loveday's defection was still worrying her seriously.

"You can find that out later on," Bride said. "I wonder if you're right?"

Julie, who had laid down her spoon with her fruit half-finished, joined in. "I wonder what school it could be? Has anyone heard of anything?"

No one had. Meantime, Bride had noticed her friend's face and turning, said in low voice, "What's wrong? You're looking a trifle green."

"Just a touch of tummy pain," Julie said in the same

69

undertone. "Don't say anything, Bride. It'll go in a minute. It's better already – though I don't think I'll risk any more fruit. It's on the cold side."

Bride gave her a quick look. "D'you think that's what it is? Not the kind of pains you had in the summer term?"

"Tummy pains are all alike," Julie said shortly. "Don't fuss!"

Bride had to subside but she did murmur, "Better do something about that fruit, then, if you don't want Matey asking questions."

Julie promptly spread it about her plate and laid her spoon across it and, as Matron was exceedingly rushed with the influx of new pupils, she escaped, which was a pity, as it turned out later.

By this time everyone else had finished, and Miss Annersley, standing, told them that when they had cleared the tables, Prayers would be followed by a few words from herself and then the Junior Middles and Juniors would go up to bed. The rest of the Middles would have another hour and the Seniors would go at their usual time.

"Grace!" she said when she had finished this, and the school rose and stood behind its chairs for grace which was followed as usual by the ordered rush to clear the tables and leave them ready for the maids to see to Frühstück. Bride, taking charge as a matter of course, noticed that while most of the new girls followed the example of the others, two or three of them made little or no attempt, and the Beauty and another girl seemed to have vanished as soon as the mistresses had left the room.

"This must be seen to," mused Bride as she watched Mary-Lou going the rounds, gathering up spare spoons and forks. "Mary-Lou, do look where you're going! And don't try to scrabble the things together like that or you'll scratch them. Pick them up properly."

Mary-Lou who had collided with a dark-haired, grey-eyed girl of her own age who was carrying a water jug in either hand, replied meekly, "Yes, Bride," before she muttered to the other, "Why'd you barge into me like that?"

"Sorry, but I didn't see you coming. Wait till I set these down and I'll help you," the other, who was Catriona Watson, mumbled in reply.

She set the jugs on the table and came to help, but Bride interfered sharply. "No you don't! Mary-Lou may do her own work. If you've finished yours, trot off to your common room. The bell for Prayers will ring in a moment."

Catriona gave the Head Girl a wide-eyed glance and hurriedly pushed the cutlery she had managed to collect into Mary-Lou's hand before she departed.

Bride was now engaged with Viola Lucy who was dropping tumblers, one into the other, in a way calculated to cause a bad smash sooner or later, and saw neither Catriona's look nor the anguished reproach she got from Mary-Lou before that young woman hurriedly picked up the rest of the forks and spoons and finally deposited them through the buttery hatch.

By the time the Head Girl had finished with Vi, the rest of the work was done and almost at once the bell rang and Bride left the room and made for Hall where she suddenly realized that she must take the very public seat of the Head Girl and also read the passage chosen from the New Testament for that night. No one had ever accused Bride Bettany of being shy with any truth, but she came very near to it just then. The night before, she had sat in her old seat, and the Head herself usually read in the mornings; but there was no escaping it now. Blushing to the roots of her smooth brown hair which she wore in a straight, short bob, Bride made her way to the chair and sat down. It would have been a good chance to identify the Beauty, but she was "feeling her position" to quote the school's favourite sayings on such occasions, too much to think of it and a moment later the Head entered with the Protestant Staff and there was no opportunity.

When the two divisions in the school were all seated in Hall after Prayers, the Head rose to make her proper beginning-of-term speech.

"First," she said, her deep, beautiful voice reaching to the farthest end of the great room, "I want to welcome all our new pupils and wish them happiness in their *new* Chalet School." – Several of the elder girls gasped at this – "I have heard about your former arrangements, girls, and I'm afraid you will find many differences here, but I am sure you will soon be accustomed to us and our methods and settle in comfortably. At any rate, everyone will try to help you, so it will be your own faults if you do not. And here, I think, I must explain to the rest what has happened." She smiled at the gathering. "Girls, I'm sure you all remember the Chalet School at Tanswick. Last term, its new headmistress died after a long illness and as there is no one to carry it on, it has had to close. We are fairly near Tanswick, so quite a number of its pupils have come on here. Luckily, thanks to the arrangements we were able to make for the Kindergarten and the First and Second Forms last term, we have plenty of room for them. This is, as some of you may remember, the second time the school has had to come to the rescue. The first was when we were in the Tirol and took in St Scholastika's from the other side of the Tiernsee. That proved a great success and we look to all of you to make this second version an equally great one."

A low murmur of agreement rose as she paused. She

72

smiled at them again and then went on: "Naturally, thirty-nine new girls has meant changes in our old arrangements. For one thing, we have had to rearrange forms, especially in the Middle School and you will find, as a result, that we now have Upper IVB – a new form. The new form lists are pinned up on the notice board and you can look at them presently. I hope those girls who find they have been moved up will do their best to work well with their new forms."

This remark caused a minor sensation. Quite a number of folk were dying to tear off to the notice board. However, discipline was good in the school, so beyond a little stirring and a few audible gasps, they remained quietly seated to hear what else was to come.

Miss Annersley knew all about it of course, and she had mercy on them.

"Just a word or two more," she said; and all eyes were fixed on her again. "The new mistress for the new form will be Miss Moore who is coming from Canada and will be here tomorrow. You will find which is your form room in the morning and, as you are in someone else's room, you will also find that there is a kind of General Post before most of you. You must have finished and settled in by ten.

"Now I will just mention that this is the term we hold our annual Sale in aid of the Sanatorium. I don't know how many of you know that there is a new branch opened in the Oberland. It is a small affair at present, but Sir James Russell and Dr Maynard, who are responsible for it, hope to extend it very soon. In order to help them, we propose to send them the results of the Sale, so please, all of you, do your best to equal last year's results if you can't beat them as I hope.

"Finally – and this, I think, will please you all, we

73

have been able to make arrangements for you to use the public swimming baths at Carnbach on three mornings in the week. This will mean that a great many more of you should be able to pass the swimming tests as soon as next term begins and so enjoy boating and swimming throughout the term – weather permitting, I'd better say."

They were dismissed after that and Miss Lawrence, Head of the Music staff, struck up a bright march and they had to leave Hall for their common rooms, while the mistresses went to the study for coffee and gossip.

"Well!" Bride ejaculated when at last they were free to comment. "This looks like being an exciting term! Come along; let's go and see who, if anyone, has been honoured by promotion to our company."

"That's not very likely," Bess Herbert observed. "Still, I suppose we might as well go and see the fun – for fun there will be, believe me!"

"You mean a riot?" Primrose struck in.

" 'Nay, Sire, a revolution'," Bride quoted. "Some of those infants had their eyes nearly popping out of their heads while the Abbess was talking."

"If they make *that* noise, they won't have any heads left for their eyes to pop out of," Julie declared with little heed for grammar. "Just *listen* to that row!"

"We must put a stop to that, anyhow!" Bride strode forward at the head of the others and stalked into Hall where a struggling mob surrounded the notice board.

"Quieter, please!" she ordered in her most masterful tones. "Do you *want* to get into a row as early as this?"

A certain quietness came over the mob and into it dropped like a stone in a pool, the excited remark, "*Ohh*! I'm moved up to Upper IVA and so are you, Doris, Vi, Gwen, Lesley *and* Catt! Isn't that simply *smashing*!"

"A little less slang, if you please, Mary-Lou!" Bride

remarked causing Mary-Lou to give a squeal. "Fines begin next week, remember. I suppose you would rather have a *little* pocket money each week?" From the vantage point of her five foot eight, she surveyed the lists over the heads of the younger girls. "Now keep quiet, if you can, and I'll read out the promotions and then you'll know where you are. Lilias Robertson, you come up to Lower VI. Congrats!"

A smothered outburst of clapping brought crimson to the cheeks of Lilias, a very quiet, retiring girl from Upper VA, and Bride, in pity, went on with the removes.

"Clem Barrass, Moira Damer and – let me see – yes, Nora Penley, you're in Upper VA. There are five names that are new to me as well."

"What about our lot, Bride?" Carola Johnston asked anxiously.

Bride grinned at her and looked again. "Quite an emigration from *your* form. Here you are! Amy Dunne, Betsy Lucy, Lala Winterton, Jean Ackroyd." She paused and Carola went pink with disappointment. Bride chuckled loudly and added, "Oh, and Carola Johnston. Did I miss you out, Carola? Dear me!"

"Oh, Bride, you do tease!" Carola declared, laughing happily.

"Shouldn't be in such a hurry," Bride told her severely. Then she changed countenance. "Sorry, Zoë; I *have* missed you out. You go up, too."

Judging by her expression, Zoë was left in the seventh Heaven and the Head Girl turned to announce that Katharine Gordon, Hilary Wilson and Blossom Willoughby were now members of Lower VA, which caused that trio of chums to grab at each other excitedly before they joined the stream of girls leaving Hall and went to their own quarters to rejoice wildly. Most of their set had been moved up the previous term and it was a great thrill to know that they were to be together once more.

The crowds round the board were very much thinner now, for all the Upper IVA girls had departed after hearing Mary-Lou's announcement. Bride glanced round those remaining, reminded them that a noise would bring down authority on them and left them to finish the lists for themselves.

Some of the prefects departed for the prefects' room; one or two others had odd jobs to do elsewhere and Bess went off to the library where the new books, ordered last term, were waiting to be catalogued and stamped before being put into the shelves. Lesley and Audrey went with her and Bride was left with Nancy, one of her special chums, to stroll along the corridor in the direction of the Sixth Form's common room with the amiable intention of welcoming Lilias in their midst. Elfie had gone to make out tentative practice lists for the next day's games since there was no match in the afternoon.

As the two prefects reached the door of that dedicated to the four Fifth Forms, it opened and Betsy Lucy came out, followed by a girl whom Bride had no difficulty in connecting with Betsy's description before Abendessen. She pursed up her lips in a soundless whistle when she saw her, for Betsy had not exaggerated about her looks and this latest addition to the Chalet School was something out of the ordinary there.

"Oh, Bride," Betsy exclaimed, "this is Diana Skelton, one of the new girls. She's to try our form for the present. Diana, this is Bride Bettany, our Head Girl. Diana was at Tanswick, Bride."

Bride gave the new girl a smile. "Hello!" she said. "Hope you'll enjoy being in our Chalet School, once you've got used to it."

"Oh, how d'you do?" Diana replied languidly. "I don't know, I'm sure. This seems to be so *very* different! Quite other ideas!"

Nancy's eyebrows were disappearing into her sunny brown hair, but Bride kept her countenance, though she was inwardly as startled as her friend. "You'd expect that, wouldn't you?" she said. "I don't suppose any two schools are absolutely alike. Still, you'll soon be used to us. Betsy doing sheepdog to you? You're in luck! She's quite good at it." Then she nodded pleasantly at the pair and led Nancy off.

"Who on *earth* does she think she is?" the latter burst out as soon as they were out of hearing. "She's out-of-the-way-pretty, but *did* you notice her voice?"

Bride nodded. The new girl's voice had struck her unpleasantly, for it was rather high-pitched and with a distinctly cockney accent. "Let's hope they don't all talk like that, for it seems to me we're going to have our work cut out this term. Didn't they have free discipline and so on at the Tanswick place?"

"I've heard so." Nancy giggled. "They're in for a few shocks here, aren't they? There aren't many rules, but those there are have to be kept or else –!"

"Oh dear!" Bride sighed. "Why on earth did Loveday have to go prancing off to South America just *this* term? I don't fancy being Head Girl in any circumstances. To have to take it over with an influx of oddities who don't know what keeping rules means won't make it a picnic!"

Nancy laughed. "My dear girl, you'll do it as well as anyone. But I'm more than thankful the Head didn't pitch on me," she added.

"You're so comforting," Bride said plaintively. "Honestly, Nancy, I hope you'll manage to avoid having any of your wilder ideas this term. I simply must have all the backing I can get."

"Don't worry; we'll all back you up," Nancy declared. "All the same, I shouldn't wonder if you were right – in one way."

"How do you mean?" Bride demanded. "I'd have said it was in every way."

Nancy stood still, her hands in her blazer pockets, her brows drawn into straight line as she frowned before she said, "Well, I may be wrong, but I rather fancy I've heard that the Tanswick place was one of those awful snob shows. If that is really the case, we're in for squalls, for they won't agree with *our* ideas one little bit."

"Mother's little comforter! I suppose you can't think of anything else to make me think this term looks like being the worst ever?"

Nancy's brows relaxed and mischief danced in her hazel eyes as she replied demurely, "Oh, I could think of quite a number – if you want it, that is. But if you ask me, I'd say we'd better live from day to day and tackle the troubles as they come. There's one thing, anyhow, Bride."

"What's that? At the moment I can't see one ray of light in the whole set-up."

"Well, we do know what to look for. We can be on the watch for any silly snobbishness and squash it good and hearty before our own crowd are infected."

Bride's face relaxed. "That reminds me; I can think of another."

"Oh, what?"

"That Mary-Lou and Co. are in Upper IVA and, in any case, always do lead most of that gang by the nose. I defy anyone to turn our Mary-Lou into a snob or Vi Lucy, or Lesley Malcolm or any of that crew. They're as wicked a set as ever annoyed a deserving body of prefects; but, thank goodness, they've never been tainted with *that* particular disease and are never likely to be if I know them."

Nancy chuckled. "How right you are! Young Vi's special friend at home is Mellie de Garis whose father is a no-good fisherman when he's anything. As for Mary-Lou, I'd as soon suspect Tom of snobbery as her!"

"And the fifths have Betsy and her pals. I begin to feel a little happier on that score," Bride said solemnly. "But this free discipline question is going to be a teaser. Somehow, I don't see that kid Diana What's-her-name knuckling under if she takes it into her head that she doesn't want to keep law and order. As that young cousin of yours remarked to me, I never saw anyone so obviously stuck on herself before. And we can't hope for much help in that line from the kids. Half of them seem to think that rules are only made to be broken!"

"I know." Nancy thought a moment. Then she said shrewdly, "Just the same, I'm not so sure that you aren't crossing bridges we may never come to. Mary-Lou and Co. mayn't be too fond of keeping the rules, but they do think quite a lot of their school and they'll be up in arms at once if any newcomer starts crying down our rules and institutions. I admit," she added, "that that won't make for peace. But it will probably mean that that crowd will be a little more careful about their own doings from sheer pride."

Bride nodded thoughtfully. "Yes; that's so – very much so. Oh well, it's all in a lifetime, I suppose! We must just be on the alert and ready to squash anything that needs it. And now, we've been breaking rules ourselves long enough, I fancy. It's a good job our room is in this corridor and not where it used to be or we'd have had to call this conversation off ages ago. As it is, you've helped me to see my way a bit. I don't feel quite so ready to go into the garden and eat worms as I did before."

"And *that's* a good thing!" Nancy said emphatically as they turned into the prefects' room. "Hello, everyone! What do you think of our latest?"

CHAPTER 6

Trouble Begins

"Hurry up, Marian! You've still got to strip your bed and say your prayers!"

Marian Tovey, one of the girls from the Tanswick Chalet School, stopped brushing her hair to turn and stare at Gwen Jones who, as prefect of Leafy dormitory, was supposed to be responsible for seeing that everyone left it on time and, furthermore, left it according to Matron's ideas of neatness and hygiene. Marian was the only newcomer to the dormitory for the authorities, knowing the regime of the Tanswick school, had seen fit to scatter its ex-pupils as widely as possible.

So far as the Juniors were concerned, this policy was bound to be a success, since most youngsters follow the rest of their clan. It was with the Seniors and Senior Middles that the Head and Staff expected any trouble. Some of these girls had been three or four years at the other school and had absorbed its principles thoroughly. It was to be anticipated that they would dislike the firm discipline exercised at St Briavel's and Miss Annersley had taken those over fifteen with great reluctance.

"I wouldn't have minded a whole bunch of under-elevens," she had confided to her secretary when they were talking it over. "Unfortunately, they had no actual Juniors. Eleven was the youngest. The eleven-to-four-teens will settle down all right in a few weeks' time.

Their little playmates will see to that! It's the girls of fifteen-plus and sixteen that are the snag."

Miss Dene had agreed with this dictum. "All the same," she had added, "there are some who haven't been there so long and have come from the more usual type of school. They should be all right and the rest must just try to realize that our ideas are different and come into line."

It had been left at that, since there was nothing else they could do.

Marian Tovey was fifteen-and-a-half, a year older than any other girl in either her form or the dormitory. It had been hoped that she could be placed in one of other of the Lower Fifths where she would have been with girls of her own age, but her entrance papers had put that idea out of the question. In fact, it was found that, with very few exceptions, the girls from the Tanswick school were a good year behind their contemporaries on the Island. Free discipline does not make for hard work unless the pupils are born students and the general tone of the Tanswick school had not made for that.

Now, at Gwen's remark, Marian shrugged her shoulders. "What a fuss! As if anyone bothered about bed-stripping and prayers nowadays! If Matron doesn't like the way I leave my cubey, she can see to it herself!"

"I don't advise you to try it on," Gwen said firmly. "I don't know what your other Matron was like, but ours is a holy terror! Don't be silly, Marian! Where's the point in getting yourself into a hectic row at the very beginning? It won't get you anywhere and Matey will be stricter than ever about your cubey. You don't want to be dragged out of Frühstück to go and clear up, do you?"

"Oh, forget it! You kids are such *good* little girls! I'm sure she'll quite enjoy a change in that way!"

At this point Mary-Lou shoved her oar in. "That's

where you're wrong!" she snapped, glaring at Marian. "We're *not* good little girls!" – This last rather as if goodness were something to be avoided at all costs – "You needn't think that! But we *have* got some sense and we don't go out of our way to break rules!"

Mary-Lou had been a small, sturdily-built creature, but last term she had taken to growing with the vim she had put into most of her doings and was becoming a leggy young thing. Even so, she was still half a head shorter than Marian who looked down at her with a superior smile as she remarked, "My dear, good kid –"

"I'm not your dear good kid!" This was more than flesh and blood could stand. "Don't forget that you're in the same form as me and I'm nearly two years younger!"

It was Marian's turn to flush and look angry. She was a very proud girl and it had been a real shock to her to find herself relegated to a Fourth Form where the average age was less than fourteen. At Tanswick, she had been in the Fifth Form and with girls of her own age. Mary-Lou had touched on a sore point and Marian would not forgive her easily.

"Stop argy-bargying, you two!" Gwen cried at this juncture. "Mary-Lou, go back to your own cubey and finish if you haven't done it already. As for you, Marian, I've warned you and I'm not doing it again. The only thing is if you don't keep the rules here you'll be for it! That's all!"

With this last remark she marched off up the dormitory to go and make sure that Verity-Anne was managing, and an uncomfortable silence fell on the room where people attended to last-minute oddments before swinging up their curtains and going to line up beside the door.

Left to herself, Marian finished her hair and dropped her brush and comb into the drawer. Then she looked at her tumbled bed irresolutely. Perhaps she had better strip it. As that girl Gwen had said, there was no use having a row at the beginning. She hauled off the clothes and dumped them down on the chair. Then, satisfied that she had done all that was required of her, she tossed up her curtains and left the cubicle, ignoring Gwen's hint about her prayers. She made for the door, but was speedily brought up short by half a dozen people who told her to go to the back of the line already formed.

"Oh, rot!" she said rudely. "I'm not going to bother about all that tosh!"

Before they could stop her, she had shot out into the corridor where a very tall girl was standing, watching the people from Wallflower march sedately through the corridor to the head of the stairs were Elfie Woodward was standing to see them down to the hall.

Tom Gay, seeing a Middle come dashing out of Leafy and preparing to break through the neat line filing out of Wallflower on the opposite side of the corridor, made a long arm and caught her back.

"Here! Where do you think you're going?" she demanded. "Go back to your dormitory and join on the line there. Prudence Dawbarn!" she raised her voice, still holding Marian. "Stop shoving like that! Either march properly or go to the back of the line and take an order mark."

"Sorry, Tom," replied Prudence in a tone that was quite impenitent. She was a twelve-year-old with an innocent face that completely belied her character.

"I should think so!" Tom retorted. "March on, Wallflower! Now then – what is your name, by the way?"

Marian had enough sense to know that impudence and defiance would not help her here, so she muttered, "Marian Tovey!" in a sulky tone.

"Oh! Well, Marian, we've too many people in this place for any girl to be allowed to go dashing about in that style. If you think it over, you'll see what I mean," Tom said mildly. "Go and tail on to your own file and march downstairs with the rest properly. You'll have plenty of chances of ramping about outside."

Seeing nothing else for it, Marian went back to the dormitory and tailed on after Penelope Drury, a sullen look on her face. Tom waited until she was there and then spoke again. "Who's prefect in Leafy this term?"

Gwen came forward. "Me, please, Tom."

"Well, please see that any new girl in your charge knows the rules in future," the big prefect told her severely. "They haven't had time to learn them all yet, and they won't manage it, either, if you dorm prees don't help."

Gwen took the rebuke meekly enough, but the rest were indignant. Meaning looks were directed at Marian who took no notice of them, so no less a person than Verity-Anne spoke up.

"Please, Tom," she said in the tiny, silvery voice that exactly matched her fairy-like appearance, "Gwen *did* tell Marian, but I – I don't think she quite took it in, perhaps."

Tom had not been blind to the behaviour of the inmates of Leafy, but all she said was, "Very well, Verity-Anne. Gwen, I beg your pardon. I hadn't understood. Now that's finished! Are you all ready? Forward – *march*!"

They marched off smartly, Marian following at the tail end and feeling furious with everyone – including herself. Tom had no right to be there! And who was she, anyhow, to give orders? She glared at the tall prefect as she passed, but Tom was keeping a watchful eye on Pansy dormitory and took no notice. Downstairs, and once they were safely in their form room, however, Leafy took care to let the new girl know what they thought of her for letting Gwen in for that undeserved reprimand.

"Why didn't you tell Tom that Gwen *had* told you?" Christine Vincent demanded indignantly. "You can't say she didn't, 'cos we all heard her."

"It's no business of yours!" Marian flared out angrily.

"It's all of our business," Mary-Lou informed her. "You let Gwen in for a ticking-off she need never have had. Only that it's the beginning of the term, Tom might have given it to her in the neck! She *had* told you and you ought to have had the decency to say so!"

"Oh, what a lot of silly *fuss*!" Marian cried furiously. "I never in all my life heard of a school where so much fuss was made over trifles!"

"What's it all about?" Vi Lucy wanted to know. She was in another dormitory, much to the disgust of her chums; but Matron was far too wary a bird to let the entire gang share the same dormitory.

Half a dozen voices promptly told her and a look of deep disgust crossed her charming little face. "What a low-down thing to do!" she exclaimed. "It's the sort of sneaky thing only an outsider would do!"

"It *wasn't*!" Marian cried desperately. "I – I didn't have time to say anything. Someone barged in before I could get round to it."

"*That's* not true!" Mary-Lou declared. "We gave you plenty of time."

"How dare you call me a liar?" Marian demanded, glaring at Mary-Lou who gave her back glare for glare.

"I didn't say that. But if the cap fits, wear it!" was the smart riposte.

Just what would have happened next, no one could

ever say. The Junior Middles did not mean to bait Marian, but she had sinned against their code and then tried to brave it out. That was something they were not prepared to stand: neither would her pride allow her to do the obvious thing – tell Gwen she was sorry and let it go.

However, there came an interruption.

"Now then, you folk," said a voice from the door, "haven't you anything better to do than stand there nattering together? Where are your books and pencil cases?"

They turned to find Primrose Day standing looking at them with a calmly inquiring air that none of them liked. As the desks were innocent of anything, they had nothing to say. Meekly, they went to their lockers to hunt for Bibles, scribblers and pencil cases which they placed on their desks in an uneasy silence. Primrose surveyed the results of their work and then desired to know if that was *all* they would need for the first half of the morning.

"Our arithmetics," Beth Lane, form prefect said, "but we're to have new ones and Miss Slater said she would bring them to the lesson when she came."

"Very well, then. Sit down in your places and make sure that your pencils are all sharpened ready. Has the ink monitress seen to the inkwells?"

Sylvia Worth who was ink monitress said that she had, so with a reminder that the bell for Frühstück would go in a minute or two, Primrose left them. When she had gone, Beth turned to Marian.

"We'll wash all that business out," she said firmly. "This is Marian's first term so she must have her chance. You've got to be fair, remember."

"Oh, *I* don't care." Marian declared in a lordly way.

This was hardly true. Besides herself, there were seven

87

more girls from Tanswick in the form and three of them at least were looking at her in a way she didn't like. The other four were tittering among themselves at the moment. Marian had not been a great favourite at her old school and they were not very sorry that she had been put in her place like this.

What happened during lessons, however, put the whole affair out of the heads of the eight. For one thing, they discovered that work at *this* Chalet School really meant work. There was no slacking permitted during lessons and the preparation awarded them nearly stunned them; especially when they learned that it *must* be given in at the proper time and not just when it suited them.

The first lesson that morning was Old Testament with the Head. Upper IVA had "done" Joshua last term and they were to read Judges this and revise both books during the summer term. Those who knew what to expect sat in their desks with Bibles opened at the right place, scribblers and pencils ready in case Miss Annersley should give them any notes to take down, and awaited her coming. When she came in, most of them stood up smartly. Hilary Bennett, Maureen Grey and Ursula Vane followed their example next moment, but the other five got to their feet after the rest and they did it noisily and untidily. Miss Annersley said nothing, though she eyed them thoughtfully. She opened her Bible, told them that they would begin to read the first chapter verse about and requested Vi in the front row to begin.

Thanking her stars for an easy verse, Vi complied glibly and the reading passed on to Lesley Malcolm. There was no trouble until they came to the sixth verse when Anne Gordon was pleased to giggle aloud at the fate that befell Adoni-Bezek. The Head glanced at her.

"That strikes you as funny?" she asked quietly. "It was

considered one of the worst humiliations of those days. A man robbed of his thumbs could hold no weapon of war and so was harmless. If his big toes went, he was lame for life. You can understand that his enemies had no more to fear from him."

"But wasn't it a horribly savage thing to do, Miss Annersley?" Beth asked in shocked tones.

"From our point of view, yes. But you must remember that those were savage times. As you will see when you read on, Adoni-Bezek had done the same thing to his own prisoners. Go on, please, Mary-Lou."

Mary-Lou read the next verse with great effect. Anne herself was next and they went on quietly until it came to Marian's turn. She had the verse dealing with Caleb's offer of his daughter Ach-sah to the man who conquered Kirjath-sepher. Reading aloud was no gift of hers and she was apt to be careless over her words. Even the Head had to bite her lips when Marian bestowed on the lady the startling name of "Atchoo!" and the form laughed outright.

"'Ak-sah', Marian," Miss Annersley said gravely, though she was dying to join the laughter. "C-H in Hebrew was pronounced like our K."

Marian darted an angry glance at the girls nearest her, but the Head was the Head, especially here. She repeated the name properly and finished the verse with a black scowl, but that was all. The next girl continued and they read on until the chapter ended – with a good deal of help from Miss Annersley over the more difficult names. Then they were told to close their Bibles and see how much they could remember of the chapter.

It should have been fairly easy for Miss Annersley was careful to frame her questions in the most helpful form. Most of the former members of the form got on well.

Those who had just come up also managed the majority of their questions, though Mary-Lou was floored when asked to name two of the tribes who did not drive the Canaanites completely from their midst. Of the new girls, only Hilary Bennett made any sort of showing, none of the rest seeming to know much about it. Even the Head who was famed for her patience began to look severe as girl after girl either stared blankly at her or else shook her head and the question had to be passed on.

The climax came when Miss Annersley asked Marian what Caleb offered as a reward for the conquest of Kirjath-sepher. A dozen hands were waving wildly before she had finished the sentence and quite a dozen more shot up the moment after. Marian sat dumb and, when Miss Annersley said, "Come, Marian, surely you can tell me that?" she only sat dumb. The Head passed the question on to Ursula Vane who gave it triumphantly, and then turned to Beth with a query as to which city fell to Caleb's lot.

At the end of the lesson, they were told to read the chapter again and prepare the next for questioning.

"And remember," she said, more for the benefit of the new girls than the rest, "I expect you to know it." She gathered up her books as she spoke and rose from her seat and the form rose with her – more or less. Five girls scrambled to their feet a few seconds after the rest and one girl remained seated.

Miss Annersley looked at them and there was a dead silence. "Sit," she said; and the form sat down again, most of them wondering fearfully if Marian would be slain then and there or merely sent to the study.

The Head did neither. She laid her books down on the desk again, leaned on it and spoke quietly to them all in a conversational tone. "I realize that you girls who are new to us may not yet be accustomed to the acts of courtesy that here are considered necessities. However, now you are here, you must try to remember that politeness is the rule. When a mistress enters or leaves the form room – and that includes my secretary, Miss Dene – you rise at once. I hope that is understood for the future." Then she continued in a rather different tone, "Please remember, girls, that we shall judge of your former school by you. If you don't wish us to think that bad manners were the usual thing, don't show us any." She picked up her books again and smiled at them. They all rose to their feet at once – even Marian, however unwillingly. Her pride would not permit her to be accused of bad manners. But she resented the need bitterly.

They were given no chance of discussing this affair. Miss Slater was waiting outside the door and she entered immediately the Head had left the room. She was followed by Audrey Simpson who was loaded with the new arithmetics and when the girls had been told to sit down and Audrey, having deposited her burden on the desk, departed, Beth and Gwen Jones were told to give them out and be quick about it.

Miss Slater was very unlike Miss Annersley. She was an excellent teacher but she had a quick temper and woe betide the girl who roused it! Half a dozen at least of her pupils regarded her with apprehension, among them Mary-Lou who was *not* a mathematical genius. However, on this occasion she contrived to distinguish herself, drawing from Miss Slater the remark that she could evidently work well enough when she chose.

Miss Slater's lesson was not new to her as it happened. That lady elected to start the girls on areas of sections and, during the holidays, Mary-Lou together with Clem and Tony Barrass who lived with the Trelawneys at present as their parents were abroad, and Verity-Anne who spent a large part of her holidays in the same place since she was motherless and her father a busy man, had spent part of the time in building new hutches for Tony's rabbits. For reasons best known to himself, the young man had insisted on knowing the exact areas of all he did and Clem, sixteen and in Upper VA, had grinned to herself and taught them how to work the sums. As a result, Mary-Lou sailed through the work easily. The same could not be said of Verity-Anne who was even more unmathematical than her chum and was nearly in tears by the end of the lesson!

As for the Tanswick girls, they were left gasping and Miss Slater departed to seek her coffee and biscuits with her mind firmly made up that whatever else the Tanswick school may have taught its pupils, arithmetic was definitely not among the subjects!

"Do you mean," Anne exclaimed when she had gone, "that we've not only got to work like this every lesson, but do those five sums and get them right as well? How simply ghastly!"

"Miss Slater *is* rather a pill," Beth acknowledged. "All the same, she does get you on and when you think of exams in a year or so's time, that's something. But as for the prep, honestly, Anne, you must do your best with it or you'll be slain."

"But I can't *hope* to do all those *and* the Scripture and whatever else we may have for prep and get the lot done before tomorrow!" Anne wailed. "It'll take me all night to do those sums alone!"

"Don't be mad," Beth said. "You can prepare your Scripture on Sunday. It isn't wanted till next Monday. And anyhow, you're not expected to spend more than three quarters of an hour on any one subject. As for you,

Mary-Lou," she went on, turning to that heroine, "break the news gently. *Are* you suddenly developing into a maths genius?"

Mary-Lou grinned and shook her head. "Not me!" she said simply. "Clem showed me how to do *those* sums in the hols. That's how I knew what to do."

"Well, all I can say is that I'm glad to hear it," Beth said.

"What about our milk and bikkers?" Vi asked plaintively.

"OK – OK! The bell's just gone. Line up at the door, you folk. March!" And Upper IVA marched out to seek their milk and biscuits and the subject was shelved for the time being.

CHAPTER 7

The Staff Air Their Views

"I've been deputed by the rest of us to invite you to coffee after dinner tonight. Do come, won't you?" Thus Miss Slater to the Head a fortnight later.

"With pleasure," Miss Annersley replied smilingly. "But why this very urgent invitation?"

Miss Slater eyed her chief thoughtfully. "How do you know that it isn't a sudden deep desire for your company?" she countered.

Miss Annersley chuckled, while her blue-grey eyes danced with mirth. "Oh, my *dear* girl! When you folk only want a gossip, someone generally comes flying down *after* dinner to suggest that I have my coffee with you. When you take the trouble to invite me so formally in advance, I know there's something you all want to discuss seriously."

Miss Slater looked startled. "Good Heavens! I'd no idea you kept tabs on us like that! You're right, of course. We have a whole bunch of problems we want to discuss and it's always easier over coffee and cakes."

"I could call a Staff meeting if it's as important as all that," Miss Annersley offered with a gleam in her eyes.

Miss Slater shook her head. "No thank you! At Staff meetings we're all so very official that I, for one, usually forget more than half I wanted to say – unless I've jotted it down, that is. When we're just gossiping idly, well, you know yourself how one thing leads to another. So we can expect you round about half past eight, may we?"

"Thank you; as I said before, it'll be a pleasure. By the way, I hope you won't all be badly offended if I contribute towards the refreshments. Joey sent me a huge box of candies which arrived this morning. I opened it after tea and they look even more luscious than usual —" The Head paused significantly.

"Then they must be ultra-luscious!" the mathematics mistress said promptly. "Oh, do bring them along. They'll be much appreciated, I assure you! Though I must say I see no reason why we should always share your Canadian loot," she added.

"Not *always*," Miss Annersley told her demurely. "You never get a sniff of what comes during the holidays. However, this is such a monster box, I'd never get through it alone. It's the plain duty of you folk to come to my rescue."

"And, as a Staff, we always try to do our duty. We'll love to help you out!" Miss Slater assured her. "Was there a letter from Jo? How are they all?"

"All very fit and well. She enclosed some snaps, so I'll bring them, too, and then you can all see for yourselves." The Head gave a glance at the pile of Sixth form essays on her desk and Miss Slater took the hint and departed to inform her peers that the Head was coming up for coffee, so they had better do something about tidying up the Staff room before dinner.

Punctually at half past eight that evening, Miss Annersley arrived bearing a gigantic box of Kelowna candies and the snaps she had promised. The entire Staff were awaiting her, for Mlle de Lachennais, Senior of the Staff, had asked Bride if she and the prefects would take charge for the rest of the evening.

So they were on duty and the Staff were free for once.

The younger members had turned to and tidied up the room which had stood in much need of it. With its bright curtains of ivory cretonne over which great red poppies sprawled cheerfully, the fire of applewood and fircones Miss O'Ryan had lit in the big grate – it had once been one of the more important bedrooms – and the bowls of hyacinths and jonquils which stood about on the tables, it had a most welcoming air. Two of the tables – each of the dozen resident mistresses owned one standing beneath her own bookcase – had been pushed together and covered with an afternoon teacloth donated by Miss Derwent whose hobby was crocheting. The cups and saucers were rather a mixed bag, since they had decided to use their own, but they made a sufficiently festive table, especially as Mlle had produced her treasured silver coffee service. Two large plates were piled high with little cakes they had coaxed Frau Mieders, the domestic science mistress, to make for them, and an Indian basket Jo Maynard had sent to Biddy O'Ryan was full of a varied contribution of biscuits.

The Head sniffed delightedly as she entered. "Applewood! How I love the smell of burning applewood! And what gorgeous bulbs! Who is responsible for those?"

Peggy Burnett, formerly Head Girl of the school and now its PT mistress, acknowledged that she had done it and the Head congratulated her. Then someone pushed forward a big armchair for Miss Annersley and she sat down and produced a letter from inside her box at sight of which most people exclaimed joyfully.

"That from Jo?" demanded Miss Everett, the gardening mistress. "What's the latest news from Canada? Are they all well?"

"Splendid, she says. The twins are breaking records and she herself hasn't felt so fit for years. She also says that Robin Humphries is not only well, but plump and, judging from her photo, that is true. Here are the very latest in snaps. Pass them round and you'll see for yourselves."

Those of the Staff to whom Jo Maynard was an old friend caught at the snaps eagerly and handed them about with frank comments.

"Jo's right about herself, anyway," Miss Burnett said with a chuckle. "The woman looks a regular tub!"

"*What*? Let me see!" Biddy O'Ryan squeezed her head under her friend's arm – there was a difference of five inches in their height – and stared at the snap. "Good gracious! What a shock you gave me! Part of that is *clothes*! Her face *is* rounder. Sure, 'tis the darlin' she is. Are those the Trips?"

"I wish Jo heard you!" the Head said severely. "You know how she bars that particular expression."

Biddy O'Ryan chuckled. "I've heard her on the subject," she said.

"All the same," Miss Everett put in, "it's amazing the way those children seem to have come on. What a size they are!"

"We'll never be knowing them next term!" Biddy said solemnly. "Look, Derwent." She handed the snap over to Miss Derwent who had been new the previous term and so had not yet met any of the Maynards except the doctor. "You'll have the pleasure of teaching those next term."

"What pretty girls!" Miss Derwent said. "Bright, too, I should say."

"Jo's children couldn't be anything else, or they wouldn't be hers." Matron twitched the photo from

Biddy's fingers. "Yes; Margot hasn't lost that wicked look of hers, I see. But what a change! She went away the most white-faced little misery you could imagine. Now, she looks as well as the other two."

"Con seems to have lost that up-in-the-moon expression of hers, I'm glad to see." Miss Slater was studying another.

"Here are the boys. But what splendid little fellows!" Mlle remarked. "Charles, too, looks very well."

"Jo is right," Miss Annersley said laughing. "Canada has certainly done something for them all. Look, Miss Armitage." She turned to the science mistress. "These ar the famous twins – Felix and Felicity."

"What lovely babies!" Miss Armitage bent over the snap. "I wouldn't mind having twins myself if I could have them like that!" And she glanced with a smile at the diamond and sapphire ring she wore.

Some of the snaps were of Lady Russell's family and, while the new mistresses exclaimed at the sight of Sybil Russell's loveliness, the rest were equally enthusiastic to see that Josette, always the frail member of the Russell family, seemed to have improved as much as her cousin Margot Maynard. The school belonged to Lady Russell, she having established it in the far-off days when she had been Madge Bettany. Even marriage and motherhood had not made a great deal of difference to her feeling for it. She identified herself with it very closely, so that what her saucy sister Jo called "the foundation stones" among the Staff rejoiced in having the photos.

When they had all seen and commented on them, Mlle called the party to order and began pouring out the coffee which the Staff "babies" carried round. When everyone was duly supplied with coffee and cake, she took her own, pulled her chair up by the Head's and then said

98

plaintively, "But, Hilda, we have done no business. We invited you tonight because we all feel it very necessary that we have a talk about the new girls; and now you have wasted all our time with Jo's snaps."

Miss Annersley laughed. "Oh, Jeanne! Do you really call it waste?"

"Well, perhaps not. I love the dear Jo and her babies. Indeed, I wish they were all back in England that we might consult her," Mlle sighed.

The Head raised her eyebrows. "What in the world has happened? You seem very depressed tonight. Is anything wrong?"

"That," Miss Everett said slowly, "is just what we can't quite make out. There's a strange atmosphere in the place. We've talked it over amongst ourselves, but no one can throw any light on it. Things are certainly different and the attitude of the girls – *some* of the girls – towards both us and the prefects seems to be altering."

Miss Slater set down her cup. "Quite apart from that – and I can feel it as well as anyone – I do want to say that I think we'll have to do some rearranging of forms. If the new bunch we've had wished on us is the result of 'free discipline', then give me good old strong-hand-over-'em!"

Miss Annersley sat up. "Are they so very bad?" she demanded.

"'Awful' doesn't even begin to describe most of them! Look here, Hilda!" Miss Slater spoke urgently. "We put Alison Grant and three others into Upper VA because they *are* seventeen and you said – and I, for one, agreed with you – that we didn't want new girls of that age in any of the lower forms. But oh, my dear, they simply can't touch my work! Alison tries – she's quite a nice girl, and she does want to get on. But she's always being let down by the fact that she doesn't know her groundwork thoroughly. Janet Overton tried at first, but I feel that she's growing disheartened and this past week her work's been going to pieces. As for Pamela Morton and Eileen Osborne, they don't even want to learn!"

"You could say the same thing about most of the new girls in the Fifths," Miss Derwent chimed in. "As for Diana Skelton, it isn't often that a girl manages to rouse in me feelings of hatred and malice, but I rarely come away from a lesson with Lower VA without feeling that I could cheerfully shake her until the teeth rattled in her head!"

Miss Annersley looked rather horrified. "My dear girl! What a confession! What does she do to arouse such vicious feelings in you?"

"Doesn't attempt to work, for one thing. Doesn't even *want* to learn. Half the time she doesn't know the first thing, and she merely looks supercilious if you try to pull her up."

"If you ask me," Miss Slater chimed in, "that girl is so eaten up with vanity and self-conceit that she regards everyone else as being slightly less than the dust beneath her chariot wheels. Her algebra and geometry are beneath contempt and even Mary-Lou knows more about arithmetic than *she* does!"

"At that rate, what about putting her down?" Miss Derwent asked hopefully.

"Diana must not go down." The Head spoke with finality. "I am going to confess to you folk that I'm sorry I ever agreed to take her. However, it's done now and she must stay till the end of the year, at any rate. I happen to know that her people are expecting us to accept her for the Welsen branch then, but I've already written to Miss Wilson on the subject, *and* had a reply and she says there won't be a vacancy. But as long as she's here, I won't have her in a lower form than she already is. Her influence isn't at all the sort of thing we want with girls in the fifteens. Lower V is full up and in B there are three or four girls of the feather-headed type like Rosemary Lambe, Felicity King and Jennifer Penrose. I'm very sorry for us all, but we must put up with her. It's only for two terms and A people will probably help her to grow a little out of her superior attitude."

"I don't have her for anything – thank goodness!" Miss Armitage spoke meditatively. "Apart from feeling that she's what Mary-Lou calls 'the cat's bathmat', what is wrong with the girl?"

Half the Staff told her together and the resultant gabble made her protest.

"I can't make head or tail of what you're all saying! Derwent, what do *you* think is the matter. I know her for an exceedingly pretty girl who spoils herself by going round looking as if no one else was fit to breathe the same air. What else is wrong? I can see there's plenty."

Miss Derwent flushed. "She's the most unutterable little snob it's ever been my ill luck to meet! Goodness knows who or what her people are, but she acts as if anyone who worked for their living weren't the same flesh and blood as herself. In my opinion it would do her all the good in the world if she had to turn to and scrub floors for her bread and butter! I gather, that that's not at all likely to happen?" She finished with a querying look at Miss Annersley who shook her head with a slight smile.

"Not in the least likely. As for who she is, this, again, is in confidence, but her father is the Skelton who manufactures glue. He's quite a decent sort of man, but he married a silly woman and Diana is the result."

"If she's Skelton's Glues, you're right. She certainly

101

won't have to stoop to earn a penny," Miss Derwent agreed. "What a pity!"

"*But*," Miss Everett spoke impressively, "if she's Skelton's Glues, apart from the fact that they must be almost multi-millionaires, I don't see why she should think she can look down on anyone else here, Staff *or* pupils. I happen to know something about John Skelton, as it chances. His father was foreman in a knacker's yard and young John, who left school at thirteen, went into the business. He was a hard-working, clever lad, and when he was older, he went to night school and then he began to experiment and the result was Skelton's Glues. I take my hat off to him, for he's made his way against big handicaps. But his daughter is a silly little nincompoop who wants taking down several pegs to make her fit to live with. I *could* do it, of course; but I'm not going to. She isn't worth the fuss!"

"I sincerely hope you won't," Miss Annersley said in some alarm. "If some of the girls got to hear of this, Diana would have a very thin time. Children can be very heartless and if she's setting any of them against her they might very well make cruel use of such information. I won't have it! What's said here is said in confidence. As for Diana, when she goes out into the world, I don't doubt that she will come up against some hard edges. Let it go at that and put up with her. After all, *you* all know that she isn't any better than anyone else – yourselves included. She's only a silly child, after all. Let's hope the school helps her to gain a little sense!"

No less a person than Mlle took up the tale. "I agree with you, Hilda chérie. But what are we to do if she cheats?"

"*Cheats*?"

"I have no real proof of it, but I am very sure that

102

she copies her exercises and translations from someone though I have never found her out yet. But I know she could not gain the marks she does through any fair means, for she has no knowledge of the irregular verbs and her grammar – oh, c'est effroyable!" In her agitation, Mlle lapsed into French.

"Well, she can't do much cheating over *my* work," Biddy O'Ryan said. "History is something you either know or don't know. She *doesn't* know and she seems quite pleased to be ignorant. What *I* dislike about her is her insolence. I warn you all, some day I shall blow up and then pity help her!"

"What do you mean? Give me an example." Miss Annersley set down her cup and leaned forward.

Biddy considered. "Well, this morning I was taking in their essays. She said she hadn't finished hers. I asked why not and she had the cheek to say, 'Oh, I was bored with it. It really wasn't worth while.'"

"And what did you do?"

"Told her that, worth while or not, unless I had that essay by tomorrow morning there'd be trouble. She didn't say anything, but she *smiled*!"

"What a piece of impudence!" Miss Derwent said hotly. "I hope you ticked her off for it?"

Biddy chuckled. "I didn't say a word. I merely smiled, too. I don't *think*," she added thoughtfully, "that she quite relished it. I made my smile as inward as I could!"

"What on earth do you mean?" Miss Derwent stared at her.

"Just that! What else would I be meaning?" Biddy said sweetly.

Miss Moore, the geography mistress, nodded. "She did the same thing to me – *once*." She spoke meaningly.

"She hasn't tried it on again. *How* I squashed her! She was scarlet before I'd finished with her."

As Miss Moore had, in one term, earned the reputation for a gift of biting sarcasm that even Miss Wilson herself, famed for her tongue, had never bettered, the rest could well believe that Diana had lapsed into confusion. So far the girl had yet to be found who did not wince under her gentle, drawling voice when she was exercising her talent. Biddy O'Ryan voiced the feelings of the rest when she said thankfully, "It's glad I am you weren't here when *I* was a pupil."

"Would anyone care for some more coffee?" Mlle asked at this point. She refilled the empty cups and then sat down again to say seriously, "But truly, Hilda, this is not all. Diana is, perhaps, the worst, but there are others who are making us difficulties. There is a girl in Upper IVA, par exemple, who is not the type we would wish here."

"Meaning Marian Tovey?" Miss Slater asked with a grin. "I flung her out this morning for playing about and making other people play about, too. I saw her after the lesson and told her that if it happened again, she would have solitary work for a week to come. She made me waste nearly fifteen minutes as it was!"

"And then," said Miss Dene who had sat silent through all these diatribes, "there are those demons in Lower IVA – where Emerence is," she added, deep meaning in her tone.

No less a person than Matron backed her up in this statement. "Untidy, lazy little wretches!" she said in her most trenchant tones. "And regular monkeys for mischief, the whole lot of them!"

"Oh, goodness!" Miss Everett exclaimed. "As if Emerence and that crew needed any help that way! They have

Priscilla Dawbarn and Peggy Harper already besides Emerence. That's more than enough for one form! I haven't had them yet – weather's been so wet and you know we agreed that it was practical gardening for those imps and not talks and so on. They've been having dictation and extra arithmetic in my time."

"Well, I don't envy you when you *do* get a fine day," Matron said. "You'll have them all over the place in less than five minutes! They're like a bunch of eels."

"How consoling!" Miss Everett grimaced across the room at Matron. "Well, if they don't behave themselves, they may understand that their bed will be taken away from them and they'll do spelling and sums for the rest of the term in place of gardening! That's all!"

"That should settle them." Rosalie Dene gave Miss Everett a laughing glance. "The majority love gardening and they *don't* love either spelling or sums. If anyone is the cause of their having their precious flower-bed taken from them, they'll make her wish she hadn't been born! In any case, Betty, I don't mean that they're *bad*. They're nothing like so awful as Emerence was when she first came and she soon tamed down. It's this beautiful 'free discipline' they've been having that has gone to their heads. Also, like most kids of their age, they're a sinful lot. There's one child there – Cornish, judging by her name – and she's the most enterprising young demon I've ever met – apart from Emerence. She beats even the Dawbarns!"

"Primrose Trevoase?" Miss Annersley asked. "Yes; I thought that was the child you meant. Her family come from Cornwall as you say."

Miss Moore suddenly chuckled. "She's a brat – but rather a nice brat at bottom, I think. There's something very charming about that cheeky little face of hers."

"And something very disarming about her innocent

manner." Peggy Burnett joined in. "You're quite right about her being enterprising, Betty. What do you think the monkey did yesterday – aided, I may say by the usual gang?"

"What?" It came in an enthralled chorus. The Staff at the Chalet School had a strong sense of humour, taken as a whole, and a naughty little girl who contrived to be funny as well sometimes escaped her due rewards.

Miss Burnett began to laugh. "I have been giving them jumping in a circle over the bag – you know what I mean. Well, yesterday, those young monkeys got at the bag, tipped out the sand it contains, and made it up with teasel-heads crammed chock-a-block and the contents of several emery cushions to give it weight. The result was that whenever it caught anyone on the ankle this morning, they were well prickled. I'd taken two classes who complained loudly and bitterly before it dawned on me to examine the bag. I guessed who'd done it – Priscilla Dawbarn was looking her saintliest throughout their lesson and when I came to think it over, I realised that she and her gang had all leapt like young goats during that particular exercise – so I went and tackled them about it. They owned up at once, and Miss Primrose added that she had thought of it! She seemed very pleased with herself, so I slew them to teach them not to play such a trick again."

"What did you do?" came in half a dozen voices.

"Set them to emptying the bag with ungloved hands. Then they had to share out the emery powder equally and sew up their cushions again. After that, I told them to learn the thirteen and seventeen times tables by heart and have them ready to say to me – *dodging about*! – tomorrow morning. Otherwise, I assured them, they would lose their games until they did know them."

"How they will loathe you!" Miss Slater exclaimed.

"I daresay! If it puts an end to that sort of prank, I shan't mind," Peggy said equably. "They'll get over it in time."

"Well," the Head set down her cup and opened her box of candies. "I think I won't worry about the younger girls. Mischief is something all you people ought to be able to deal with. I should do as you suggest, Betty," she spoke to Miss Everett. "Tell them that if they don't behave themselves they'll lose their flower bed and their gardening. That will settle them. As for Primrose, her father is a friend of my cousin's, so I know the Trevoases quite well. When they came to arrange for her to come here, her father begged me to do my best to reform her. She'd had one term at Tanswick and I gathered that her manners and conduct when she came home for the Christmas holidays left her parents bereft of breath." She gave a sudden peal of laughter. "Her father earnestly asked me to buy a cane and *use* it!" She stopped short to hand round her candies. Then she went on, much more gravely. "I don't like what you tell me about the elder girls. As a school, we have always frowned heavily on snobbery of any kind and I won't have it now. All of you, please keep a firm eye on the Fourths and Fifths and be ready to trample heavily on the least sign of it. So far as the cheating is concerned, Jeanne, I think we may leave that to the girls themselves. If it goes on, they will see it soon enough and they'll drop on it at once. We've never had much trouble that way in this school. It *is* only Diana, isn't it?"

"She is the one I most suspect in that form," Mlle replied. "I am not sure of Laila Semple or Sylvia Peacock, but I feel very certain of Diana. There has been a little in some of the lower forms, too, but I am not troubled about that so much. Already, there has been trouble with Mary-Lou and that new girl, Anne Gordon. Then the rest joined in and I do not think that Anne or anyone else in that form will commit that sin again." She suddenly smiled and the rest smiled with her. They could well imagine the scene!

"Very well, then," the Head said briskly. "We'll leave that question to the girls. I'm certain it will be safe enough in their hands. Finally, if any of you have cause to complain of impertinence of the kind Diana seems to be guilty of, you are to report it to me at once. That is another thing I will not have. Now I think we've been serious long enough. Have another candy, all of you, and I'll read Jo's letter to you. She seems to be enjoying life as usual!"

CHAPTER 8

Julie Creates a Sensation

The prefects were in their own room. It was Friday night; therefore, an easy night for them. It had seemed good to Bride to call an informal meeting to discuss what they should arrange for the next day, since there seemed every likelihood that the rain, which had streamed down with very few breaks for the past ten days, would not ease off *that* night.

February was a very wet month that year – "One of the wettest on record, I should imagine," Elfie Woodward had said only that morning when she woke up and went to the window to gaze out disgustedly. "This means cancelling the Sacred Heart lacrosse. I can't *think* what's happened to the winters lately. We used to have snow; but we generally got some jolly decent days in February. But here we are: February 16th, and most of the time it's been raining. Anyhow, the pitches will be seas of mud, so that's that!"

"Perhaps it's all these atom bomb explosions," Bride had suggested as she pulled on her stockings.

"It wouldn't surprise me. Well, I must go and bath!"

As a result, Bride had put up her notice after Mittagessen, calling the prefects to a meeting at 5.30 p.m. in the Prefects' room, and here they all were in conclave, looking very serious over their business.

"The morning won't worry us," Bride said. "Prep – mending – Guides; that will keep the whole lot busy until twelve thirty and then they have to go and change. The question is what are we doing with them in the afternoon? Got any ideas, anyone?"

"What about calling an extra meeting of the Hobbies Club?" This was Audrey Simpson's suggestion.

Tom Gay shook her head. "No fear! They haven't been across the doors since Wednesday morning and they're all fed to the teeth. You'll have to think of something a lot more active than that, let me tell you, my love!"

Primrose listened to the rain as it splashed sharply against the window panes. "Surely it can't go *on* like this! I don't believe it's ever once let up since it started – except for that break on Wednesday morning. I know I woke up in the middle of the night and it was coming down full tilt then. Don't you think Guides will take off some of their energy, Bride? They'll have a certain amount of exercise then; and Hobbies is fun, you know."

Bride set her elbows on the table and cupped her chin in her hands. "Years ago," she said solemnly, "when we were at Plas Howell and in Lower Third, we nearly had a tragedy, as some of you may remember. We'd had a week of this sort of weather and what happened? Most folk went completely haywire. I was one of 'em myself and you were another, Prim. Lavender Leigh and Joy Bird had a stand-up fight and it finally ended in Lavender having an accident, thanks to Joy's temper."

"That was snow – not rain," someone remarked. "Joy shoved Lavender down into the dip by the Scarp when we were having a snowfight and it was full of drifted snow and she was buried. What a scare we all got!"

"Oh well, the *principle's* the same and it's the principle that matters," Bride said easily. "The whole point is that we've all been kept mewed up for the last few days and it never agrees with kids to be shut in day after day. Their

110

little tempers begin to rise and then – look out for squalls!"

"What are we doing with them tonight?" Bess Herbert asked.

"Dancing, I suppose. It's no one's night particularly." – By which Bride meant that no form in particular would act hostesses – "There won't be any special programme. Dancing and games will be best."

"Well, they can work off some of their superfluous energy that way," remarked Tom Gay. "What do you say, Julie?"

Julie nodded indifferently. She was not feeling well just now. The old tummy pains had returned, rather badly this time. After that first evening, they had been dormant and she had forgotten about them; but if she had told the truth, she would have said that they had been nagging at her all the week. The sensible thing would have been to go to Matron, but when they had occurred during the summer term, that lady had made remarks about a grumbling appendix. Julie had taken fright at once. She was a very highly-strung girl and she dreaded the thought of an operation. So far, they had been bearable, so she had held her tongue, coaxed a couple of aspirins out of Nurse whom she had happened to meet and hoped for the best. Matron herself had her hands full with a fine crop of flu colds among the Junior Middles and had had little chance of noticing that the girl was a bad colour, with heavy shadows under her eyes, and that she played with her food at mealtimes.

Bride had been attending to Tom. Now she shifted her gaze to Julie. "You don't seem awfully interested," she said.

"My dear, I'm bored stiff! I'm as bored as any kid you –" Julie suddenly stopped short as a sharp pain stabbed through her. She turned very white.

111

"What's wrong with you?" demanded Bride, jumping to her feet. "What is it, Julie?"

The pain had vanished again and Julie sat up. "Nothing!" she said with a touch of defiance. "What *should* be wrong? I'm all right – just a touch of indigestion, but it's nothing really."

Then she bit her lip to keep herself from crying out, for the pain stabbed again, and much more sharply this time.

"A *touch*?" Bride was stooping over her by this time. "You're *green*, my child! Here – oh, you, Madge – scoot and fetch Matey! Julie's pretty bad. Help me to get her to the sofa, some of you."

The meeting broke up in confusion as Madge Dawson went flying to seek Matron while Tom and Bride lifted the doubled-up Julie and carried her carefully to the old-fashioned sofa at one side of the fireplace. They laid her down, but that was the limit of their ideas. Bride said later that she felt sure Julie had appendicitis and, as she didn't know the first thing about it, she thought it would be wiser to wait for Matron.

Meantime, Madge had not come back and time was passing. Julie, all attempts at stoicism given up perforce, was uttering little cries and her face drawn with pain, frightened them badly.

"Let's get her to bed," Anne Webster suggested. "She'd be more comfy in one way, especially if we got her clothes off. Could you walk that far, Julie? It's only four doors along."

Julie was beyond talking at the moment. All her courage could not prevent a smothered scream coming from her as the pain stabbed more fiercely than ever through her side and the frightened girls acted at once.

"Go after Madge and tell Matey we're taking Julie

112

to bed," Bride snapped at Audrey Simpson. "We can't take her to San – too much flu there – Tom, you and I are the heftiest. Let's fetch her mattress and put her on it and carry her to bed that way. Scoot, Primrose, and yank off the sheets and things. We can put them over her once she's safely in the dorm. Lesley and Nancy, go and fill all the hot water bottles you can find. Oh, and someone find the Abbess and tell her." Then she bent over the moaning Julie. "Poor old girl!"

"Keep your chin up," Tom added. "We'll have you in bed in a brace of shakes now. Here comes Primrose with the mattress."

Very carefully they lifted Julie from the sofa to the mattress which Primrose had contrived to carry with the undersheet and blanket more or less undisturbed. Then, with Tom and Bride taking the head and Bess and Anne lifting the feet, they bore her through the corridor and set her down carefully on the bedstead.

Bride set to work to take off her shoes and stockings while Primrose unfastened her frock. Among them, they contrived to get her into her pyjamas by which time Madge had returned to say that Matron was nowhere to be found, so she had braved rules and gone to San where she found Nurse busy with Norah Fitzgerald who was violently sick. She had sent word that they were to try to get Julie to bed, but to do nothing else. She would come as soon as she could leave Norah. She knew Matron had gone across to St Agnes', the Junior school. One of them was to find Miss Dene and ask her to ring St Agnes' and tell Matron to return at once. Then she was to get on to the doctor and ask him to come, too. The last ferry had gone, but the doctor had a motor boat and would cross very quickly. Finally, as the Head was out, they were to inform Mlle.

"Anne went for the Abbess as soon as we'd got

113

Julie here," Bride said from her post beside Julie, who was gripping her hand and moaning pitifully at intervals. "OK, Julie, poor old lady! You'll be better presently. Nursie's coming and she knows what to do."

Mlle was the first to arrive. She took Bride's place and bent over the sick girl, deep concern in her little dark face. She asked one or two questions and Julie managed to gasp a word or two in reply. Then Madge, who had gone to Miss Dene, arrived to say that the doctor was picking up Matron and they would both be here shortly. Miss Dene had now gone to see that the big school car was filled up with oil and petrol and run her round to the front door in case, as she expected, the doctor ordered Julie to the cottage hospital at Carnbach.

"Very good," Mlle replied in her own tongue. "Then we can do no more at present. Girls, all of you but Bride go back to your own room. She may stay in case I want a messenger. Say nothing to anyone else about this until we give you permission."

A fresh cry came from Julie and she turned back to the bed, though there was nothing she could do. Then Nurse appeared at the door and gave them a look that sent them flying before her order, "Be off with you! We'll send for you when we want you! Now, Mlle, what's all this? Let me see." And she drew back the clothes to examine Julie.

It took Nurse a bare three minutes to diagnose the case. She pulled up the sheets and blankets and nodded at Bride. "We must wait for the doctor. Meantime, you go and see that Betsy and Vi don't hear of this. Time enough later on. Mlle will stay with me, and Matron and Doctor will be here shortly. I'll come along to you as soon as there is anything to tell."

Bride went at once, casting a pitiful look at the patient. But she had sense enough to know that the

114

fewer people there were in the room the better just now.

It was fully an hour, and the Middles had gone to bed, before Nurse finally came along to the Prefects' room where the anxious girls were sitting about, too worried to settle to anything. They brightened up when they saw her buxom form and Bride jumped up at once.

"What's wrong with her, Nursie?" she asked, her face tense with anxiety.

Nurse looked at them. Like several of the Staff, she belonged to Tirol days and she remembered something Matron had said when Mlle Lepâttre, one of the school's first Heads, had collapsed as the result of serious illness which had ultimately proved fatal.

"The elder girls must know the truth," she had decreed on that occasion. "I think they should be told how serious it is. I don't believe in trying to shield young things from *all* sorrow and trouble. We want to make strong, helpful women of them, not spineless jellyfish!"

Julie was clearly dangerously ill and Nurse felt that her friends should understand something about it.

"It is certainly appendicitis," she said, therefore. "We shall have to wait and see what the doctor says when he comes; but it will definitely mean an operation, and she is gravely ill at the moment. Miss Dene is trying to get her people on the phone as we ought to have their leave for her to be given a general anaesthetic, and I expect Mrs Lucy, at any rate, will come as soon as she can. Isn't there a baby, by the way? Who can tell me?"

"Kitty's nearly three now," Bride said. "Auntie could leave her all right if that's what you mean."

"Oh, good! Julie will have to go to the hospital at Carnbach, you know. We haven't facilities here – not what may be needed."

They looked at her with horrified faces. Bride as the niece and Nancy as the daughter of doctors knew more than the others. They guessed that, though Nurse had not said so, she was afraid of peritonitis. Furthermore, Nancy was Julie's cousin and they were very fond of each other. She went very white, but she said nothing and Nurse, who had forgotten the fact and, in any case, was very anxious about her patient, never noticed. Bride did, though, and she slipped a comforting arm round her friend's waist.

"How long will it take Auntie J. to get here?" she asked. "They live in Guernsey, you know. How will she manage it?"

"She'll fly, I expect, as soon as there's an available plane," Nurse told her. "Now I must go. Matron is with Julie. She will go with her to the hospital when they take her. But I can't stay here. I've got my hands full with the flu colds and that wicked imp, Norah Fitzgerald, making herself sick with gorging peanuts. I must get back to San. By the way, which of you sleep in Julie's dormitory?"

Three hands went up and Nurse nodded. "Bride, Elfie and Nancy. Thank you. It's nearly time for you people to go to bed, but we want the dormitory clear until they have moved Julie, so you had better stay here until someone comes to tell you. I don't suppose it'll be much longer now. The doctor ought to have got the ambulance at the other end fixed up. He's given Julie an injection so she isn't in so much pain and, mercifully, he has his motor boat, and can take her across in that. The worst will be over in a very few hours now. Try not to worry, girls. That won't help anyone. Far better think of Julie when you say your prayers. And you might do the last dormitory rounds for Matron as she can't see to it and I certainly can't spare the time. Now buck up and stop looking like a set of Dismal Desmonds!"

She nodded at them and left the room with a rustle of starched uniform and the girls were left alone.

"Sit down, Nance," Bride said gently, lowering Nancy on to a convenient chair.

Primrose gave the girl a hasty glance. "Good gracious, Nancy! You aren't ill, too, are you?" she said urgently. "Shall we bring Nurse back?"

"Talk sense!" Bride retorted. "Nancy's all right, only it's been a nasty shock for her."

Nancy caught a quivering lip between her teeth. "We – we're almost like twin sisters," she said unsteadily. "We've always been together since we were mere infants and Julie's pretty bad when Nurse can talk like that. And Auntie J. such miles away, too!"

"I know." Bride's tone was still gentle. "All the same, Nance, you'll have to buck up. Someone will have to stand by Betsy and young Vi, you know. You're the obvious one to do it. Aunt Janie won't have much time to come over here to them just at first and they'll need you to – to hold their hands, so to speak."

"I hadn't thought of that. The poor kids!" Nancy's voice was very pitiful. "It'll be a horrid shock for them –"

"Car!" Tom broke in. "Are they taking her off now?"

"Shouldn't think so," Primrose said. "Nurse talked as if it would be a little while yet before they moved her. Much more likely to be the Abbess coming back from wherever she's been. I say; hadn't we better be doing something? Didn't Nurse ask us to take over the dormy rounds? Come on; let's start in on them."

Bride stood up. "Best thing to do! Prim, will you see to this floor of the wing? Tom, you and Lesley might take the same in the central block and Bess and Madge, Anne and Audrey go upstairs. Rosalind, you and Nancy

117

and Elf and I will see to the other wing. Scram, the lot of you! Go quietly, though."

They scattered to make the rounds of all the dormitories. It was Matron's job, but Julie needed her and they knew Matey well enough to be sure that she would not leave their friend. Halfway through their task, they heard a steady tramp-tramp-tramp and Bride, coming downstairs from the south wing, drew back as she saw two ambulance men with a stretcher between them. Julie's black head was very still on the pillows. Behind came Miss Annersley and Matron in big coats with caps and scarves. The doctor had gone on ahead.

Bride turned to Nancy who had followed her. "They've been waiting for the ambulance," she said in a low tone.

"She – she looks very *still*," Nancy replied shakily.

"Well, you'd expect that, you goop! Didn't Nursie say Doc had given her a shot of something to dull the pain? Much better for her that way. I expect she's practically asleep and knows nothing about all this."

"Oh, if that's it!" Nancy said in relieved tones.

"Well, you ought to have guessed that! There! They're down the stairs now and into the hall, so we can go on. Come on! We can't hang over the rail to watch. I don't think Matey or the Abbess would like it." And, very wisely, Bride drew her friend along to the Prefects' room.

When they heard the big hall door close, however, Nancy turned.

"I'm going to find someone to tell us," she said firmly. "Mlle will be about somewhere. Let's go and find her."

She hurried off and the rest followed. As Nancy had suspected, Mlle was there, making the door secure for the night. The Head and Matron would stay in Carnbach, for little Mrs Lucy could not hope to arrive from Guernsey until the next day and they would not leave her girl until she was there. They waited until Mlle had bolted and chained the door. Then Tom ran down the stairs noiselessly and the rest followed.

"Mlle!" Tom spoke urgently. "Tell us the latest, won't you?"

Mlle nodded and her eyes went to Nancy. Nurse might have forgotten the bond between her and Julie, but the Head had not and she had left a special message for the other cousin.

"Nancy, petite, I have a message for you from Miss Annersley. She bade me tell you that Julie is very ill – but *very* ill at present. She is to be operated on as soon as possible. Your uncle and aunt have phoned leave for the anaesthetic. Miss Annersley bade me tell you that nowadays, when medical science has made great advances, once the first two or three days are over, all will be well and Julie should recover quickly. This is not such a terrible thing as it used to be. And she asked me to ask all you who are Julie's friends to pray for her safety, for that is the one thing you can do for her just now and the best thing."

"Thank you, Mlle. Is – is Aunt Janie crossing tonight?" Nancy asked tremulously.

Mlle shook her head. "That would be impossible. It is too late and she has your baby cousin for whom she must arrange. But a friend of your uncle's will fly her to Cardiff tomorrow morning early and Miss Dene will meet her there with the car and she should be with Julie by early afternoon."

Nancy nodded. "Mr la Touche. He has his own private plane. I'd forgotten about him. He'd be sure to bring them. He and Uncle Julian are great pals. Oh, I'm so glad!"

119

"But yes; it is a real blessing," Mlle agreed. "And now, what have you been doing?"

"Nurse told us to do the last dormy rounds," Bride explained. "We've just finished and everything is all right."

"Ah, c'est bien! Then, mes enfants, you must go to bed and to sleep. Julie is in good hands and, as I have said, once the operation is over, we may hope that she will make speedy recovery."

Tom went darkly red and swallowed once or twice. Then she said, "I say, Mlle, before we go, d'you think we might – might say a prayer together for her? You know what it says about two or three gathered together. I – I mean it would seem more – more urgent together."

For reply, Mlle opened the door of the study. "But I am very glad. That is a good thought, Tom. I will join, if you will permit. Come in here, girls."

They went in and knelt down and Mlle repeated two or three prayers before beginning on Our Father. The little quiet interval helped them and when they finally stood up, most of them felt stronger to face the night and next day. Nancy's eyes had lost their look of strain and though she was very grave, Mlle felt easier about her. They said, "Goodnight" and went to bed very quietly. All of them addressed very fervent prayers to the great Father of all before they lay down. Whether she knew it or not, Tom had taken the first step in her chosen career that night.

Before she slipped between the sheets, however, Bride went into Nancy's cubicle. She found her friend just rising from her knees. She was still white, but her lips were steady and her eyes hopeful. Seeing this, Bride said nothing; only she kissed Nancy before she went back to her own domain – and that meant a great deal from unsentimental Bride as Nancy knew. She smiled at her chum and Bride went off.

An hour later, the rising moon shone into the Rose dormitory and found all the occupants sleeping quietly. They slept until the rising-bell sounded when Miss Annersley, who had come back shortly before, leaving Matron in charge until the Lucys could arrive, came to the Prefects' room to tell them that the operation was safely over.

"It was a very bad one, girls," she said. "Julie couldn't have lived if it had been postponed twelve hours longer. But, though she is still in danger, the doctors and nurses all hope and expect that before long she will be on the mend and all will be well."

CHAPTER 9

Betsy

"Betsy, the Head wants to see you in the study as soon as you're dressed."

Betsy Lucy turned round from the mirror where she was engaged in putting a gloss on her bright brown hair and stared at Bride who had brought the message.

"*What*? Go to the study at once at *this* time in the morning? But – but I've done nothing! – Anyhow, nothing that needs a Dilly-dilly-come-and-be-killed sort of order like that!"

Despite the gravity of the situation, Bride was unable to refrain from a chuckle. "Horrid conscience you do seem to have! Oh, it's nothing you've done; nothing of that kind at all. You buck up and finish dressing and hop along to the Abbess and you'll know all about it," she added. "I'll see to your bed for you." And she began to strip the little bed deftly.

Betsy hurriedly tossed down the brush, rammed in the grips that kept her thick, straight locks from falling over her face, picked up her blouse and, as she pulled it on and fastened it, said, "Look here, Bride: what *is* all this in aid of?"

"Vile construction!" Bride said austerely. "Has no one ever told you *never* to finish a sentence with a preposition?"

"Oh fiddle!" Betsy began to wriggle into the skirt that was de rigueur now that she was fifteen. "There's something behind all this. I'm awfully grateful to you for fixing my bed and all that, but I'd a lot rather know what's behind it all. I haven't a single sin on my conscience – or not so that you'd notice it, anyhow! – and *why* are you fussing about my bed? You prees aren't in the habit of saving our crowd from trouble that I've ever noticed!"

"Your English," Bride said dispassionately as she "humped" the bed in the middle to let the air pass under the mattress, "is getting worse and worse. Never use repetition, my child, unless it's for the sake of emphasis. And how do *you* know that we aren't in the habit of saving you kids trouble, may I ask? That's all *you* know about it! Anyhow, the fact remains that the Abbess told me to send you to her. I wonder –" Bride paused and Betsy, engaged in a mad hunt for a handkerchief, never noticed that however light her tone might be, her eyes were very sombre.

"*What* do you wonder? – Oh, got him, thank goodness! – Go on, Bride! What do you wonder?"

"Oh, just if the Head's been wondering exactly how long you folk take to dress after the rising bell and –"

Bride was interrupted by a perfect squeal of horror as Betsy swung her curtains aside and shot from the cubicle at full speed. The Head Girl was left gasping but Betsy's next door neighbour volunteered an explanation.

"It's all right, Bride. Bets hasn't suddenly gone crackers. It's just that she does rather dream over her dressing and Matey ticked her off for it last week. *Is* that why she's been sent for to the Head, d'you know?"

"The Head didn't take me into her confidence," Bride replied gently before she left the room, and Lala Winterton stood gaping after her with open mouth for a full five seconds before she remembered that she was none too far on in her own duties and hurriedly turned to strip her bed.

Meanwhile, Betsy had gone scuttering downstairs and along the corridor to the study where she found her thirteen-year-old sister Viola standing by the Head. Miss Annersley gave the elder girl a smile as she bobbed her curtsey at the door and called her to come to the fire.

"Come and sit down, Betsy. It's a miserable day!" with a glance out of the window at the rain which was coming down as steadily as ever. "That's right. Now, dear – and Vi, too – I'm afraid I have some rather bad news for you."

Betsy was quick-witted. She saw that their elder sister was not present and she promptly leapt to a conclusion. "It's Julie! What's wrong with her, please?"

The Head's arm had gone round Vi who was looking frightened and she held out her other hand to Betsy who grabbed it and clung to it as if it were a lifeline.

"I think you know that Julie's been having a return of her old tummy pains?" she said. "Last night she had a bad attack and when Nurse saw her, she sent at once for the doctor. He ordered Julie into hospital at Carnbach and operated at once for peritonitis."

A cry broke from Vi at this and the Head held her close. "Don't be frightened, Vi! Julie has been very ill and it was a bad operation, but it's over now. When I rang up the hospital just before you came, the Matron told me that she is going on as well as could possibly be expected. No one could expect more so soon after the operation. It means that they are quite satisfied and, please God, Julie will soon be on the high road to recovery."

Betsy stared into the fire, trying to pull herself together. Then Vi's frightened sobs roused her from the dull sense of terror that had overwhelmed her on hearing the Head's news. She pulled her little sister towards her and held her tightly.

"Don't howl like that, Vi. The Head says she is doing well. It's over now, so we've nothing to be afraid of." She looked at Miss Annersley over Vi's golden-brown curls. "Is Mummy here?"

"We expect her before long. Your father's friend, Mr la Touche is flying her to Cardiff and Miss Dene has set off in the car to bring her from there."

Betsy nodded. "He would, of course. He and Daddy are great chums. That's splendid, Vi! We shall see Mummy soon – perhaps even, tonight." She turned to the Head again. "Who – who took Julie to the hospital?"

"Matron and I; and Matron is staying with her until your mother arrives. I shall go back as soon as I can be spared from school."

"And – when did it all happen? Please, Miss Annersley, we'd rather know everything."

"So you shall. Sit down, Betsy; and Vi, come and take this pouffe. Dry your eyes, darling. It's been a nasty fright, hasn't it? But we may hope that that is all over now."

Vi scrubbed her eyes violently and squatted on the pouffe near the Head's chair and Betsy sank into the fireside chair indicated, her bright brown eyes fixed on Miss Annersley's clear-cut face.

"Julie hasn't been well for some days," the Head began, choosing her words carefully. "She has had attacks of pain and Bride tells me she had one at the very beginning of term. But I'm afraid it goes farther back than that. Do you remember, Betsy, that she had one or two bouts last summer term?"

Betsy nodded. "She was in bed with one the day of the tennis match between Campion House and us – the day that silly ass Jennifer Penrose locked Blossom into the art room and Katharine had to take over her place as reserve when Nita Etringham dished her shoulder – I – I mean *injured* her shoulder!" Betsy reddened under the sudden twinkle in Miss Annersley's eyes at the slang. "But, Miss Annersley, I know she hadn't any more goes after that. At least if she did, she said nothing to any of us about it."

"No; I think you're right there. But Matron did speak to your mother about those attacks at the end of the term. Your own doctor at home examined her during the holidays, your mother told me, and he could find nothing. The mischief must have died down for the time being. But it flared up again this week, and last night what had been a 'grumbling' appendix became an acute one and she had such bad pain that Nurse came to see her and sent for the doctor at once. When he came, he ordered her off to hospital immediately and she was operated on at eleven o'clock last night. Matron and I were there all night, but I had to return this morning for a few hours. We couldn't tell you when it happened – it was too late to rouse you, so we had to leave it till this morning. Now you know everything."

"Wh – when can we go and see her?" Vi asked with a gulp.

"Not for a day or two. She was very ill and, of course, the operation has left her very weak. She must be stronger than she is now before you can visit her, Vi; but I hope we can manage it by about Wednesday next week. She ought to be much better then."

"Will they let Mummy see her at once?" Betsy asked abruptly.

"Oh yes; your mother will go to her as soon as she arrives." The Head thought of that moment the night before when the men were bringing the stretcher into the room and she had been sitting by Julie, holding one hot, weak hand in hers, and the girl had said with difficulty, "I – I want – Mummy – please."

Betsy was replying to the last remark. "Oh, good! Julie would want Mummy. We always do when we're ill or anything. I – I was – afraid they might say it – would be better – if Julie didn't see anyone at all!"

Miss Annersley smiled. "Mothers don't come under that heading as a rule, Betsy, though I'm afraid sisters do. Not that Julie is likely to know much about it for a day or so," she added. "They will have given her something to dull the pain and she will be too drowsy to notice much about her. But your mother will be with her and she'll see her when she rouses."

Vi was satisfied. In some ways she was very childish for her thirteen years and she was pleased to think that Julie was sleepy and out of pain now. The Head had said that she would probably be well enough to see them in a few days, so that must mean that she was all right, even though she had been so ill and was too weak to see anyone but Mummy. She gave her eyes a last scrub with her handkerchief and rewarded Miss Annersley for her remarks with a wide smile. Betsy, however, was nearly sixteen now, and she understood far better than her young sister what might lie behind the Head's words. She glanced at Vi and Miss Annersley saw it and guessed that the girl wanted to ask her questions but preferred to say no more while the child was there.

"Vi," she said, "you know now that it's going to be all right. Suppose you run upstairs and sponge your face. You don't want the others to see how you've been crying, I know. And I think you had better get another hanky. That one is finished, I'm afraid. Run along, dear.

You can go up the front stairs for once." She stooped and kissed the flushed and tearstained face, and Vi got up and left the room laggingly. She had had a shock, even though it had been greatly softened by her own ignorance and her elders' thoughtfulness. But she was beginning to cheer up. The hope of seeing her mother shortly – for surely Mummy would be able to visit them once Julie was really better! – helped her enormously.

When she had gone, the Head turned to Betsy. "What else do you want to know, dear?" she asked in that beautiful voice of hers.

Betsy waited a moment to steady her own voice. "You – you're *sure* Julie really will get all right, aren't you? I've heard that people sometimes come through an operation all right, but – but have a bad time afterwards because of the shock."

"So far as anyone can say, Julie should make progress once the next day or so is over. You shall ring up the hospital yourself and ask at teatime how she is."

Betsy cleared her throat before she spoke again. "Peritonitis is a bad thing, isn't it – worse than appendicitis, I mean?"

"Very bad, Betsy. But the doctor says she came through the operation itself in good shape and she's very strong and sturdy as a rule, you know. And then there was no delay – or none once we knew how ill she was." Miss Annersley thought, but did not say that if only Julie had gone to Matron when she had the first bout of pain that term, much of this might have been avoided. It was useless to speak of it at present and even cruel with the girl in the state of anxiety she now was. "Finally, you have to remember that medicine has made enormous strides of late years. With all the wonderful new drugs they use nowadays, even the worst operations are much less dangerous than they used to be. I have kept nothing back from you I promise you that. She will be very weak for a few days and they will keep her absolutely quiet until her strength begins to come back. You can understand that. But once she is over the first few days, she ought to make headway very quickly."

Betsy turned and stared into the fire again and the Head left her to herself for a minute or two. She got up and went to her desk where she busied herself with tidying her papers. Presently, she came and laid a hand on the slender shoulders. "Listen to me, Betsy. I know you've had a horrible shock, but you mustn't upset yourself if you can help it. If you make yourself ill with fretting, you won't be able to go to Carnbach when Vi does. If Vi visits her and you don't she may begin to wonder and ask questions. I know how close you all are as a family, and Julie might do her share of fretting if she thought you were miserable. That would be a bad thing for her; it might even set her back a little. No one – you, least of all! – wants that. For her sake you must try to cheer up and be as hopeful as you can. She has your mother with her and she will get the best of care. No one can do anything more but pray for her and you know that we shall all do that." The Head paused a moment. Then she told the girl of that little meeting in her study late last night and Betsy flushed and then smiled a rather watery smile.

"How lovely of them all! I – I'll try not to worry or fuss. But – but it's been rather – a shock, you know."

"I know, dear. But the worst really *is* over. I mean that, Betsy," she added as the girl gave her a keen look. "I wouldn't lie to you nor even equivocate. You know that, I think. Now, wouldn't you prefer a quiet breakfast alone? Or is there anyone you'd like to have with you?"

Betsy fished out her handkerchief and dabbed her eyes. "Oh, Miss Annersley, you do understand! Yes, I don't want to go to Frühstück, please. But – but if I may, I'd like Nancy."

"Very well. Do you want Vanna and Nella as well? I'll ask you to leave Vi with her own crowd. It'll be better for her. But if you want your cousins, you can have them."

Betsy uttered a queer sound, half-laugh, half-choke. "The entire family, in fact! No, Miss Annersley. It's awfully decent of you to think of it, but Vanna and Nella are just kids in lots of ways. I know they're nearly three years older than I am, but they *are*! They're five months older than Julie and seven older than Nancy, but where those two come in they're utter *babes*! Why, I often feel years older myself! I'd rather have just Nancy, please. They'll be awfully sorry and all that, but they won't help and Nancy will. Besides, she and Julie have always been such chums."

Thinking of the pretty Ozanne twins who were cousins of the Lucys and the Chesters, the Head fully agreed with this. They were the youngest of their family while Betsy and Nancy both had a long string of brothers and sisters after them. They were in the same form as Betsy, but while she was always among the first three, they cheerfully adorned the lower end of the lists. At seventeen, they were little older in outlook than Vi, and neither wanted to grow beyond it. Life had always been very easy for them. Their father was a wealthy man who could give them all they wanted and their mother had tended to keep them much younger than their age. Not even school had done much to mature them so far, and Miss Annersley felt that they would always slip through life happily unless circumstances changed. The Chesters were a very long family and a poor one into the bargain, and the Chester girls had known hard struggles. As for the young Lucys, there was no lack of money there, but their parents had brought them up to help with the younger ones and take responsibilities as they grew older. Betsy was right when she said that her Ozanne cousins would not help much.

"Very well, dear. You and Nancy shall have breakfast by yourselves in here. I'll see that it's sent in. But after that, Betsy, I want you to take up the day's work again. It will be better for you than having nothing to do but think of Julie. Yes," as she saw the mutinous look that flashed over Betsy's expressive face at this. "You feel that you can't settle down to maths and French and all the rest and I'm very hard-hearted to insist on it; but I do know what I'm talking about. I want you to try to think only of your work during lessons –"

"But," Betsy pointed out demurely, "this is Saturday. There *are* no lessons."

The Head looked at her and began to laugh. "Well! You've caught me out this time, Betsy, and no mistake! I'd forgotten that. The fact is with all the rush I'm completely muddled. Well, if there aren't lessons, there are prep and mending to do. Guides come after that and I'm sure you won't want to let down your Patrol. You are PL for the Cherries, aren't you?"

Betsy nodded. "And how!" She was beginning, despite herself, to cheer up under the Head's wise treatment. Suddenly she caught that lady's eye and blushed. "Oh, I beg your pardon! I didn't mean to talk slang!" she added hurriedly.

"I'll forgive you this time," the Head assured her. "But do try to remember. You girls still use an appalling amount of slang and the rules against it are going to be tightened up, so I'd advise you to be careful how you speak in the future. After all, there should be no need to use it. English is, perhaps, the richest language in the world. I don't ask you to express yourselves like Jane Austen young ladies," she added with a twinkle, "but I do beg that you will try to avoid the worse excesses. Now I will send for Nancy and you can have a quiet time together until Prayers. But after that, my dear, you must come back to the workaday world. Remember, Betsy, that 'Laborare est orare'. The biggest thing you can do for Julie at present is to pray for her and you can offer your work to God as part of your prayers."

With this, she left the room and presently Nancy arrived. A somewhat subdued Nancy she was, but she was a part of home, and as she laid her hands on her young cousin's shoulders, giving her a gentle shake, Betsy somehow felt better still.

"Well, Bets, my lamb!" she said. "Julie has certainly managed to create a sensation this time! But she's getting better now."

"Was – was she very bad last night?" Betsy asked anxiously.

"Well, she wasn't too good. You aren't when you've an outsize in tummy aches; but she might have been a lot worse," Nancy said judicially. Not for worlds would she have let the younger girl know of the agonies of pain Julie had endured. She heard the rattle of crockery outside the door and turned with a thankful, "Here comes brekker! Bacon, to judge by the odours! Oh, my one and only Aunt Sempronia! Bacon *and* eggs! Here's richness, Betsy! Gladys, Cook is a star of the first order! This table, please. Come on, Bets! You can serve the bacon while I pour the coffee. I don't know about you, but I'm simply ravenous!"

All the same, it was with an effort that she cleared her

plate; and only the fact that the Head had warned her that Betsy must be persuaded to make a proper meal forced her to toast and marmalade after. She was rewarded for her own efforts by seeing her cousin eat a good meal and a little colour come into the small, quaintly puckish face that had looked so wan when she first entered. She kept up a flow of light chatter the whole time, but she was a very thankful girl when she heard the first bell for Prayers ring and knew that they must go.

"I don't think I'm cut out as a comforter for the young," she confided to Bride much later on.

CHAPTER 10

Bride in a Difficulty

"Well, Julie seems to be coming along all right now, thank goodness! After all our alarums and excursions that's something to be thankful for! She's had a doing, poor kid! Let's hope this *larns* her – and everyone else, too – not to sit on any odd pains but go straight to Matey about 'em! However, the Abbess says that when she rang up the hospital this morning, the matron there told her that Julie had slept all night and Doc says she's on the right road at last. It's only a question of time now before she's convalescent. Meanwhile, have you folk ever thought what a hole we are in?"

It was Bride who spoke and the occasion was a full prefects' meeting. It was rather more than ten days since that eventful night when Julie had given them all such a shock. Since then, they had been kept very anxious, for the girl had been dangerously ill for the next few days from the shock of the operation. The first grey hairs had shown in Mrs Lucy's bright brown head during the time, for, though the younger members of the school had not known it, there had been one long day and night when Julie was so weak that it seemed as though she must slip away from them. Even when she had turned away from the Gates of Death, she had healed slowly and the hospital folk had been afraid of complications. However, that was over now and, for the first time, Bride had had time to realize that they had been one prefect short in

134

any case and now they would be without a second for the remainder of the term. Julie was Head of Netball as well as Staff prefect. She had had her full share of supervision duties and someone must take over those – a good many someones, in fact. Hence, this meeting!

Nancy, who had been allowed to visit her cousin the day before, looked up the table at Bride and said, "Julie was talking about that when I saw her yesterday. She asked me to tell you, Bride, that she thought that so far as the netball was concerned, it would be best to put Dora Robson in her place. She said would you and Elfie talk it over, and if you agree, will you see what Burnie thinks?"

Bride looked at Elfie. "What about it, Elf? You know better than I do and you *are* Games pree."

Elfie considered. "Yes; I think Dora would be as good as anyone – much the best, in fact. I know Julie consulted her a good deal. If Burnie says it's OK – I mean all right – that would certainly solve *that* problem. And Dora has been running the netball since Julie was taken ill."

"Well, that's something settled, anyhow!" Bride said thankfully. "We'll have to see Burnie about it, but I don't suppose she'll object, especially as Julie suggested it herself."

"Oh, she'll agree all right," Elfie assented. "What are we to do about Staff pree, though?"

Bride knitted her brows. "I haven't the foggiest! I'd take it on myself, but I honestly haven't a moment to spare. What about the rest of you? Any offers? Speak now, or for ever hold your peace!"

No one spoke, for no one felt she could manage any more than she already had.

"We'd best see the Abbess about it," Primrose Day

135

suggested. "When it comes to duties, though, I'll take over one of her preps."

"Will you? Then I'll take the other evening prep – it had best be evening, I think. I'll put us down for them at once. Which days did she have?" Bride leaned backwards in her chair to twitch the duties timetable from the board behind her and study it.

"I could do her two afternoon preps if you like," Madge Dawson offered. "I'm not in any of the school teams, so I can be spared from games and it won't interfere with the music-room jobs."

"Yes; but haven't you an exam shortly?" Bride asked. "I thought you were supposed to be doing extra prac in the afternoons this term?"

"I could get up earlier those days and put it in before Frühstück. I'm sure Matey would give me leave as it's for an exam."

Despite her worry, Bride grinned. "Are you? It's a lot more than I am, let me tell you. After Julie's affair, I don't see Matey giving anyone leave to be down a whole hour earlier at this time of year. Oh, you can try, of course – no harm in trying. But I rather think you're in for a disappointment if that's your idea."

Madge subsided. There was too much truth in what Bride said for her to dispute it. Besides, once Matron had put her foot down, they all knew that it was *down* and no amount of coaxing would move her.

"What else have we to think of besides the preps?" Bess Herbert asked.

Bride looked at the timetable again. "The Thirds' Break on Tuesdays and Fridays. It won't matter so much once they can go out, but with the sort of weather we've been having all this term, that's about once in a blue moon! D'you think we'll *ever* see the sun again?"

"You're telling *me*!" Elfie spoke with some bitterness. "Do you people realize that so far we've had to cancel five matches this term? And I *mean* cancel – not postpone! There simply isn't time to fit them in now, even if the rain stopped today and the pitches dried up and were playable on by Monday – which they won't be!"

"Well, hardly! D'you want a miracle?" Primrose asked. "Thank goodness February is nearly over. March may be a lovely month. At least we haven't had much snow this winter."

Quite unexpectedly, Lesley Pitt suddenly quoted,

"'February fill the dyke,
Fill it with either black or white.
And if it's white, so much the better.'"

"What on earth do you mean?" Primrose demanded.

"It's an old saying. And there's that other one about a green February making a fat churchyard," Lesley said.

"It's a green *Christmas*," Audrey Simpson interjected. "*And* we had it in our part of the world! On Christmas Day the rain simply poured down all day and we went to church in raincoats and wellies."

"*We* had fog," Tom told her cheerfully. "The foghorn went all day – like a cow mourning its lost calf. It didn't go at all well with 'Oh come, all ye faithful'!"

"Oh, do stop yattering!" Bride spoke crossly. "This is a Prefects' Meeting; not a yatter party nor a weather discussion. You stop it and give your great minds to our problems, if you can!"

The weather gossips looked slightly ashamed of themselves and the meeting came to order with due meekness.

"The question is," Bride said when they were all sitting, looking expectantly at her, "what are we to do about filling

137

up Julie's duties? She won't be back this term, you know. After a doing like hers, she'll probably need all the time till next term to pull up. Even next term it wouldn't surprise me if she had to take things easily. What do you all think? Should we go to the Abbess and ask her to give us a new Sub pro tem. and shove one of our Subs up to full pree? Nancy, you're the only one of us who's seen her. How did she strike you? I *am* right about her not coming back till next term?"

"Dead right!" Nancy spoke with emphasis. "She's horribly weak, and 'skinny' doesn't begin to describe her! Nurse told me that she really was beginning to make headway and, judging by what the Abbess said today, there's no need to worry about her any more. But she definitely won't come back this term. Auntie J.'s hoping to be able to take her home the week after next. That will bring it into March. When do we break up? April 8th, isn't it? And this is February 19th. How long does that make, anyone?"

"Six weeks or so," Primrose said. "No; if they aren't taking her home till the week after next, you're right, both of you. She definitely won't return *this* term."

"She'll be all right for next, though, won't she?" Elfie asked in sudden alarm. "We come back on May 1st, don't we? That would be nine weeks, anyhow."

"Oh, I should think she'd be fit again by that time," Nancy agreed. "They all said that once she definitely turned the corner she'd steam ahead like anything!"

"Ye – es," Bride said thoughtfully. "Nine weeks is a long time. Though I don't know," she added. "Mummy's op was done in November and even now she isn't getting up for all the day."

"No, but Auntie Mollie's heart was dicky," Nancy said quickly. "And besides, it was a different thing, Bride. I've heard Dad say that most people recovered fairly quickly after an appendectomy."

"After a *what*?"

"That's the correct name for the op. However, there's one thing you mayn't know and that is that all the lot of us – Chesters, Lucys *and* Ozannes – come up jolly quickly once we start. I expect Julie will be pretty well all right by May."

"Well, that's something to know!" Elfie heaved a sigh of relief. "Julie came on a lot at cricket last year and I don't want to be missing those patent twisters of hers in the team."

"I don't suppose you will," Nancy said easily.

"Then at that rate we needn't worry too much about next term." It was Bride's turn to sigh relievedly. "I must say I think we've enough on our plates without that. Well, what do you think of my suggestion? We certainly must do something. We've managed so far but it's been a scramble and I loathe a scramble."

"Look here!" Tom had been chewing things over. "You're proposing to put Dora into Julie's place for netball. Why not ask the Head if she couldn't – Dora, I mean – take over the whole shoot of Julie's jobs? She's got sense and she can handle the kids all right. They all like her and *we* like her. Why not go to Burnie and see what she says about the netball? Then, if she's agreeable, I should say send a deputation to the Head to ask if Dora can be appointed pro tem, as Bride says. Julie will be back next, from what Nancy says, so it would be for the rest of this term only. She'll take on her own chores when she *does* return. And anyhow, she won't have to fuss with the netball as that's off for the summer."

"That's a jolly good idea, Tom," Anne said with enthusiasm. "It's certain we shall have to have someone, and

Dora would be the very one for it. I was rather surprised she wasn't appointed in the beginning," she added.

"So was I." Pretty Rosalind Yolland, the youngest of the sub-prefects now spoke up. "You could have bowled me over with a feather when the Head read out my name and Dora's was left out."

"I can guess the reason for that," Bride said shrewdly. "You and Audrey are having another year here after this and the idea is that you get practice in being a school pree. Dora will be leaving. She's eighteen now and she's going into nursing. She's only marking time until she goes to her hospital – Bart's, I think it is. She told me so herself."

"Oh, I hadn't thought of that," Rosalind said. "I say, we shan't be so badly off next year, after all. Tom says she's giving Switzerland a miss, and Audrey and I will be here. That'll be three of us former prees. These last two years, it's meant having a complete new set."

Bride fixed her with a stern eye. "You give chat about next year a miss! It's this term we're discussing! I'm going to put Tom's idea to the meeting. All who think it's the best we can do, hands up! Unanimous! Well, that's all right."

"Who's going to be the deputation and when shall we go?" Lesley Pitt asked. "You and Elfie will tackle Burnie. Not that that need worry you, I should think she'd fall on your necks and weep with relief at having *that* problem so neatly solved for her."

"What a vision!" Bride began to laugh. "Oh yes; Elfie and I will go and see Burnie about the netball. As for when we go to the Head, the sooner the better. Let's take another dekko at the timetable. I have a horrid feeling that tomorrow Julie had a mid-morning walk." She studied the big sheet. "Yes; she had the Thirds after church. Of course, if this rain goes on, it won't matter,

140

for there'll *be* no walk. But we'd better get things settled just in case. I propose we vote for the deputation to the Head so as to be ready. We'll have to do that after tea. There's just time to vote and let Elf and me go to Burnie. I'll be thankful to have things fixed up. We've managed, but it's been a bit of a nuisance."

This was agreed to. They voted and the deputation finally resolved itself into Elfie, Nancy and Lesley with Bride leading it, ex officio, as she remarked.

"You're very Latinized today," Primrose teased her. "What's the why of that?"

"I only use terms that express what I mean very shortly," Bride retorted with dignity.

"When do we go?" Elfie asked. "It's nearly teatime now. Can we manage it just after, before prep begins?"

"Well, we must see to it tonight," Bride agreed, studying the timetable once more. "Elf, if you and I go at once, we should be able to see Burnie at once. Then we can see if we can fit the deputation to the Head as you suggest. If not, I suppose we must leave it till just after prep, but I'd like to get it settled as soon as possible. It's an awful bother having to arrange from day to day."

They got up and left the room to return five minutes later with the information that they had met Miss Burnett at the head of the stairs and she fully agreed that Dora should take over the netball for what was left of the term.

"So *that's* all right," Elfie said jubilantly. "I'm almost certain the Head will agree to making her a Sub and either Audrey or Rosalind can be shoved up to full pree."

"Oh, not me, I hope," Rosalind said in some alarm. "I find Sub quite enough for my modest taste, thank you!"

"It isn't our pigeon. You'll have to do as the Head says," Bride told her austerely. "There's the first bell! Come on, everyone! We'll have to fly or we'll be late for tea and *wouldn't* the kids chortle if that happened?"

They had a rush, for there was only a ten minutes' interval between the first and second bells. None of the Staff ever came to tea, the prefects being in charge of that meal, and Bride herself was on duty at one of the big urns, while Nancy and Bess had the other two. Usually, whoever was on duty went to the dining room when the first bell rang and started to fill the cups at once so that there was no delay. Today, when the rank and file marched into the dining room, the three prefects had just begun and the girls had to wait, rather to their surprise.

This meant that the tea itself was slightly delayed and Diana Skelton, who was a slow eater felt distinctly annoyed when Lesley urged her to hurry up a little as the rest had nearly done. She said nothing, but she made no effort to hasten, and the two or three others who were also behindhand and who had literally choked down their last mouthfuls, looked at her meaningly as she took dainty bites out of her cake and sipped her tea.

"Oh, *come* on!" Katharine Gordon said in an impatient undertone. "Don't be all night over it! The rest of us want to get off if you don't!"

Diana stopped eating to reply in dignified tones, "I see no reason for gobbling my food down. It's not only bad for the digestion; it's very ill-mannered."

What Katharine might have replied to this snub will never be known, for at that moment, Bride called for Grace and they all stood up and Diana found that she must either leave the greater part of her cake, or else do as Mary-Lou at the next table was doing – cram the whole piece into her mouth at one go and try to swallow it as soon as possible. The younger girl, who had overheard Katharine's remark and most of Diana's answer, looked across and winked cheerfully at the elder girl before she

142

got to her feet and stood with hands devoutly folded and head bent, her cheeks bulging and her jaws moving rapidly.

"Disgusting little *pig*!" Diana exclaimed audibly. She reseated herself. "*I* shall finish in a ladylike manner."

"OK; that's up to you," Carola Johnston returned, picking up her plate and cup and marching off with them to the hatch.

Bride, watching the Juniors for any monkey tricks, overheard and looked across the room. "Aren't you finished yet, Diana?" she said.

"Not yet," Diana replied, raising her cup elegantly to her lips. "I object to bolting my food like *some* people here!"

"That meant for me?" Mary-Lou grinned, having disposed of her mouthful at last.

Bride was in no mood to stand nonsense. "If you've been bolting your food, you ought to be ashamed of yourself!" she snapped at Mary-Lou. "You've plenty of time to eat all you want if you don't waste it by chattering so much. Take your crocks to the hatch and then be off with you! As for you, Diana, hurry up, please! I've something better to do than stand about here waiting for you folk to finish just because you choose to chatter instead of eating!"

Mary-Lou gave Bride a wide-eyed stare before she fled before the storm. Then she scuttled off to join her peers and wonder to them why Bride was so short-tempered today.

"Oh, they've all been worried over Julie, I expect," Doris Hill said. "That does make people cross. And Diana's enough to get anyone's goat! I do dislike that girl!"

Meanwhile, Diana herself had flushed under Bride's

undeserved rebuke, since she had not done much talking, and flared out. "There's no need for anyone to stand and watch me. I'm not a baby!"

Bride glared at her. "Finish that cake and take your things to the hatch and hurry up. And another time, kindly don't answer back like that!"

Primrose, on the point of leaving the room, looked back and saw what was happening. "Diana last again?" she queried, coming back. "All right, Bride. You get off and I'll wait and see her out of the room. The rest will be waiting for you, and she's a regular snail over her meals at the best of times!"

Bride was about to go when Diana's temper suddenly gave way. She jumped up, flung the remains of the cake on the floor and stamped on it. "How dare you! How dare you talk of me like that! I'll take as long as I like and not ask *your* leave!"

"Oh no, you won't," Primrose said with imperturbable good temper. "You'll learn to hurry a little. In the meantime, you can go to the kitchen and ask someone for a brush and dustpan. Then you can come back and sweep up this mess. And for goodness' sake stop dancing jigs on it! Talk of not being a baby!"

Bride suddenly found her voice. "And after that," she said, "you can come to the Prefects' room and apologize to Primrose for speaking and behaving to her like that! You must have taken leave of your senses, I think!"

Diana gave her an impudent look of defiance. "What d'you take me for? Think I'm going to be ordered about by girls not a year older than myself? You can whistle for your apology – *and* your brush and dustpan!"

"Don't talk rot!" Bride told her sharply. "You'll do as a prefect tells you. Age has nothing whatever to do with it. Stop making all this silly fuss. Run along and get that brush and dustpan and don't be a silly young ass!"

"Guess again!" Diana retorted.

The two big girls looked at her and then at each other.

Bride spoke first. "I've told you not to be silly. You'll do as Primrose told you. *You* made the mess and you must clear it up. The maids won't do it. Now hurry up and do as you're told."

"Not if I have to stay here all night!"

"Oh, it won't come to that," the Head Girl said drily. "For one thing, the maids will be in shortly to lay the tables for Abendessen and I imagine you don't want *them* to know you've been behaving like a KG baby! Do as Primrose told you and then come to the Prefects' room and be done with it!"

Diana wavered at the mention of the maids. She was a very silly, snobbish girl and she certainly disliked the idea of their finding her in trouble. Besides, as she knew, they all disliked her for her manner to them and she could just see them chuckling over it. She relaxed so far as to go for the brush and dustpan and give the floor a cursory sweep. But that, she found, would not do. Bride had vanished to join her deputation who had been nearly dancing with impatience; but Primrose was still there and she insisted that every crumb should be taken up before she let the girl go. Diana might have defied her again, but she could hear the noise of rattling cutlery being put on the trolley to bring in and nothing would induce her to let the maids see her in such an undignified situation, so she obeyed resentfully.

"Now take those things back and then come to the Prefects' room as Bride told you," Primrose said.

She wanted no apology for herself, but Diana had been rude to a prefect and Primrose knew that she must not be allowed to get away with that. Besides there was

145

the Head Girl's authority to back up. The prefect watched the culprit vanish behind the baize-covered door that led to the kitchen regions and then raced off upstairs, never doubting that Diana would do as she was told and shortly follow her to offer the apology, however scanty it might be.

The deputation was still closeted with the Head, but most of the others were there, waiting for the prep bell to call them to their duties. They either laughed or shrugged their shoulders when they heard the story Primrose told them in reply to their queries as to what on earth she had been doing since tea. Like her, however, they all expected that she would turn up shortly.

No Diana appeared however by the time the bell had rung, and they had to scatter to take various preps, or else settle down to their own work, deciding that one of the Staff must have kept her for some reason. The prefect system was so much a vital part of life at the Chalet School that it never dawned on them to doubt that she would defy one of them. So far as they knew, no pupil at the school had ever done so and they hardly thought Diana was the girl to do it.

However, the deputation came back from the study to say that the Head agreed with them and would announce Dora's promotion after Prayers that night, and still she did not come. Bride got out her book and prepared to do her best with a French essay while the others, who had duty, picked up the first lessons they needed and hurried off to relieve their deputies.

Bride wrote her name and form on her paper and the title of the essay. Then she suddenly remembered and looked up. "I suppose that little ass has apologized, Primrose?"

146

Primrose shook her head. "She hasn't been near. Probably one of the Staff nobbled her. I expect she'll turn up after prep."

Bride said no more and soon the only sounds in the room were the moving of pens over paper and the turning of leaves.

When the period ended and the others had rejoined them, they waited, but still no Diana, though she had plenty of time now.

"The silly little ass isn't coming," Bride said at last. "Well, she'll come and apologize to Primrose after Prayers or my name's not Bridget Mary Bettany!"

"Somehow," said Primrose herself as she packed the last of her books neatly away, "I don't think it's going to be so easy as all that. If you ask me, she's decided to dig her toes in and hang the lot of us! However, time will tell!"

"Time *will* tell," Bride retorted. "Diana apologizes for her impudence to you or she'll be sorry for it, and that's that!"

CHAPTER 11

Advice from Jo

Nearly a week had passed and, so far as the business between Diana and Primrose was concerned, things were at a deadlock.

"I see nothing for it but reporting her to the Abbess," Bess said one evening when the prefects were in their room as usual, waiting for the prep bell to ring. "We can't let this sort of thing go on. The kids are beginning to pick it up. Look at the way Emerence sauced Audrey last night! And Audrey's a full pree now! It's ruining our discipline."

"It's not going to the Abbess yet," Bride said, frowning blackly. "I want us to settle it ourselves if we can. In any case Audrey got the best of that affair and Emerence has gone round like a pet lamb all today. All the same, I quite agree that we must take steps. I'm going to."

"What are you going to do?" half a dozen voices demanded.

"Write to Aunt Jo, of course!"

There was a minute's silence as they digested this. Then Tom strode forward and gave her friend a buffet on the shoulder.

"Well done, you! That's the best notion yet! Mrs Maynard ought to be able to advise us if anyone can. She's been a Head Girl herself – *and* when the school was half full of foreigners! I'll bet she had some jolly rum knots to cut; and then she's always kept up with the school."

"For Heaven's sake don't knock me about!" Bride protested. "Anyway, it's not a new idea. I've been thinking of it the last two days. I *don't* want us to have to go to the Head. It'll be pounds better if we can settle the thing for ourselves. At the same time, if it goes on much longer, we shall have to. But that's to be a last resort. Anyhow, we'll see what Auntie Jo has to say."

"When are you writing?" Lesley asked.

"Now," Bride said firmly. "If you folk could manage to stop yattering for half an hour or so, I could get down to it at once. But you all *talk* so, and I can't think. I want to give her a clear picture of the set-out, so that she'll know exactly how things are. If only she'd still been over at Carnbach, I'd have asked leave to ring her up about it days ago. I'll be thankful when they all get back again! She's always been such a stand-by and it's been awfully difficult having to do without her all this time."

"It seems odd, doesn't it?" Primrose mused. "Mrs Maynard must have left school – as a schoolgirl, I mean – about twenty years ago –"

"Well, she didn't. She isn't thirty-eight yet, you know, nor anything like it. She was only twenty-one when the Trips were born and they've not eleven yet – or no; I'm wrong. They were eleven last birthday –"

"You were right first time," Nancy corrected her. "They were nine when they went away. That makes them ten last birthday, so Auntie Jo is thirty-one. It's only thirteen years since she was at school. But why d'you want to know, anyhow, Primrose?"

"Nothing much, really. What I set out to say was that lots of people wouldn't understand, but she does. She's part of the school, even now, in a very special sort of way – Oh, I know what I mean, but I can't explain it.

Anyhow, she *is*!"

Bride nodded. "OK – I mean, all right. I see what you mean and it's only what I've always felt myself. Anyhow, shut up, all of you and let me get going on the letter."

"Very well. Are you going to read it to us before you send it? You're speaking for all of us. I think we ought to make sure you've left out nothing that matters. We've got to put a stop to this sort of thing and do it at once," Elfie argued.

Bride nodded. "Yes; I'll read it to you – after Prayers. Now, for pity's sake be quiet and let me get on with it. I've got to squeeze in German and history and a spot of literature somehow as well and the sooner I finish this, the sooner I'll be able to get down to my work."

They all saw the force of her argument and stopped talking. Elfie turned to making out the lacrosse team for Saturday's match – the rain had stopped at last and the field was drying up under a strong east wind – and having a trying time since none of the new girls knew anything about lacrosse, though some of them were eager to learn. She had tried two or three people in Loveday's place, but no one had done much good so far and there were times when she told herself she was really thankful that the weather had been too consistently bad so far for any matches to be played.

The rest attended to odd jobs until the bell sent them off to take prep, depart for the library or else sit down at the table and begin with their own work. Dora Robson was one of them, still rather shy over her unexpected promotion. She was a very quiet girl, but, as Bride had said, full of sterling good sense and with an unexpected gift of humour which made her a welcome addition to their numbers. She kept glancing at Bride, whose smooth brown head was never raised from the letter she was

150

scrawling at a great rate. Sheet after sheet was filled with her small, rather angular script. Dora counted seven pages and then glanced at the clock, wondering when the Head Girl proposed to attend to more lawful work. Bride paid no heed to the time, and when Primrose came back at half past six from supervising Second Form prep, she was still busy.

At long last, she signed her name, gathered up her pages and began numbering them. When that was done and they were lying in a tidy pile before her, she stretched luxuriously and then looked at the clock. The squawk that burst from her startled the rest.

"Merciful Heaven! Look at the time! Ten to seven and I haven't touched a single book! Here, someone, shove this lot into the cupboard till later on and let me get cracking!"

The less said about her work the better. She skimmed through the chapter Miss O'Ryan had given them to read, and then concentrated fiercely on her German idioms. These were something that must be learned. It might be possible to produce something that would pass in history, for Bride had the memory of her Aunt Jo and could glean a certain amount of information from a rapid run-through of history or literature; but things like idioms had to be properly learned. She fixed the whole of her mind on that great pageful that Miss Denny had told them to learn and contrived to get about a dozen into her memory before the bell rang and books had to be put away.

"What on earth will you do?" Nancy asked sympathetically.

"Get up early tomorrow and learn as many more as I can and trust to luck that Sally calls on me early in the lesson. As for the lit, I'll just have to trust to luck again. Thank goodness I like reading poetry, anyhow, and I do know something about *Gareth and Lynette* as it is. So long as the Abbess doesn't sail in with contexts, I should be all right there. If she does though, I've had it!"

"We'll try to keep her off contexts," Audrey assured her. "I don't know it any too well myself, so I shan't be sorry."

To the prefects, it seemed as if Abendessen and Prayers would never come to an end. They finished at last, however, and once they had left Hall, the grandees of the school tore upstairs to their own room, thankful to remember that except for "Lights Out" their duties were done for that day. Lesley produced a box of fudge and they settled down round the table to listen to Bride's screed.

"I'll read it straight through," she said as she sat down. "When I've finished, you can all make any comments you like and if you think of anything I've missed out, we can put it in then. No, thanks, Lesley, not just now. I can't read aloud with my mouth full of fudge. You can save my share for later. Ready? Right! Here goes!" And she settled back in her chair and began to read.

"Dearest Auntie Jo,

I know you always tell folk to stand on their own feet and avoid trampling on other folks' if it can be helped and I've honestly tried to stand on mine, but it just can't be done. Not in this instance, anyhow. I could ask Peg, but she never had anything like this to deal with and anyhow, you're a lot older and have had yards more experience, so I'm asking you. Do be a lamb and tell me what you think I can do – short of going to the Abbess which none of us wants. It would look so feeble!

"Here's the yarn. Do you remember the Chalet

152

School at Tanswick? It was a frightfully modern school where you seem to have worked or not, just as you chose. And that goes for Juniors as well as Seniors! They also adopted our colours which I call frightful cheek, though I'm bound to say that they interpreted them in the weirdest way. Last year at this time, for instance, they went in for *orange* tunics! You should have seen them!

"Games don't seem to have been compulsory, either, and though a lot of them did a fair amount of tennis, they didn't worry about much else. Sally Winslow, one of the best of them and quite a decent kid, really, says that when she went to the school last Easter, she was awfully browned off because they didn't play hockey officially. Not that it mattered then, but they had the Christmas term at Tanswick and though she did her best to scratch up two elevens, they were mostly Juniors and it wasn't much fun for her as she's fifteen.

"Well, that was the last term for Tanswick. The school's closed now, for the old Head had to give up to go and look after the family of some relatives who died and the new one died about the middle of the term. She'd been ill for ages first, poor soul! She, by the way, was the one who brought in a lot of their madder ideas and the old one had had a few to start on.

"No one wanted to carry on, for which I don't blame them. The result was that there were sixty or seventy girls let loose on the world, and you know how it is with vacancies at present. About forty of them were drafted here, and five or six were leaving in any case, so three or four more joined them and the rest went to other places. One of the girls who came here is a young beauty – that's true, by the way, in every sense of the word! – called Diana Skelton. Who she thinks she is, we don't know, but she puts on the airs and graces of a princess when she isn't cheeking prefects right and left. She really is a pain in the neck! And I know that's slang, but nothing else is strong enough to say what I think of her! She's sixteen and a half, but brains are *not* her chief point, so she's been placed in Lower VA along with kids like Betsy Lucy – and while I remember, Julie's going on fine now and they hope to take her home some time next week. Auntie J was over yesterday and told me so when I saw her – and Carola Johnston who are both just a month or two over fifteen and can make rings round her when it comes to lessons. She is also a horrid little snob. Young Sally says that at Tanswick there was a little bunch of them, Diana being head and chief. They called themselves 'Nous Autres', if you please, and, so Sally says, looked down on everyone else. Five of them left when the school closed but, for our sins, we've been landed with the remaining eight *and* Diana.

"Don't worry about the school. We're all keeping an eye open and if we see any signs of that particular idiocy coming up, we'll stamp on it heavily."

"I should *think* so!" Elfie interjected at this point.

Bride glared at her. "I told you folk to be quiet until I'd finished. If you don't want to hear the rest, say so and be done with it."

"We do – we do!" rose in eager chorus round the table. "Go on, Bride, and let's hear it all! It's OK so far."

"And you dry up, young Elf!" Tom ordered.

Elfie blushed and hid her head and Bride, after an awful glower round the table, condescended to go on.

154

"So far, they don't seem to have made much impression on the others – haven't had the time, of course. But we *have* got one or two very much inclined the same way and, by all unholy chances, two of them are in Lower VA and I've seen them about with Diana this past week or so. Not that that was what I set out to tell you, but it's as well for you to have a full picture of the position.

"The real trouble is this. One day last week we (by which I mean the prefects) were late for tea-duty. We'd been having a meeting to decide what to do about Julie's supervision and so on for the rest of the term as she won't be back till after Easter. As a result, most of the cups hadn't been done when the rest came in and the kids had to wait. I did give them five minutes extra, but some of them were on the natter all the meal – as usual! – instead of getting on with it. Mary-Lou was one, of course; and the great Diana was another. When I did stand up to say Grace, neither of those two had got very far with their cake. Mary-Lou shoved the whole lot into her mouth at once – I got this later from Clem Barrass who said she'd ticked her off well for bad table manners, so I did nothing more about it – Goodness knows how she got rid of it without choking! I expect you remember the great chunks of school cake they dish out? However, she got away with it as you might guess, knowing our one and only Mary-Lou.

"Diana didn't attempt to do anything of that kind. She goes in for 'elegant' manners. I've seen her cocking her little finger in the air when she holds her cup myself! She went on nibbling daintily and sipping at her tea like someone's maiden great aunt, so Lala Winterton says. As a result, she still had more than half her cake left when I stood up. After Grace, she sat down again to finish. Carola had something to say about it and I went to hurry her up. She cheeked me over it and Primrose, overhearing us, came back and said she'd wait with her until she finished as she – I mean Primrose – knew I wanted to go to the study with a deputation to ask if Dora Robson could take Julie's place all round for the rest of the term and time was getting on. She said that Diana always *was* a little snail over her meals which wasn't exactly tactful, I'll admit, but then Primrose often isn't."

At this point Primrose flushed up and looked as if she might say something, but her next-door neighbours nudged her, so she bottled up her wrath for the time being and left it till later.

Bride, sublimely indifferent to this, continued reading:

"Anyhow, Diana lost her temper and behaved like an infant of your Mike's age. She chucked the cake on the floor and danced on it – literally. Primrose choked her off pretty sharply and told her to fetch a brush and dustpan and clean up the mess at once. I topped it off by telling her that when she had done that, she could come to the Prefects' room and apologize to Prim for cheeking her.

"She said she wouldn't and I rather think she meant to refuse to clear up her mess, but we stopped *that*, anyhow. When she had finished, Primrose left her and came upstairs. We waited and waited for her to come, but she never did. We waited until after tea next day and then, as she

156

still didn't come, we sent for her. – Mary-Lou, as it happens. She was passing our door when Nancy went to look for a messenger. She *would* be! That kid contrives to be up to her neck in every single thing that goes on! She went and came back ten minutes later with eyes like saucers. Diana had flatly refused to budge. I rather think Mary-Lou expected the heavens to fall!

"Now, Auntie Jo, you know yourself that you can't allow that sort of thing. If you do, it's 'Goodbye!' to any sort of order so far as *we* are concerned. I wanted to go for her myself, but the rest wouldn't hear of it. They said it would be letting down the dignity of the Head Girl. It's really just as well, for Madge went in the end, and she came back raging mad to say that the young ass had said to her, 'You can tell Bride What's-her-name that if she wants to speak to me, she can come and find me and *perhaps* I'll speak to her then.'

"This, if you please, before a bunch of Junior Middles who were goggling their eyes nearly out of their heads, so Madge says.

"Now I know I could report her to the Abbess and she'd jolly soon make her apologize and do it in public into the bargain; but we don't want to do that if we can do it in any other way. For one thing, it would make us look so feeble, as if we had to run to the Head to get our orders obeyed and you know that's not so. At the same time, young Diana can't be allowed to go on defying us like this. It's awfully bad for the kids, especially if they think she can get away with it. To give you one example of what's happened since, that bright specimen, Emerence Hope, cheeked Audrey right and left over leaving her locker looking like a hurrah's nest. It's true Audrey nearly took the skin off her and she caved in and tidied the locker _in her free time_ as meek as Moses, but we can't have that sort of thing going on. You know that for yourself. All the same, we're at our wits' end to know what to do about it. Do put on your thinking cap and send us some good advice! You ought to be able to after all your experience! I may add that Emerence hasn't been the only one to try it on. Write as soon as you can.

"I hope the kids are all well and your twins going ahead. Have they started to teeth yet? They're going on for seven months, aren't they? I thought they were ducks when I saw them at Christmas.

"By the way, you'll be interested to know that Dora goes to her hospital after Easter, so this is her last term. Jolly, isn't it, that she's got a chance to be a prefect before she leaves?

"Maeve sends her love. I'm thankful to say that she's toeing the line for once in her life and, as a result, all her gang are doing the same, even the Dawbarns, for which I'm devoutly thankful. Luckily Diana's line of country doesn't appeal to them in the least and they _have_ some sense of what's done or not done over a thing like that. Funny as it may seem, that crowd are actually _shocked_ at Diana!

"Well, here endeth the lesson!

"Tons of Love.
Bride."

Bride finished and looked round. "What have I left out?"

There was a pause. Then Elfie replied. "Nothing, I should think. At least, I can't think of a single thing myself. Honestly, Bride, I knew you could write a decent letter, but I never imagined you could get off a screed like this!"

The rest agreed with this dictum, so Bride folded her sheets, slipped them into a foolscap envelope which was ready addressed, and then went off to ask Miss Dene for an airmail stamp. She came back to say that the secretary had offered to take it to Cardiff in the morning and post it there.

"So that's all right!" Bride wound up joyously. "Aunt Jo will get it very shortly and she's safe to reply as soon as she can."

Then she found herself embroiled with Primrose who demanded to know what she meant by accusing her friend of being tactless.

"*You've* no room to talk," Primrose finished up. "You're as tactless as they come, yourself!"

It took Bride a good ten minutes to pacify her. But they were too good chums to quarrel, so it ended with Bride apologizing and agreeing that there were times when her best friend couldn't say *she* was always tactful. After that, the prefects settled down to await Jo Maynard's reply, meanwhile putting down any incipient rebellion with a firm hand. All the same, they devoutly wished the deadlock would end. There was an uneasy undercurrent which did not make life go any better. Luckily they had not long to wait, for Jo replied by return.

Warned by what had happened over her own letter and Primrose, Bride carefully read the screed through first. She was lucky enough to be free the second period that morning, so she escaped to the library, ensconced herself in one of the wide window seats and tore open the envelope. Then she buried herself in her aunt's advice.

"My poor lamb! What a nasty position you do seem to be in! I can't say I ever had to tackle anything quite like that when *I* was Head Girl, though I certainly had some strange problems to solve in my time. However, I've thought long and hard and here's the result. I hope it helps you.

"You say that this Diana-child refuses to fall into line with the rest of the community. That sort of thing is definitely anti-social behaviour. If she refuses to abide by the rules decided on by the majority, there's only one thing for it. Neither can she enjoy the privileges of the majority. Now what are your privileges? You think that one out and decide accordingly. Where certain rules are in force they must be kept or the end will be anarchy. It is against the rules for Junior girls to be impudent to prefects who are, in a sense, the Head's representatives. This Diana certainly owes Primrose and Madge an apology and until she has the decency to make it then, so far as the pleasant things you prefects run are concerned, she should be an outlaw.

"Mind, you are not to bully or lecture her. That's just as anti-social as what she is doing. But see her and explain exactly how she stands and what will happen if she won't give in. Be firm about it, but be kind. It's no use putting people's back up. You only make them dig their toes in harder than ever and make up their minds never to knuckle under. See that she apologizes properly and, since it's all been so public, you would have every right to make her

160

perform her amends in public. However, I'll leave that question to you. But once it's over, forget it. That's my advice and you can take it or leave it as you choose.

"I'm glad to hear that Julie is recovering at last. Poor kid! She certainly has had a doing as you say. And it's been hard lines on you to have a situation like this to face. I'm glad you've decided to hand over the whole job to Dora, especially as she is leaving at the end of this term. I remember her quite well and what a jolly girl she is. She'll be glad to think that she has had a chance to be prefect, even if it's only for a few weeks. And it really comes very conveniently that she is leaving as now she won't have to sink back into being one of the rank and file again when Julie comes back next term.

"Now I'm going to be aggravating. There are quite likely to be big changes in the school presently. I'm not going to say anything more about it except that I rather think you'll like our latest ideas. This hint will serve to whet your appetites for what is coming. And *don't* you all wish you could get hold of me!

"Yes, the twins have started teething, but, thank goodness, it's been very easy so far. You remember what a time we had with Mike? And Stephen was even worse! But beyond a little fretting, both Felix and Felicity have produced three teeth without any bother.

"My love to Maeve. I'm glad she's playing up and being a little sport. As for the Dawbarns, they were both born to be hanged! It's quite refreshing to hear that they're behaving themselves for once in a way!

161

"Now cheer up, all the lot of you, and think over what I've said about Diana. But don't get down in the mouth. If all else fails, you can remember that *I* shall be back next term!

Much love to you all and especially to Bride.

Jo Maynard."

Bride handed the letter round at Break, and by the time morning school had ended everyone had seen it.

"When can we have a meeting?" Nancy demanded in the Splashery where they were all making themselves fit to be seen for Mittagessen.

Bride ran her comb through her hair and thought. "Not this afternoon. We have games till three thirty and then some of us are on prep duty. And Madge isn't here, either, thanks to that exam of hers. She won't get back till after six, will she? Better make it after Prayers, then, and ask if some of the other Sixths will take over our duty for once. They ought to. We haven't worried them all this term, so far."

So it was arranged and the prefects went about their work for the rest of the day with minds considerably lightened.

CHAPTER 12

Diana is Dealt With

"Well?" Bride, sitting at the head of the table in the Prefects' room, with the rest seated down the sides and all looking solemn, glanced round them as she held up Jo Maynard's letter. "What do you think of the idea?"

"It's far and away the best," Nancy said. "I quite see Auntie Jo's point. But what exactly are the privileges we can debar her from? We'd better make a note of that first."

"There's Hobbies," remarked Tom, who was prefect for the Hobbies Club. "Not that she seems to be over-keen about it, anyhow, but if she's debarred from coming, she'll have to amuse herself as best she can alone which I don't suppose will appeal to her."

"No books from the Fiction Library," added Bess. "What about being in the teams, Elfie?"

"She isn't in one," Elfie said, "and you know she has to have her ordinary practices. Those aren't our business. Anyhow," she added, "she hates laxe and hockey and hasn't much more than a mild liking for netball, so you won't hurt her overmuch there."

"But, bless me, what does the silly thing go in for?" Primrose exclaimed. "Not keen on games or hobbies – and I don't suppose she's much of a reader, either. How does she – er – recreate?"

"She likes tennis," Elfie said doubtfully.

"But that's only for summer. What does she do for the winter?"

"I can tell you that one," Madge Dawson said unexpectedly. "She plays cards. She's simply mad on Bridge and Canasta."

"How on earth do you know that?" Bride demanded sharply.

"Well, she plays mainly with Sylvia Peacock, Sarah Lomax and What's-her-name Morton from Upper V. Young Sarah was in San three days last week with swollen glands which left them one short and Diana actually had the nerve to ask me to make up."

"What did you say?" Lesley asked with real curiosity.

"Told her I hadn't either time or inclination. I like Canasta very well; but Contract Bridge doesn't appeal to me in the least. We play ordinary Auction at home – when we *do* play."

"It was downright impudence on her part!" Rosalind spoke hotly. "The very idea of asking a prefect to join their silly game!"

Bride had been looking startled. Now she dropped her aunt's letter on the table and called the meeting to order. "That's enough about that. I must make inquiries into this presently, for I don't see how that crew could play Contract in their common room with all the row that usually goes on there and I want to know where they *did* play. But we'll deal with that later. At present, all I want is a list of the privileges we can cut out. Then I'm sending for her to tell her what will happen. There isn't any too much time, so just drop the cards business for the moment and see if you can think of anything more or if that's all."

"Saturday evenings?" Lesley suggested.

"All those that go by invitation, of course. Just

164

the ordinary dancing and games evenings belong to the school. It's our own affairs that we control that matter."

"What will you do about the Sale if she still refuses to apologize?" Dora Robson asked. "That is certainly very much our affair."

"I hope she'll have the sense to apologize before then," Bride said curtly. "If she doesn't, she's out of it, naturally." She glanced over the lists she had been scribbling down. "This OK?" She read it out: "Library – Hobbies – Invitation evenings – Sale. Anyone think of anything else?"

No one could.

"Very well, then." The Head Girl took a fresh sheet of paper and wrote on it. Then she folded it and looked round. "We'll have her in and ask her to apologize –"

"*Publicly*," Nancy interrupted. "She was publicly rude to Audrey – before a whole crowd of Juniors. She must apologize before them or they won't realize that you can't do that sort of thing here."

"She'll loathe that," Bess said.

"Audrey didn't like it when Diana cheeked her before the kids. Anyhow, you can't let that sort of thing go on, or goodness knows where it'll end," Elfie pointed out. "We can't leave the kids to think she's got away with it – and that's what would happen if you let her apologize in private."

Bride sighed. "Oh, I do agree. We can't sacrifice the morals of the young for the sake of one girl! All the same, I have a horrid feeling that we're going to have a tussle before she gives in."

"What have you written?" Nancy asked.

"Just the usual summons – 'Diana Skelton to appear before the prefects at once' – and signed my name. Prim,

165

would you find seeing if you can get hold of someone to take it – *not* Mary-Lou, by the way. Best catch someone from Upper V or one of the VI."

Primrose took the note and vanished to reappear in a few minutes and say, "All right. I bumped straight into Clem Barrass. She'll see that the note gets safely to its destination and add a few words of wisdom off her own bat into the bargain. Clem is one of the most level-headed we have. I should say that she's definitely slated for a prefectship next year."

"Talking of Clem Barrass," Bride turned to Elfie, "I've had an idea about that Second Home you're missing in laxe, Elf. What about trying young Clem there? I know she only began laxe last term, but she's picked it up amazingly. She has a marvellous eye and throws dead straight, not to mention her level-headedness that Prim spoke of just now. I should say she might quite well fill the breach, shouldn't you?"

Elfie pondered this. "It's an idea. I hadn't thought of her because she *is* so new at it, but I shouldn't wonder if she would do quite well in that place. Look here, get this Diana business over and then we'll have a meeting of the Games committee and I'll put it to them. Then we can send for Clem and tell her and she can come for team practice tomorrow afternoon. Thanks a lot, Bride."

"I wonder we didn't think of her sooner," Nancy, captain of the lacrosse team, said thoughtfully. "She's amazingly good considering she hasn't had two terms at it. And she's got drive as well as all the rest and that's what we're rather lacking in the team this year. It really is a brainwave, Bride."

Bess had been keeping an eye on her watch. "It's taking Diana a jolly long time to get up here," she said. "I hope the little ninny isn't going to refuse, for

166

that means the Head, whether we like it or not; and if the Head takes over, there'll be trouble."

"Don't worry," Bride said with a grin. "Clem will have rubbed *that* point of view well in. Diana will turn up all right, or I miss my guess. She *may* think prefects don't really count – from all I can gather, they didn't at the Tanswick establishment – but Heads, however idiotic they may be in their ideas, do. Diana will come, even though she may take her time over it."

Pat on her last sentence came a sullen knock at the door and the prefects, who had been lounging anyhow round the table, promptly came to attention and when Bride called "Come in!" and the door opened to admit Diana, it was a very severe-looking assembly that met her eyes.

She trailed in, a sulky look on her face that spoiled all its prettiness, and when she finally fetched up at the foot of the table which had been left vacant for her, the eyes she directed straight at Bride Bettany were dark with rage.

When Clem Barrass had handed her the note in the common room, her first reaction had been to refuse flatly to attend to it.

"I'm not going," she had said. "You can tell them I said so. If they want me, they can come and find me. Who do they think they are to order me about like this, I'd like to know?"

Clem eyed her curiously. "I wouldn't send a message like that to the prefects if I were you," she said slowly.

The rest of the crowd in the room backed her up at once.

"You can't possibly send a reply like that to a prefects' summons!" Iris Drew protested in shocked tones. "There'll be a most awful row if you do. I know you've stuck out against them, Di, and I know you don't think

167

they matter; but honestly you *can't* go on – not after an official summons like this."

Diana's lip curled in a sarcastic smile. "I suppose *you* would go with a run," she said disagreeably.

"Well, what do you think? Come to that, I would never have let it come to a prefects' summons," Iris replied. She was a pretty, empty-headed girl, who had been attracted by Diana's undoubted good looks, not to speak of the charm that young woman could exert when she chose. She had giggled over the snub administered to Audrey, though even then she had said in rather horrified tones, "Really, Di, you are the edge! Audrey's a full prefect now, you know." But she had been in the school four years now and she knew well enough what a formal summons to appear before the grandees of the school meant. She knew, too, what would happen if Diana remained stubborn about it.

So did Clem and, though she disliked all she had seen of this new girl, she felt she must stop her from making a fool of herself if she could. So she added on her own account, "Iris is quite right, Diana. If you send a message like that to the prefects, you'll find yourself in the Head's study in short order."

Diana looked rather startled. She had gleaned enough from the talk of the rest to know now that the prefects at *this* Chalet School were not the nonentities the ones she had previously known had been. She had thought they would never report her to the Head for she was shrewd enough to guess that they would expect her to regard such a proceeding as a sign of weakness on their part. But she was not going to give in without a struggle.

"Oh, so the dear little prefects finding they can't force me to do as they wish by themselves are calling on the big guns?" she sneered. "Dear me! Whoever would

168

have thought such important persons would climb down like that?"

Clem stiffened. She slowly looked the new girl up and down from head to foot before she spoke and Diana wriggled despite herself under that cool regard. Then the Sixth-former said icily, "Hardly! It happens to be a rule that *if* any girl is so silly as to refuse to obey such a summons, then she is automatically reported to the Head for deliberate defiance. The prefects have no choice in the matter."

Something in Clem's measured tones added to that chilly gaze of hers weakened Diana a little. She glowered up at red-haired Clem who was half a head taller and bit her lips. And then Vanna Ozanne chose to add sweetly: "And if it comes to the Head, I wouldn't be *you* for all the tea in China!"

"What do you mean?" Diana demanded sharply.

Nella, who had come up to the group, answered for her twin. "Because whatever the prefects may do to you, the Head will do – but a dozen times worse, of course. And *then* she'll order you to do whatever it is the prefects want. I don't suppose you mean to go cheeking the Head. No one here will advise you to try *that* on!"

Diana glanced round and saw by the faces about her that every one was in full agreement with Nella. Even those who had come from the Tanswick school with her clearly would not support her in any rebellion. They might laugh over the way she had spoken to quiet Audrey, but no one was going to have anything to do with defiance to Miss Annersley. And when she thought that, it suddenly dawned on Diana that that sort of thing was rather beyond her.

"Oh well," she said with her most jaunty air, "if

there's going to be a major fuss, I suppose I'd better go and see what they want."

"I should think you had!" Carola Johnston remarked.

Jean Ackroyd, who was form prefect, proceeded to give point to what had been said by adding, "And take my advice and behave decently to them for once. If you don't, you'll precious soon wish that you had! Anyhow, we're sick of the way you're behaving, getting the entire form a bad name! Take her along, Clem, and try to din some sense into her as you go!"

Jean turned on her heel and marched off to pick up her knitting when she had said this. Diana went crimson and the look she cast at the unmoved Jean boded no good for that young lady. All the same, she did follow Clem from the room. At the foot of the stairs, the senior girl paused and turned to her.

"Look here, Diana, take Jean's advice and don't give the prefects any more sauce. They *are* the prefects here, and that means something, if it meant nothing at your old school. Empty-headed little Junior idiots may laugh at you and think you've been daring; but people of your own age won't. They're near enough to being prefects themselves not to like it overmuch. We all realize that our behaviour now will help to make things hard or easy for us when our turn comes. That's one of the things we get rubbed into us at intervals."

"Oh, *stop* preaching!" Diana flared out. "I'm sick of it!"

The grave kindliness in Clem's grey eyes changed to an icy distaste, but she only said briefly, "Up the stairs, turn to the right and it's the end door on the corridor. Hurry up!" Then she, too, turned away and went off on her lawful occasions, leaving Diana to mount the stairs and walk along the corridor with steps that grew more and more reluctant. However, by this time she knew that there was no help for it, so she tapped and when she heard Bride call, "Come in!" went in. But the anger Jean and Clem had roused in her was boiling up and the prefects were in for storms, had they but known it.

When she was standing at the foot of the table, she gave Bride a glare that startled that young lady. Then she said, "Well, here I am. You sent for me and I've come."

Her rage accentuated the slightly common accent Bride and some of the others had noticed in her voice before, and Lesley and Nancy exchanged glances. Bride, however, was too worried to think of it for more than a passing moment.

"We've sent for you, Diana," she said, "to tell you that we have talked the matter over and decided to give you one more chance. Either you apologize to Primrose and Audrey at teatime tomorrow when all the Juniors are present, or you'll be barred from all the out-of-school things that the prefects run. That means you won't come to Hobbies or Saturday night invitation shows. Neither will you be allowed to take books from the fiction library. And, of course, if you still haven't apologized by the time we hold the Sale, you won't be able to take part in that. So now you know how you stand."

Diana stared dumbly at her. She really did not know what to do. She hated the idea of being turned out of all the fun and the loss of the fiction library would be a real deprivation to her. She troubled the reference library little enough, but she devoured anything and everything in the shape of a novel that she could lay her hands on. Besides, if she were not allowed to turn up at Hobbies and the invitation Saturday evenings, the younger girls would soon notice and begin to talk. And yet her pride

171

would not allow her to make that public apology that Bride demanded.

"You – you can't do that sort of thing," she said at last.

"Oh yes, we can," Bride assured her. Then her tone changed. "Don't you see, Diana, that you can't go about talking to prefects, who are the Head's representatives, in the way you have done? It's – er – anti-social behaviour. You are living in a community," this with a sudden recollection of Jo's letter, "and you must keep that community's rules or else forfeit your privileges. The way you treated Primrose and Audrey is setting the Juniors an awfully bad example. There are always little idiots among them who may think it clever to do the same sort of thing. Then they'll get into fearful rows and it'll be partly your fault because they'll say – and quite truly – 'Well, one of the big girls does that sort of thing so why shouldn't we?' Don't you understand?"

Diana stared at her, wide-eyed. It is safe to say that this point of view had never struck her before. Dimly, she realized that Bride was trying to help her out. She also realized that there would be no backing down where the prefects were concerned. She felt that she was in a cleft stick. Either she must apologize – which was unthinkable; or she must forfeit all they had told her – which was equally unthinkable. She wished heartily that she had never been sent to this stupid school. But wishing wouldn't help. Her mother spoilt her completely but every once in so often her father put his foot down, and when it was down no power on earth could make him move it. He was ambitious for his only child. Very proud of her prettiness and charming ways – when she chose to exert them – he had made up his mind that she was to have the good education he had missed. He had never liked her former school and had been delighted at the chance

172

to send her to St Briavel's. She knew that no amount of coaxing would persuade him to send her elsewhere. And yet – the future looked very black for proud, silly Diana who had been a leader in the school at Tanswick.

She stood there, gripping the edge of the table, and stared speechlessly at Bride. The prefects were all looking at her, wondering what would be the outcome of it all. They were quite decided that something must be done to put an end to the impertinence that was growing among certain of the wilder Juniors. There had been none of it until Diana had been impudent to Primrose and Audrey, therefore, they set it down to her example. She must make amends for it one way or another. The leaders of the school were quite determined about that.

Tom moved restlessly. Why didn't the silly little ass hurry up and say what she was going to do? Standing there pussy-struck wasn't going to solve the problem for her. The big prefect decided to hurry things up a little.

"You've asked for it, Diana," she said bluntly. "It's a nasty impasse for you, but you've got to take one way or the other. If you don't, it'll have to go to the Head. I don't suppose you want that."

Diana took no more notice of her than if she were a fly on the wall. She still stared at Bride, who made a little sign that Tom rightly interpreted to mean, "Pipe down!" The big prefect nodded slightly and said no more and there was silence again.

Finally, Diana spoke. "If – if I don't do *either* of the things you say, what will you do?" she asked in bewildered tones.

Nancy and Lesley gasped aloud, taking this as a fresh example of impudence; but Bride was quick to jump to the real meaning.

"In that case," she said quietly, "it will go to the

Head, I suppose. But I don't advise you to try that, Diana. You wouldn't like the consequences at all."

Again there was silence. Then, just as two or three of them were beginning to lose patience utterly and wish Bride would hurry up and tell the girl that her sentence went into practice then and there, Diana spoke again.

"You haven't given me any choice," she said sulkily. "Very well. I'll apologize to – to Primrose and Audrey at teatime tomorrow." She stopped and gulped something down. Her pride was bitterly hurt at having to give in, and if she had dared she would have flung some sort of defiance at the Head Girl, even then. But the memory of what she had to face on the morrow for just that very thing restrained her.

Bride nodded. "Very well. You can do it before Grace is said after tea. And for goodness' sake, don't let yourself and us in for such a stupid scene again!" she added. "*No* one is looking forward to it – I can tell you that! Now go back to your common room, and don't be such an ass again. We've had more than enough of you."

Diana left the room, seething at this, and Bride would have been wiser to omit her final remarks, but she, too, was beginning to lose patience. She very much doubted if there would be anything more than the form of words in that apology. However, Diana had given in, which was something gained. Jo had scored as usual.

"Well, that's that," Nancy said. "Tom, why didn't you hold your tongue? I don't suppose you made it any easier for her. And she'll loathe us all after this."

"I can't see that she loved us awfully much before," Elfie remarked. "Personally I'd have been just as glad if she'd never come to the school. How are you going to deal with the card business, Bride? You don't want to yank her here again, I hope?"

174

"Most certainly *not*!" Bride spoke with emphasis. "I'm not saying anything at present. The Sale's coming on and I'm going to ask the Head if we can begin our usual extra Hobbies meetings next week. That will give them all something to think about. In the meantime we must keep our eyes open, and if we see any of them sneaking off we must put a stop to it at once. Oh, dear!" She caught herself up short.

"Why?" Bess asked, seeing that she was saying no more.

"Just I wish we could go along smoothly for a while without any more fusses. I'm more than sick of this last one!"

But Bride's two closest friends, Elfie and Nancy, knew that there was more in it than that. They left her alone, however, and Elfie called on the Games' Committee to decide when they should have their meeting, so the subject dropped.

CHAPTER 13

Diana Apologizes

Next day, it seemed to Diana as if the hours simply raced ahead to teatime. Even now, if she had dared she would have refused to make that apology – but she didn't dare. Whatever she did about it, she knew that she would lose ground and standing in the school, for if she had chosen the alternative Bride had offered her, the younger girls could not have failed to understand that she was being shut out of their out-of-school activities by the prefects and, with all her hardihood, she dared not gatecrash on them. As a result, she went about the whole day in a state of suppressed fury which made her so unapproachable that even Iris and Sylvia, usually her boon companions, gave her a wide berth. As for her work, *that* went to pieces completely. She had never given anyone at her new school any reason to believe that she was overburdened with brains. Today, as the Staff complained in the privacy of the Staff room, she seemed to have reverted to a state of utter ignorance!

"I never thought much of that school at Tanswick," Miss Slater said after Mittagessen, "but Diana Skelton seems to be only one stage removed from Wordsworth's idiot boy! She can't even add nine and seven together today!"

Miss Derwent looked up from the basket she was weaving for the Sale. "All that crowd – the Diana Skelton crowd, I mean – seem to be in a ferment about something.

176

Oh, don't ask *me* what it is; but it's been going on for quite a few days now. My own impression is that things have come to a head somehow and Diana is well in it and that's why her work today would disgrace a member of Lower IIIB. Not that it's ever a great deal better than that," she added as an afterthought.

"Well, I only hope they manage to clear up whatever it is before my next lesson with them," Miss O'Ryan said crossly. "Sure, I never trained to be a teacher of semi-idiots and I don't like it at all, at all!"

Thereafter, the conversation moved to some other topic and the Staff dismissed Diana and her doings from their heads for the present.

At teatime, Bride attended to her urn as serenely as if she had not also spent most of the day in a semi-ferment, too. Only she was older and also had been trained to put first things first. So, though teatime's ordeal was never far from her thoughts, she had managed not to disgrace herself at lessons. All the same, as she filled up cups and passed them along, she was occupied in wondering if Diana would come up to scratch or whether, when it came to the point, she would try to back down.

"And if she does that," the Head Girl thought, "she'll have made the most utter fools of us and we'll be in for a sweet time with the kids! Oh, *hang* Loveday's old uncle! Why on earth couldn't he have left whatever he had to leave to her father and let it go at that?"

No one, least of all Diana herself, imagined how churned up were Bride's feelings during the meal. She pulled herself together and chattered with the rest much as usual; but her two chums, Nancy and Elfie, eyed her askance more than once. They knew their Bride after ten years of close friendship, and both thought that she was feeling by no means as insouciante as she appeared.

The last Junior drained her cup. There were only crockery and crumbs on the tables and the girls sat gossiping and waiting for Grace. Knowing that she had put the ordeal off as long as she could, Bride struck the bell she had taken from the Staff table and rose to her feet with a gesture which kept most of the school in its seats. Mary-Lou and Co, who had not been paying much attention to their elders, stood up as usual and then sat down again hurriedly when they saw that the majority were sitting tight. Everyone stared up at the prefects' table, where Bride, making the most of her five foot eight, stood looking very dignified, but inwardly quaking. As she had told herself a moment before, there was no saying what Diana might take into her silly head to do at the last moment! However, there was no help for it, so Bride spoke.

"Diana, come up here, please. Girls! Diana has something to say which we wish you all to hear. Get on with it, Diana!"

Tall fair Primrose and quiet Audrey stood up at this, Primrose turning very pink, and Audrey rather white and biting her lips. She was not only quiet, but very reserved, and she hated being the focus of all eyes.

From her table at the other end of the room, Diana had also risen and was making her way to the prefects, her head held high, her lips set in a thin straight line. If Audrey was whiter than usual, she was like a sheet and Bride was moved to wonder for an instant if she would faint. Then, as the girl reached them, she realized that she was not faint, but simply so angry that for a second or two she stood perfectly still without saying a word. Only she lifted eyes like pieces of glinting steel and glared at the Head Girl who looked back at her seriously.

"Go ahead, Diana," she said gravely.

Diana swallowed once or twice. Then she said absolutely tonelessly, but in a voice that reached them all, "I apologize for being rude to you, Primrose and Audrey." Then she stopped dead, her lips once more in that hard line and her eyes on the floor.

In mercy, Bride waved her back to her seat, saying curtly, "Thank you. That's all we want. You can go back to your place."

"Finished with us?" Primrose asked. "Good! Come on, Audrey!"

They went to their seats thankfully. Bride stood waiting until Diana, head still high, though she carefully looked at no one on her way to her seat, had reached it and sat down. Then the Head Girl spoke.

"I'm not going to rub anything in," she said, her clear tones carrying to the farthest corner. "I just want to point out to you that when you are impertinent to the prefects, you are impertinent to the Head. I hope you all understand that prefects are the Head's representatives amongst us as a body. We aren't going to allow that sort of thing for one second, so please be very careful – everyone. That's all I have to say. Now stand for Grace."

They rose to their feet as one girl. Bride had made a deep impression on them. One or two of the Senior Middles had wondered how she would tackle the situation, and some of them such as Iris and Sylvia had declared that she would have to give in or else report to the Head. That she had brought Diana to an apology, however much lip-service it might be, made a feeling of respect rise in them where she was concerned. As for the younger Middles, Mary-Lou and her gang were aching to get off to their own common room where they could loose their tongues comfortably. Most of the others were in much the same case. The sinful Dawbarn twins having,

179

for once in their lives, been out of it, were looking almost unbearably smug; and Emerence Hope, Peggy Harper, Jocelyn Fawcett and Susan James, who *had* been in it, were realizing that Diana's punishment might be theirs unless they were careful.

Grace over, the school cleared the tables and then all under the prefects marched out. The prefects watched them go, standing in a solid clump by their table. When Joan Fitch of Lower IIIB finally left the room, most of the grandees of the school looked relieved, but Elfie and Nancy were remarkably serious for them.

"Well, thank goodness that's over!" Lesley said. "Now, perhaps, we can hope for a little peace and quiet and a chance to get on with work for the Sale. Bride, we still haven't decided what we are going to do this term. Have you any ideas?"

"We'll have a meeting tomorrow morning before Guides and discuss it then," Bride promised. "Well, thank Heaven that's over!"

"I couldn't agree more!" Primrose fanned herself with her handkerchief. "And oh, may I nevermore be fated to be the recipient of a public apology! I felt a complete ass! Thank goodness you made it as short as possible, Bride!"

"That wasn't on our account," Audrey assured her. "It was to give Diana a break. Not that I wasn't thankful you cut it off as you did, Bride," she added feelingly. "I agree with Prim. I'd rather be excused such another experience! I bar luxuries!"

"Well, we'd better get cracking," observed Tom as she moved to the door. "Coming, Anne?"

Anne Webster, another quiet girl, went with her, and the rest of the prefects gradually drifted out of the room in twos and threes until at last only Bride herself and her two great friends, Elfie and Nancy, were left.

"Bride," the former said very seriously, "I rather think you'll have to look out for that girl."

Bride stared down at her – Elfie was on a miniature scale – and then demanded, "What on earth do you mean?"

"I mean Diana. No; listen, Bride! You've got the better of her and made her apologize after she'd said in public that she never would. She's not going to forgive you for that in a hurry. I saw the look she gave you just before she spoke and honestly, I think she'll have a jolly good shot at paying you back for it."

"Oh, well, I expect she does rather loathe me at the present," Bride said lightly. "I'd expect that. If she only knew, though, it's Auntie Jo she should loathe and detest. I don't think I would ever have thought up what she did. She's a useful sort of aunt to have around, isn't she? However, I don't suppose Diana will carry on with a wholehearted hate for very long. She'll simmer down presently and then she'll more or less forget about it – though I must say I hope she doesn't forget to the point of having to go through that sort of thing again. Like Prim and Audrey I don't like it at all and I'd rather be excused. Don't worry, Elf."

Nancy took her turn. Sitting on the edge of the table, the early March sunset glinting on her golden-brown hair, she said gravely, "*That* won't simmer down – don't you believe it! She's the kind that broods over things and you've given her something to brood over in all conscience! Don't forget that you've made her humiliate herself in public – before the whole school, in fact – and a girl of her type isn't going to forgive or forget such a thing in a hurry, if at all."

At this point, one of the maids came in to lay the table for Abendessen. The girls saw her and went out, Bride saying, "It's all right, Olwen. We were just going." She turned to the other two. "Come along to my study, you two. This must be straightened out at once. Diana hasn't an easy time before her and you two mustn't get mad ideas into your heads about her. She's just a silly young ass that can't stand corn, as Dad says. I don't think she's vicious."

Laughing, she tucked a hand through an arm of each and led them to the tiny cubbyhole that was the Head Girl's study – the only one here, though at Plas Howell all the prefects had studies. But then, Plas Howell was a mansion on the grand scale, and though the Big House on St Briavel's was quite large enough to house the school comfortably, there was no room for extras like prefects' studies.

Bride lit the gas fire tucked away in a corner, and then dropped into the armchair at one side of it. Nancy sprawled in the deckchair at the other side and Elfie perched on the arm of Bride's. The Head Girl snuggled down comfortably and then glanced at her watch before saying, "We've only about ten minutes left before prep. Look here, you two, what do you mean? Surely," she began to laugh, "you don't imagine that Diana will try to carve chunks off me with a breadknife?"

To her amazement, they remained quite serious. Elfie said, "Of course we don't mean that! Don't be a bigger idiot than you can help! But I do think – and I know Nancy agrees with me – that she'll go all out to get her own back on you somehow."

"But, Elfie! What do you think she could do?" Bride argued. "She won't try cheeking me in public – not after today's business anyhow. We aren't in the same form, so she can't very well upset my work. She's not even in the hockey team, so she can't bash me with her stick. What *do* you think she can to to me?"

"I don't know," Elfie said steadily, "but I'm as certain as I am of anything that she'll do her level best to get back at you."

"Oh, my dear, what utter rot!" Bride laughed again. "You two have been reading too many thrillers! Snap out of it, both of you! The one way she *could* hurt me will be knocked flat by what has happened today – I mean if she'd got any hold on the Juniors. I don't mind owning now that I *was* really afraid of that." She continued on a graver note. "That's why I stuck out for the apology business. I'm not going to have the Lower School messed up and, you know, she *is* the kind to appeal to brainless kids. She's pretty and she says smart things and she has quite a way with her when she likes – not that she's ever tried it out on me. Still I have seen her with other folk, so I know about that all right. We have our share of feather-headed idiots and – well, 'Evil communications corrupt good manners', you know. I don't mean anyone to have any excuse for letting the school down if *I* can help it."

"I think you're right there," Nancy acknowledged. "She's come a nasty cropper now and the Juniors won't forget. You've put a spoke in her wheel there. No; what I think is that she will try to do something personal. Oh, do be sensible, Bride. Of *course* we don't think she'll go for you with a poker or anything like that! Is it likely? But she *will* – oh, yes, she *will*! – do her best to injure you in some other way. So you'd better mind your eye!"

"OK," Bride agreed easily. "If it'll make you two any happier in your minds, I'll keep a lookout. All the same, I don't see what she can do and I think you are both fussing most unnecessarily. Now come off it! There

183

goes the bell and I'm on duty with Upper Second, so you'll have to excuse me. Let's see: I'd better take my German trans. Where's my *Kinder der Welt* got to?"

Elfie was on prep duty, too, and Nancy had a pressing engagement with Mlle in the Staff room over a French essay, so they had to separate. But after Prayers that evening, when Bride was in the Head's study, seeking permission to hold a prefects' meeting about the form the annual Sale was to take, the other two, alone in the Prefects' room since the rest were joining in country dancing, discussed it again, and with great seriousness.

"Bride may laugh as much as she likes," Nancy remarked, "but that girl has it in for her. I saw it in her eyes when she gave Bride that glare at teatime."

"So did I," Elfie said soberly. "But you won't convince Bride of it by talking. We shall just have to keep watch ourselves." Then she added, "I owe Bride a lot for all she did last term when Marmee died. It was she who kept me going when I thought my career would have to come to an end. Besides, we've been pals from the word Go! *You* know that, Nance. We three have come up the school together and if anyone had a good pal we've had it in Bride. She's so decent herself, she'll never see what Diana is getting at until it's there. I hope you understand what I mean?" she added. "I do myself, but it's a bit hard to put it into words."

"Oh, I know. I rather feel the same myself," Nancy nodded. "I haven't forgotten how decent she was, writing to me every week to keep me up in school news that term I had to miss because I'd smashed my ankle. She's doing the same by young Julie, too, you know. Yes; Bride's a top-notcher all right. Wish we had more like her in the school!"

"And then," Elfie went on, pursuing her own line

of thought without paying much attention to this, "she's had a fairly stiff time this past four or five months. Her mother was so ill and it wasn't as if Peggy was here. Peg was in Switzerland and you know what pals she and Bride have always been for sisters! Then she had to step into Loveday's shoes at a moment's notice and that wasn't easy. And then there was Julie's illness and though Dora is really very good, it's not quite the same thing. The Sale comes off in a few weeks' time and there's all the summer term to go after that. I may be head of the games, but Bride's head of the cricket and I mean her to have a free hand there. If I can prevent Diana Skelton from messing up the end of her last year here, I jolly well mean to do it."

"Oh, so do I," Nancy agreed heartily. "She certainly doesn't believe it herself. In fact, if you ask me, I should say she thought you and I were a bit touched on the subject. But I'm positive that wretched girl means mischief somehow or other. I wish to goodness her folk had never sent her here! Since they have, however, and, as things have turned out, it looks as if you and I must look out for tricks. I don't like the beauty and I would trust her as far as I could chuck her!"

As Elfie was of the same mind, she joyfully agreed to a compact with Nancy to keep an eye on Diana since Bride herself had only laughed at their warnings. In this, they were far more justified than they knew at the moment. Diana smarted under the indignity she had suffered that afternoon as she had never smarted before. Accustomed to being looked up to and admired at the Tanswick school, she literally writhed when she thought of the indignity of having to give in and apologize publicly to girls she despised as being much less pretty than herself, far poorer and therefore, to her way of thinking, very much beneath

185

her. She blamed Bride alone for what had happened, and she was already setting her brains to work to think how she could best revenge herself. She was not without plenty of shrewdness, and she knew that whatever she did she must wait a week or two. Let time and crowding school events help to wipe the memory of today's incident off the minds of most of the girls. Then she would think of something that should hurt Bride and pull her down from her high place. If only she could have known that the Head Girl was suffering the same feelings of degradation as she herself was feeling now, Diana thought she might be able to forget it all. But until then, look out for yourself, Bride Bettany!

CHAPTER 14

Settling the Sale

The Head proved complaisant and the prefects held their meeting after Prayers next morning. It was growing difficult to decide on a new form for their annual Sale of Work, and they would all have scorned the idea that they should just have the stalls and entertainments and wear their afternoon frocks. To them, half the fun was in planning a fresh arrangement and dressing up for it. All the same, after all these years, it was not easy to find a novel idea.

In Tirol, the spotlight had been a Fairy Tales Sale when Jo herself had been Head Girl. Since then, among other things, they had done Many Nations, The Willow Pattern, A Dutch Sale and a Shakespearean Sale. They had had quite a time the year before in deciding what they should do and, so far, no one had made any proposals this year that met with any success. But the Sale was due in a very few weeks now and something must be settled.

Matron had insisted that the mending must be done as usual. It was a fine day, and there was a lacrosse match at the school in the afternoon and the netball team had to go over to play the Sacred Heart Convent at Carnbach as well, so she declined to allow the girls to put off darning and so on as Bride had begged. Therefore, they all arrived in the Prefects' room, complete with workbaskets, workbags and mending, and before they opened the meeting, all settled down to their chores.

187

Bride made a face at a long ladder in one of her evening stockings, heaved a deep sigh, and then looked round.

"Well, folks, I know we've got to finish our mending somehow, but just remember that the Sale's the really important thing this morning. We want to try to outdo anything that's been done before, so I hope you've all come armed with ideas – I've got some pale pink wool, Bess, if that's what's worrying you. Here you are – catch!" She tossed a ball of pale pink darning wool down the table to Bess who had been trying to decide whether beige or white would pass muster with Matron when darned into a pink vest.

Bess nodded her thanks, threaded her needle and set to work before she looked up to say, "What about an *Alice in Wonderland* Sale?"

"Nothing – except that we did that years ago when mot of us were in the Third," Nancy responded. "Bride, I was wondering if we could manage a Jane Austen Sale?"

"We'd have to make most of the dresses," Bride said, hooking away at her ladder for all she was worth. "We could manage the women's, but what about the men's? Didn't they wear tailcoats and knee-breeches and stocks and things like that? Or was it long pants strapped under their insteps? I'm a bit waffley about it."

"We couldn't possibly do it," Primrose declared. "Oh dear! I'll have to rebuttonhole this buttonhole and if there's one thing I do *not* like doing, it's anything to do with buttonholes! – Yes; about clothes for Jane Austen. It's out of the question. We could do the women's things all right, but we'd be sunk if we tried to tackle the men's. It's a pity though. We could have made it awfully attractive."

So that idea had to be dropped.

"I'd thought of Dickens," Madge said, "but you'd have the same difficulties there. Frock coats and tight trousers, to go by the illustrations! We couldn't do it!"

"What about an Egyptian Sale?" offered Dora. "*Those* dresses wouldn't be hard, except for the head-dresses. Anyway, there'd be only one Pharaoh at a time. I should think most other people just wore headbands."

"Have you thought of how the women dressed?" Bride asked sweetly. "I don't see the Abbess or Matey or any-one else, for that matter, letting us float round in skirts under our arms and strings of beads and precious little else! Certainly not at the beginning of April, anyhow. It would be draughty, to say the least of it!"

They all shouted at the picture, even Dora who had looked rather offended at first. No more was said about it and they had to try again.

"What's wrong with making it a Garden Sale?" Lesley suggested. "Deck each stall with one different kind of flower and have all the pot plants we can beg, borrow or steal as well. Then we could be dressed as flowers, too. You could use crinkled paper for that and it wouldn't take much time *nor* cost such an awful lot."

"It would cost the earth," Tom said gloomily. "Have you *bought* any crinkled paper lately, may I ask? Besides, where would *I* come in? You can't say there's anything in the least flowerlike about *me*!"

Several people grinned broadly as they surveyed tall Tom of the square face, snub nose and honest grey eyes. She was quite right: you *didn't* think of flowers in connection with her, though Dora murmured something about, "You could always be a sunflower."

"Yes; and a nice sketch I'd look, got up in crinkled paper and art muslin, wouldn't I?" Tom said emphatically. "Oh no, thank you! Not for me!"

"Well, what about a Fruit Garden, then?" Lesley persisted. "That might be better. Tom would be a – a banana. She'd look well in yellow."

Shouts of laughter greeted this last attempt. Then Bride rapped the table with her scissor handles and brought the meeting to order once more.

"We've only till half past ten for this," she said severely. "Stop wasting time, do! It's half past nine already!"

"Why not try Nursery Rhymes?" Anne Webster proposed. "Elfie would make a sweet little Miss Muffet and Tom could be The Man All Tattered and Torn out of *The House that Jack Built*. And you could have Mary-Lou and Verity-Anne for Jack and Jill and then we could use the Dutch costumes."

This was viewed with much more favour. It was certainly the most feasible suggestion that had yet been made. They had plenty of dresses that could be used and there were any number of nursery rhymes to choose from. And then Lesley elected to put a stop to it by insisting that if they did that she would be the Cow that Jumped Over the Moon. Nothing else would satisfy her and, as Bride said despairingly, even if they managed her and The Little Dog, they could do nothing about The Dish and The Spoon. Lesley remained sweetly impervious to all argument and, in the end, Bride had to call once more for order. When they were all at their mending again, she implored them not to rag as there simply wasn't time for it. She proposed that they should all think hard for five minutes and at the end of that time try to make *possible* suggestions.

A portentous silence ensued after this, broken by Bride herself. She leapt up with a cry of, "Eureka! I believe I've got it!" and dashed out of the room, upsetting her workbasket and leaving a trail of pins, needles, reels of cotton and balls of darning-wool as she went.

"What on earth's taken her?" exclaimed Bess as she went to pick up pins and needles while Elfie and Nancy set themselves to winding up the sewing cotton and wool.

"A sudden fit of insanity," Nancy sighed. "So sad in one so young and fair!"

"Can we cope with it by ourselves, do you think?" Elfie asked, her big blue eyes gleaming with mischief. "Or should we send for Nurse or Matey?"

"A warder from the nearest luney-bin and a strait-jacket would be more appropriate if you ask me," Tom grinned.

"I hope she's *safe*!" Madge joined in the fun. "Hadn't we better provide ourselves with weapons in case she goes for us?"

"Good idea! So we will! Bags me the tongs!" And Tom made a wild dive for them and brandished them wildly, nearly braining Primrose as she did so.

They rushed to grab whatever might be called a "weapon" that was in the room, giggling madly at the thought of the shock Bride would have when she returned with whatever it was she had gone to seek. They had had a very sobering time of it lately and the reaction had set in. As a result, the grave, responsible prefects of the evening before had become a set of featherheads, ready for any joke. Therefore, when Bride came haring back, waving a small old-fashioned book, her cheeks flushed and her straight brown hair worn in a short bob, flying wildly, she found all her friends clustered together in a corner and all brandishing weapons of some kind or other.

She stopped dead at the sight and her jaw fell. "What on earth do you mad creatures think you're doing?" she demanded.

"Don't come any nearer," Tom said in a deep, manly voice. "You aren't safe, and if you get too excited you might turn homicidal and we don't want any tragedies, thank you!"

Bride tossed her book down on the table and stared at them. "Have you all gone completely crackers?"

"No; it's you that's gone crackers," Nancy said with a giggle.

"What on earth are you talking about?" The incensed Head Girl strode up to the corner and was warded off by Tom and the tongs and cries from the rest. "I'd advise you to pipe down on the yells or Matey'll be on your tracks. I saw her in Pansy when I went past the door just now."

That sobered them. Matron was dearly loved by most of the Chalet School members, but she contrived to keep them in wholesome awe of her at the same time. No one wanted to bring her in on a prefects' meeting like the present one. She would certainly have had something to say in that case!

"Are you *sure* you're all right?" Elfie asked as she laid down her blackboard ruler.

"Of course I'm all right. Though I shan't be for long if you folk go on like this. Put those things away and stop making bigger asses of yourselves than Nature has already made you," Bride said with cheerful insult.

"D'you think it's safe?" Tom asked the others with a grin.

Bride suddenly jumped to what had caused all this, dropped into her chair and began to giggle in her turn. "Did I startle you? Oh, you idiots! I had a sudden idea and rushed off to ask Nursey to let me have the book – it's kept in the San library, and you know what a fuss she is about *those* books! Luckily, she was in a hurry, so she only told me I might have it but it's to be returned on

Monday at the latest. There isn't any too much time to waste, anyhow, and here the lot of you go wasting what there is as hard as ever you can! Shove those things away and come and sit down and listen while I expound."

They hurriedly put away their weapons and came back to their seats. Bride's reminder about the time had speedily brought their nonsense to an end, and they were prepared to listen attentively to her since she seemed to have a real idea.

"Well, we're all ready," Nancy said as she subsided into her chair. "Bring on your bears. We're all ears!"

"First of all," Bride said, "how many of you have read *The Crown of Success*?"

Most of them had at one time or another. Some years ago, an elderly lady at Howells village had been turning out her house, preparatory to going into a much smaller one. During the process she had discovered on the bookshelves of a rarely-used bedroom a collection of the stories she and her brothers and sisters had loved as children. Miss Annersley, who was an acquaintance of hers had been bemoaning the fact that books for the San library had to be few and far between since at that time books were not only dear, but scarce. Old Miss Blake had promptly had the lot packed up and sent to Plas Howell where the school then was. The Staff on receiving them had shrieked with laughter over them. Then they had weeded out the worst of the lot and handed the rest over to Nurse. Had the girls been asked to read such stories as a general thing, they would have been indignant; but when they were in San for a day or two, they rather enjoyed the quaint old tales especially the allegories of that once well-known children's writer, A.L.O.E. Only Bess Herbert and Rosalind Yolland did not know *The Crown of Success* and Bess instantly stretched across the table and picked it up to look at it.

"What priceless illustrations!" she exclaimed. "*Four Heads to Furnish!* What's it about, Bride? Can I keep it to skim through it? I've never even heard of it before."

"You mean 'May I?'" Bride said wickedly. "Oh yes. We've got it till Monday, so you can have it tomorrow. It won't take *you* long to read it. It's rather a pet. I've always loved it."

"But how can it help us with the Sale?" Elfie asked plaintively.

"Why, just this. I thought we could use it for our plan. For instance, the kids in the story got their grates and other ironmongery from Mr Arithmetic. And they had their wallpapers from Mr Reading – Oh, and he had a dwarf Alphabet which they had to pay with hours and minutes from their Time-purses before they could go into the shop," explained Bride who, as a small girl, had loved the story and read it at least half a dozen times. "Then Mr Geography helped them to lay out their gardens –"

"But *how*?" demanded Rosalind Yolland, opening wide eyes. She was a matter-of-fact young person and was puzzled by all this.

"It's an allegory," Bride explained briefly. "The cottages were their heads and you have to furnish your head with lessons. The people who kept the shops were called Arithmetic, Reading, History, Natural History and so on. *Now* do you see?"

"Ye-es; I think so. But how could we manage all that?"

This was something that most of them had been wondering, but Bride was ready for them. "Well, we could have the flower stall as Mr Geography's place. I thought whoever did it could bag a corner of Hall and rope it off

194

and then arrange the flowers and plants so as to make a map of the world. And then –"

Bess had been glancing over the story. "We could manage things like history and so on, but I don't see how you would wangle Mr Arithmetic's establishment," she objected. "What would you put in it, for instance?"

"Well, I hadn't thought it all out in detail, of course," Bride owned. "We'd have to go into it properly."

Nancy leaned forward and plucked the book out of Bess's hands. "Let me take a dekko! O-oh! I'd forgotten Mrs Sewing! She'd be lovely for the needlework stall! Look here, Bride!" she turned to her chum. "Bess is quite right in one way, but I do see how we could use this as a basis for our ideas. Only I'm afraid you'll have to cut out the maths part of it. I can't think of a single thing we have that you could put there. But why not make it a Sale of Learning? For example, we could put all the knick-knacks and er – er – bijouterie on the French stall –"

"Yes; and let the people who run that talk either French or broken English!" Elfie chimed in eagerly. "That would be fun!"

Nancy nodded. "And we could use that cottage affair from the acting cupboard for Mrs Sewing's cottage – but *who* would be Mrs Sewing herself?"

"Elfie!" Bride retorted promptly. "She'd look sweet as," she snatched the book from Nancy, found the place and read aloud: "'A prim little dame, dressed in a curious garment of patchwork with a necklace of small, round pincushions hanging almost as low as her waist. Instead of her own hair she wore a most singular wig made entirely of skeins of cotton and wool which was a long way down her back.' There!" she shut the book and looked at Elfie. "And Mrs Sewing always talked in rhyme. We could make up piles of rhymes for you to learn to say. The kids could be dressed the same way and have some of the rhymes, too."

The rest were in fits of laughter at this, but Elfie looked aghast. "What a simply *poisonous* idea! I'll have nothing at all to do with it! Someone else can take that on – you, if you're so keen on it. When do you imagine I'd have time to learn your wretched verses, may I ask?"

"All right – all right, if that's how you feel about it," Bride soothed her. "You shan't do it. We'll find someone else. Madge, perhaps. *I* couldn't do it. No one in their sense could describe me as 'little'!"

Madge laughed. "I don't mind learning by heart, but I think you'd better cut that part out. You can't possibly know *all* the answers, and it would be mad for Mrs Sewing to talk sometimes in rhyme and sometimes in plain everyday prose!"

"It's quite decided that we take on the stalls and shows in groups and not forms, is it?" Lesley asked.

Bride nodded. "You know how some of those little idiots in the Thirds scrapped last year as to whose stall was best. The Head was fearfully angry about it and she said that shouldn't happen again, so we're going back to the original idea and dividing everyone up into groups – so many Middles and Juniors with one or two prefects in charge. That will put a lid on any Form fusses."

"Much better scheme if you ask me," Tom remarked. "Some of those young demons don't *need* an excuse for scrapping. By the way, my village is nearly finished. Where do you propose we should put that? Oh, and what about the competition for it?"

"The competition part must wait. As for where we'll put it, we'll call it the Handcrafts department, I think.

196

There's some more woodwork this year – boxes and trays and things like that."

"How on earth would you dress the people at that stall?" Anne Webster wanted to know.

"Oh, that's easy! They can have white aprons and square paper caps like the carpenters of a hundred years or so ago used to wear. Then there's Grammar's Bazaar. I thought we could divide the stall into eight and put dolls and things like that into the noun division; dolls' clothes for the adjectives, and so on. And – let's see." She hurriedly turned the pages of the book. "Yes; all the pictures and things like scrapbooks could go to Pronoun and then Preposition could see to all the parcelling up. I think we could make a jolly good show of it. What do you all say?" She looked anxiously round them as she spoke.

"It would certainly be something quite fresh," Audrey said thoughtfully. "We've rather gone in for the pretty side of things. This would be more than that. I don't mean that parts of it couldn't be really pretty," she added, "but we could also show a – a *graver* side, which we don't generally. Yes; I like it."

"So do I" – "Me too!" Agreement came from everyone.

"Then, shall we try it? Shall I call the Committee and discuss it?" Bride once more looked at them anxiously.

"I'm agreed – so long as you don't expect me to be that ghastly Mrs Sewing," Elfie said.

"You shan't, darling! *You*," said Bride earnestly, "shall be dear Duty! I'm sure you'd do it awfully well!"

"*Help!*" Elfie had no more to say.

For the matter of that, no one had a chance to say anything more about the Sale just then, for there came a tap at the door and when Bride called, "Come in!" it opened to show Clem Barrass.

"Hello, Clem, what do you want?" Bride asked.

"Miss Derwent sent me," Clem explained. "She wants to know if you haven't heard the bell for Break? It rang more than ten minutes ago and everyone else has finished their cocoa or milk and what-have-you."

Bride gave a glance at her watch and leapt to her feet. "Mercy! Where *has* the time gone to? And I've never even finished that awful ladder! Matey will talk! All right, Clem; we'll be down in a minute. Please tell Miss Derwent I'm awfully sorry and, but this is off the record and you needn't say it to her, we'll have some news for the school by Monday, I hope. However, you'll hear all about that at the proper time. You pop off and give Miss Derwent my message, will you – just that we're awfully sorry and we didn't hear the bell and we'll be down to apologize as soon as this place looks something like the prefects' room."

Clem said nothing, though her eyes were nearly popping out of her head with curiosity. She departed to give the politest version she could manage of Bride's message to the irate Miss Derwent who had some excuse for her annoyance, since she had heard a noise in the dining room and on going to inquire what was happening, had found the bulk of the school there, but not a single prefect.

Meanwhile, Bride turned round to her prees and said, "Oh, bother! Now we'll have to go and eat humble pie! But before we do, just tell me – do you all think it'll do?"

"Rather! It's a corker notion, isn't it, you chaps?" Tom said heartily. "We'll have to go into it in Committee, of course; but honestly, I do think you've rung the bell this time, Bride."

"So do I!" Nancy said. "And Audrey's quite right about it being something utterly fresh and out of the common. There'll be heaps to arrange, of course, but we've still got three weeks and if we all hoe in we should be able to do it in that time."

As the others hurriedly cleared away their sewing materials, they agreed with fervour. Then, having left the room tidy enough to pass muster with Matron, they scuttled off to put their mending away in their drawers, hoping that Matron would be too busy to insist on seeing it. That done, they went downstairs to make the best amends they might to Miss Derwent before they got their cocoa and biscuits, after which, it was a case of fly, for Guides began at eleven and, thanks to their chatter, they had none too much time to see that all was in readiness before the Guiders came.

CHAPTER 15

Shock for Bride

The Sale Committee were quite thrilled with Bride's idea. They worked it out with eager chattering and hoots of laughter and finally asked for an interview with the Head. Miss Annersley's lips twitched when she heard all they had to say, but she managed to keep a straight face before them.

"Yes, I see," she said when Bride, as spokesman, had explained what they wanted to do. "I like the idea, but isn't it rather ambitious? It will be difficult to do, won't it?"

"Oh, do you think so?" Bride looked crestfallen and the others also seemed deeply disappointed. "We thought we could manage it, though we'll have to cut out Mr Arithmetic's shop, I'm afraid. I'm sorry about that, but we simply don't see how we can work it in. I mean there's nothing we could sell that would fit."

"Isn't there?" Miss Dene, who was also present at the interview, gave a chuckle. "*I* can suggest something. I remember the yarn – I doted on it when I was a small girl. We had it at home; it was one of Mother's old books – and it was one of my Sunday books for years as a kid."

"Well, how can we do it?" Elfie demanded. "It would be a real miss, because arithmetic is one of the things you've simply *got* to learn."

Rosalie Dene chuckled again. Then she said, "Have you forgotten that Mr Arithmetic had a partner, my dear?

200

Mr Mathematics was his name and his share of the place was full of problems. Well, have a competitions stall and there you are!"

Loud applause broke out at this inspiration. Even the Head joined in for a moment, though she speedily stopped the clapping. Her time was always very well filled and as it was she had had to put her letters to one side to give the girls this interview.

"That's a real brainwave!" Nancy said appreciatively. "Lesley can be in charge of it as Mr Mathematics and Dora can be Mr Arithmetic. They seem to be our only mathematical geniuses this year."

Bride had been gazing dreamily into space for a minute or so. Now she suddenly spoke. "I've had another brain-waggle. What about clearing out the prefects' room and having it there? Then people would have to go upstairs – the Multiplication Staircase, you remember. It would keep it still more like the tale."

"Oh, *wizard*!" This was Elfie. "Miss Annersley, can we do it?"

"You certainly *can*," the Head responded promptly. "The question is *may* you? Really, Elfie! At *your* age!"

Elfie went red. The loose use of "can" for "may" was as a red rag to a bull where Miss Annersley was concerned, as all her pupils very well knew. Usually, they were careful when in her hearing, but the present excitement had made the Games Prefect slip for once.

The Head laughed and relented. "Oh, you may, of course. I shall be interested to see how you manage to carry out all your ideas. You had better tell the school this evening before Hobbies. You shall have Abendessen at 6.45 and I'll take Prayers immediately after. That will give you extra time for Hobbies. Bride, if I were you I'd arrange to have a show of everything you have ready as

201

soon as you can. Then you will know just what is finished and what remains to be done. Don't let anyone begin anything large after that, for there won't be time to do big things. In any case, you should have most of what you need done by this. Now let me see what day would be best. Bring me the time-table, Miss Dene, please."

Rosalie Dene went to her office to bring the great sheet and the Head bent over it consideringly. Presently she looked up. "Yes; I think we might make it Wednesday. I see that neither of the Sixth Forms has any lesson after 3.15 that afternoon. I propose that you set up the trestles in the Hall then, instead of doing prep, and clear out all the cupboards and put everything out. There are twenty-eight of you, so you should be able to finish before tea. Lock the doors when you have done and after tea we'll all come and see what there is. Prep shall be cancelled for that one night and you may have Hobbies most of the evening. I know everyone works twice as hard after the show. How will that do?"

"Oh, gorgeous!" Bride went pink with pleasure. "That's a – a marvellous idea, Miss Annersley. Isn't it, you folk?"

They all agreed with fervour and the Head laughed. "We do it every year as you ought to know by this time. Very well, then; that is settled. Now, is there anything else you want to ask me? No? Then you had better go back to your work now or you'll get nothing done tonight."

They departed in high feather and when Madge, the last of them, had bobbed her curtsy and closed the door behind her, the Head leaned back in her chair, looked across at her secretary and broke into peals of laughter.

"Aren't they an enterprising set? I would like to know who was responsible for *that* idea. It will be interesting to see what they make of it; for you know, Rosalie, it won't be at all easy to carry out. Do you suppose they mean to bring in *all* the characters of that immortal allegory – Pride and Miss Folly and all the rest?"

Rosalie joined in her laughter as she said, "I wouldn't put it past them as the saying is! I wonder who they'll pick for Folly? As for carrying it out, we've done harder things than that in our time. But I'll make *one* suggestion off my own bat and that is that they have a room for Geography's department. They can't possibly do it properly in just a corner of Hall. A map of the world indeed! 'Ambitious' doesn't begin to describe them!"

"That's true. Well, there can be a right ambition as well as a wrong one, and though I seem to remember that A.L.O.E. made it a handsome cage meant to kill the bird Content, she forgot that there is a divine discontent which has always helped to better things. Well, I really must do something about my letters and it's time you were free. You've had a heavy day of it. By the way, I hope you're prepared to help them out over the competitions? You'd better run along and think up a few teasers so as to be ready for them!"

"I can do that all right," Rosalie said as she picked up the timetable to carry it back to its proper place. "It isn't an original idea, you know. We had a Competitions stall at our last parish Sale of Work. They'll have to see about the prizes, by the way. I can give them a box of handkerchiefs for one, anyhow."

"I'll find them something, too. I expect, among ourselves, we can provide prizes enough for that. And they must have a special prize for whoever gets most marks on all the competitions – two, in fact, for they'll have to divide their competitors into two classes; over fourteen and under. That will only be fair. Very well, dear. We'll see about that later. Run along now."

Miss Dene went off to make out a list of the competitions they had had at the Sale at her home, and the Head reached for the great pile of letters in her desk-basket and began to go through them and answer them, though now and then she broke off to chuckle over the latest idea for the School's Annual Sale.

Meanwhile, the prefects had gone to their room, taken out their books and settled down to hard work. The Staff were taking prep this evening, so the grandees of the school had no need to worry over their juniors. The tradition of the school was one of hard work during working hours and an unusual amount of freedom otherwise. With very few exceptions the girls had always shown that they were to be trusted and, as Jo Maynard had once remarked, you *must* have a few exceptions to prove any rule!

Normally, preparation went on from five to seven for the Seniors and five to half past six for the Juniors. When, therefore, the bell rang a good quarter of an hour earlier than usual, the school at large was filled with curiosity to know what it meant. The Head, standing at the Staff table at the end of the big dining room, saw it and judged it wiser to explain that they were to have the extra time for the Hobbies Club tonight. She said grace and then, when they were all sitting down, rang her bell for silence and explained.

"Just a moment before you begin, girls. Our Sale is coming very near now and I know you want to make it even better than last year. We will have Prayers as soon as Abendessen is over and then you may have the rest of the evening for your work. Juniors may sit up till half past eight for once, and Middles till nine. The rest, of course, will go at half past nine as usual. Now you may begin your meal. If I were you, I wouldn't waste time in idle chatter and then you will be able to get down to work all the sooner."

She sat down amid the fervent clapping of the girls, but everyone was too eager to be at work to spend much time that way and, for once, the meal was over in about twenty five minutes. Grace was said and they hurried to clear the tables before going to take their places in Hall and the big drawing room for Prayers. But once the Staff had left Hall, Bride took charge. Mounting the daîs, she clapped her hands for attention.

"Just a minute before you go to Hobbies, girls! I want to tell you that this year we have decided to make it a Sale of Learning. I'll explain just how in a moment, but before that, I want to tell you that Miss Annersley says we must have an exhibition of our work on Wednesday evening so that we can see how much we have ready and what has to be finished and so on. Now I'll tell you how we propose to arrange the Sale."

She explained their ideas as lucidly as she could and the girls listened in silence. Most of them were thrilled with the idea and if it had not been that they were anxious to be at work as soon as possible, there would have been volleys of questions. The prefects had foreseen this, so Bride wound up with: "And now stand and go to your form rooms and begin. We are coming round presently to see if you want any help and if there's anything else you want to know, you can ask us then and we'll tell you – Mary-Lou! Come back! Who gave you leave to rush off like that, I'd like to know?"

Mary-Lou, standing at the end of the line, had made a dive for the door as Bride ended. She came back, very red, and took her place with an air of resignation while Bride gave the order to turn and Madge, who had sat down at the piano, struck up a lively march and they all swung out, form by form, until only the prefects were left.

Those important young ladies waited until the last of the Sixth had departed. Then they hurriedly decided who should go to each room before settling down to their own work, and parted.

Bride had undertaken the two Upper Fourths who worked together. She found them ready with any number of questions and the first one, which came from nearly a dozen people at once, was who was to be Mr Learning? As neither she nor her fellows had given that notable sage a thought, she was rather floored by this. However, she contrived to look her stateliest as she replied that so far that point had not been discussed.

"You ought to be it yourself," said the irrepressible Mary-Lou.

"Oh, I don't think so!" Beth Lane cried. "It ought to be Tom. She's taller than Bride and Mr Learning ought to be the tallest of the lot!"

"I'll mention your ideas to the Committee," Bride said pleasantly. "Or your representative on it – you, isn't it, Gwen? – can do so. Don't forget when we have our next meeting."

Gwen Davis, who always sat mum at the meetings and voted whichever way the majority went, flushed and glared at the pair who had brought this on her. She hated being in the limelight at any time.

"Which will be our stall, Bride?" Vi Lucy asked.

"I don't know yet. Anyhow, we aren't going to have stalls by forms this year. Have you forgotten what happened after the Sale last time? Miss Annersley says that we're to go back to the way it used to be run in Tirol and make up groups out of each form."

Upper IVA, who had been Upper Third last year,

looked down their noses at this reminder. They had been out of the trouble which had arisen with the two Lower Thirds and felt very complacent in consequence. Certain members of Upper IVB who *had* been in went red and tried to make themselves smaller.

Bride grinned to herself, but she only said, "Any more questions?"

"Yes, please." This was Hilary Bennett, a new girl who had had only one term at the Tanswick school and had, accordingly, slipped into Chalet School ways with greater ease than some of them. "What exactly is a Competitions stall?"

"Just what it says. We're going to have it up in the prefects' room and there'll be a dozen or so competitions of all kinds, I expect. We'll give prizes for each and you'll pay so much to enter for any one – about sixpence a time, probably."

"What a super idea!" Lesley Malcolm observed. "Where are you getting the prizes, Bride?"

"We haven't had time to settle all those details yet," Bride told her.

"Oh, well, then, I can give you one myself. I was going to give it to be sold, anyhow, and it really would make a decent prize."

"What is it?" Bride asked cautiously. There was no knowing what these imps might think of.

"It's an umbrella. My godmother gave it to me for my birthday and I've got two without it. Mummy said I might give it to the Sale if I liked, and I jolly well *do* like!"

"Are you *sure* your mother said that?" Bride asked dubiously. Upper IVA, as a form, were noted for hating umbrellas and never using them if it could possibly be avoided. Mary-Lou, for instance, had conveniently "lost" at least three. She only had her present one because her grandmother had told her that if it went missing, she must buy herself a new one out of her pocket money. Knowing that "Gran" not only could but *would* see that this was done, Mary-Lou had kept an eye on the hated thing and still owned it after two terms – which was a record for her!

Lesley eagerly assured the Head Girl that her mother had indeed said that she might pass on the umbrella.

"Mummy said I didn't really need it and Godmother lives in Ireland and isn't likely to be coming to see us for ages. I've got it here so I can give it to you any time."

"Well, if you're *sure* it's all right," Bride agreed. "Thanks very much, Lesley. That'll make a really decent prize."

"What sort of comps are we having?" Verity-Anne asked.

"We haven't thought that out yet. If any of you have decent ideas about it – and I mean *decent*, mind! – you can write them down on a slip of paper and let me have it."

"Julie *will* be made at missing all this!" Vi said wistfully.

"She certainly will," Bride agreed. "How is she getting on, Vi?"

"Oh, much better now. I had a letter from her this morning and she says she's pretty well all right, though she gets tired rather soon still. But she'll be all right for next term. I've got the letter here." Vi pulled it out of her blazer pocket. "You can read it if you like."

Bride took it. "Thanks awfully. I'd like to see it. I owe her a letter myself, so she won't write till I've written. I'll try to fit it in at the weekend. Ask me for it when you go to bed."

Vi nodded. "OK, I will."

"And don't say 'OK'!" Bride scolded. "You've been told scores of times that it's slang. Now let me see how you're all getting on."

She made the round, commending here, criticising there and giving any help that was asked. On the whole, Upper IVA had done remarkably well, considering that their average age was only a couple of months over fourteen. When the Head Girl finally left them to go to her own work, she reflected that they were a very *young* IVA. Quite a number of them would be in one division or the other of Lower V next year, too. Of course, it was mainly owing to the unexpected influx from Tanswick that Mary-Lou, Vi and the rest had won their promotions; but even so, the girls were nearly a year younger than usual. By this time, she had reached the prefects' room. She took out the elaborate bedjacket she was knitting and thought no more about it in the lively chatter that all those present were holding.

Bess and Madge were both hard at work and presently Nancy and Primrose entered. Elfie had taken her own work and accompanied Anne to the Lower Thirds who could never be trusted to keep the peace without some sort of supervision. Tom Gay had asked leave to work in the handwork room. For some years now, she had been responsible for a very superior dolls' house which had been the prize of a competition. This year, she had decided to vary things a little. She had been hard at work ever since September in making a model village. Katharine Gordon and Nella Ozanne from Lower VA had been roped in to help. Both were keen on woodwork, though Nella preferred fretwork and carving and was really gifted that way. Katharine, like Tom, had a genius for carpentry and between them they had produced ten cottages, three larger houses, two shops, a church, a school and what purported to be the parish hall. The actual buildings were finished and they were hard at work now with the finishing. Usually, the dolls' house had been furnished, but this year they were leaving that alone. Five of the cottages had roofs made of raffia to simulate thatch. The rest of the buildings had wooden roofs and the three had set their hearts on painting in the tiles tonight. They had insisted on keeping the whole thing a dark secret apart from the fact that it *was* a village. Tom merely held her tongue about it, but the other pair gave maddening hints every now and then, rousing the curiosity of most folk to fever pitch.

"I wish those three would let us *see* their blessed village," Madge said suddenly as she sorted out her embroidery silks. "What are we going to do about a competition for *that*, by the way?"

"Naming it," Bride said firmly. "It's the only thing we *can* do. Tom said something about asking for names to compile the list soon. I believe Miss Dene asked her to do it as she'll have to type copies and she's up to the eyes in work, anyhow, most of the time."

"It seems a pity they're not going to furnish this time," Nancy observed. "We always have before – or no; not the first one."

"My good girl, where do you think we would have found the time?" Bride demanded with point. "Now don't talk for a minute. I've got to count my stitches."

They fell silent, but the moment the anxious knitter had finished, Bess began again.

"Tom's a real genius at that sort of thing, isn't she? I should think that when she really starts out as a missionary it'll give her a tremendous pull with small boys."

"She helps with the Wolf Cubs when she's at home. I.

know that," Nancy said. "She was telling me about them the other day when we were over at Carnbach. She seems fearfully keen on them."

Bride, having reached a part where she did not need to keep her full attention on her work, looked round the table at them. "You know, when she first told us, I just couldn't take it in. Tom as a missionary! It didn't seem possible! And yet, the more I think of it, the more I see that it's exactly what she's cut out for."

Primrose nodded. "I agree. She'll do it awfully well. And, you know, though Tom doesn't talk much, she's – well – she's really awfully religious at bottom. Not pi – I don't mean that –"

"I should think you didn't!" Bride grinned. "If Tom is ever pi, may I be there to see and hear her! But I know what you mean, Prim. Yes; she'll do it all right and make good at it, too."

Madge, who had been working absorbedly, suddenly cut off the end of her embroidery silk, tossed her afternoon teacloth down and stretched widely. "There! That's finished, thank Heaven! Now it's only to iron and then it's done. That makes the fourth for this year and I doubt if we can sell more than that. I've a couple of tray-cloths that'll finish up these silks and then I'm not putting in another stitch of embroidery for the next few months."

"Let's see." Bride laid aside her knitting, leaned across the table and twitched the cloth towards her. She spread it out carefully and they all stopped work to admire it. Madge was renowned in the school for her beautiful embroidery and this was a real work of art.

Bride voiced the feelings of all of them when she exclaimed, "Oh, Madge! How simply marvellous! It's the best you've done yet. How *do* you get your filling-in

211

so smooth and even? That shading is – is – well, 'super' is the only word for it! Those daisies and pansies look as if you could pick them up. Honestly, I should think we ought to mark it at least £5!"

"Don't you wish you may get it!" Lesley grinned, while Madge sat blushing under the wholehearted praise. "Halve that and we might find some millionaire who would rise to it. But if you think anyone has £5 to throw away on one article at our sale, you've another think coming, let me tell you!"

They were still admiring it when there came a tap at the door and then Clem Barrass entered, looking startled and rather shocked.

"Bride, will you please go to Matey in her room? She wants you at once."

"What on earth can I have done now?" Bride demanded as she hurriedly rolled up her knitting and pushed it into her workbag. "All right, Clem. I'm coming at once."

Clem disappeared and Bride went after her, wondering what was wrong. Her conscience was quite clear. So far as she knew she had committed no sin against Matron's code, so she entered that lady's sanctum with an airy tread. Matron was standing waiting for her.

"Come with me, Bride," was all she said and there was a tone in her voice that was not only odd, but gentle, if Bride had only noticed it.

The Head Girl, however, noticed nothing. She fell in beside Matron and they went downstairs to the entrance hall where they turned off down the narrow passage that led to the kitchens – and the Head Girl's study.

"Oh, Heavens!" thought Bride in a panic. "What have I left undone? I thought it was all reasonably tidy."

Matron threw open the door and stood back and Bride took a step forward. Then she checked and stared aghast, a horrified cry breaking from her at what she saw. She had left it tidy enough after tea, as she had been sure, but now it looked as if a hurricane had struck it.

It was in the wildest confusion. Someone had turned all the furniture upside down. The cushions were hurled into a corner and the curtains, torn down from the windows, had been tossed on top of them. The table had been overturned on top of the deckchair and, as Bride found later, one of the supports had snapped as a result. The bowls of flowering bulbs had been emptied of their contents which lay in a pathetic heap of drooping flowers, broken roots and compost on the window-sill. The books had all been yanked out of the bookcase and flung down anyhow, so that some of them had doubled up, and crumpled leaves and one ancient treasure in much need of repair had half its pages scattered over everything else. The pictures had been thrown here, there and everywhere and the glass of one, at least, was cracked right across. The vase and photos of her parents which had stood on the mantelpiece were lying inside the fender and the ink bottle had been turned upside down over them. The ink was meandering across the hearth and some had even seeped through under the fender and was staining the pretty handmade wool rug she had done herself with such pride.

All in all, short of a tornado or an earthquake, only a cageful of monkeys from the Zoo could have made as much havoc.

The Head Girl stood looking at it in stunned silence while the colour ebbed from her face and her grey eyes, usually full of laughter, grew icier and icier. Matron stood beside her, waiting for her to speak, but for once Bride of the ready tongue had nothing to say. This wholesale ragging of her study left her so amazed and angry that she was utterly speechless.

213

CHAPTER 16

Diana Has Her Revenge

Never, in all her life, had Bride Bettany been so angry as she was at that moment when she stood looking round her wrecked study and slowly taking in all the damage. Matron waited in vain for any outburst from her. She just stood there, speechless, her eyes darkening ominously with the rage that was nearly choking her. Suddenly she swung round, brushed past Matron as if that lady had not existed, and made off along the passage, paying no heed to Matey's call of, "Bride! Where are you going? Come back!"

She was still so furious when she reached the study that the good manners which had been drilled into her all her life went to the winds and she burst in on the Head without either knocking or curtsying.

Miss Annersley looked up, a sharp reproof on her lips; but it died away, unspoken, when she saw Bride's face. She sprang to her feet and came swiftly to the distraught girl.

"Bride! What is the matter, child? Is anything wrong?"

Bride swallowed once or twice and even then she actually had to force the words out. "Come – with me – please."

Then the Head realized that Bride was not upset in the sense that she had first imagined, but simply so angry that she could scarcely speak. Wondering what on earth could have happened to enrage sunny-tempered Bride like this,

214

she silently went with the girl to the little room where Matron was still standing. She had guessed Bride's goal when that young woman had pushed past her and she quite agreed that this was something the Head must be told, and the sooner the better. This was no silly practical joke that the prefects could have dealt with themselves. There was real malice and ill-feeling behind it.

The Head reached the doorway and looked in. She gasped audibly when she saw the wreck before her, and, like Bride, was robbed of speech at first. The old words from the parable, "An enemy hath done this," came to her at once and she grew almost as angry as her pupil. Whatever the Head Girl might have done to annoy someone, this was beyond everything and prompt inquiry into it must be made. But first she must find out if the girl could give any reason for such an outrageous piece of revenge.

She stood looking at the holocaust for a minute or two in silence. Then she turned to Bride who was still standing wordlessly beside her. "I see," she said slowly. "You were quite right to come to me at once. I must see to this immediately. Matron, have you the key? Then will you get it and lock the door please. Say nothing to anyone at present. Now, Bride, come to the study with me."

She swung off, leading the way and Bride followed her, still in that frozen silence. When they were in the study again with the door shut, the Head took a good look at her Head Girl and realized that her first task must be to bring her to something more like herself. Bride was as white as a sheet; her eyes looked black and they were gleaming with anger. Then Miss Annersley saw that she was actually trembling with the force of her feelings. She pulled up a chair before the bright little fire and gestured towards it. "Come and sit down, child. That's better!" as

215

Bride obeyed, still voicelessly. "You're cold, Bride. I'm going to make you a cup of coffee first. When you have drunk it, we can go into this disgraceful piece of impudence."

She went to a cupboard where there was a small basin and cold-water tap with shelves above on which she kept the materials for an odd cup of tea or coffee. On the floor was a tiny gas-ring. Miss Annersley busied herself for a few minutes, putting on the percolator, setting out cups and saucers, filling a little dish with fancy biscuits, heating the milk. In about ten minutes' time the little meal was ready and she poured out the coffee and carried it over to the silent Bride and pulled up a little table before her.

"Here you are, dear. Drink this – yes; all of it! Come, Bride, I insist!"

She held the cup to the girl's lips and Bride drank perforce. The coffee was hot and sweet and comforting. It completed what that brief space in the peaceful room with its atmosphere of sympathy had begun. Bride finished the coffee and, when the Head went to refill the cup, she suddenly laid her arms on the table, buried her head in them and burst into a storm of tears and sobs.

Miss Annersley left her to cry for a minute or two. She knew that the outburst would relieve the girl better than anything else. But when the sobs threatened to grow out of control, she came over and laid a firm hand on the heaving shoulders.

"Bride, you must stop crying now. Yes, I mean it. Stop at once. You aren't a baby now, you know. Come! Stop this – and quickly, or I shall send for Matron!"

Thus adjured, Bride made an effort and presently she was able to sit up and wipe her eyes though she still shook. The storm had been violent while it lasted and, in any case, tears were so foreign to her, that the reaction was a sharp one. Once she had regained control of herself, the Head left her to it and went to drink her own coffee. She felt the need of a stimulant almost as much as Bride for she, too, was exceedingly angry, though she had far greater powers of self-control, naturally. Presently, she brought a fresh cup of coffee to the girl and the biscuits as well.

"Drink this, dear, and try some of my special biscuits with it. You'll feel all right presently. Better now, aren't you? Finish that cup and then we'll talk about it."

Bride blew her nose violently and then took the coffee with a hand that was still shaking. "Th-thank you, Auntie H-Hilda."

The Head went back to her seat and, presently, seeing that the coffee was finished, removed the china and then came to sit down beside Bride.

"Now, dear, do you feel you can talk about it? It must be seen to at once, you know. Mischief is one thing, but sheer hooliganism like this is another."

Bride sighed. "Oh, how tired I feel! Auntie Hilda, I – I was simply raging! I – I couldn't have talked at first if you'd paid me! And I've been awfully rude to you and Matey, too. I'm most awfully sorry."

"Never mind that now. Matron would understand, and you know that I do." She paused while Bride hunted for a dry spot on her handkerchief. There was none. The Head saw and fished out her own fresh one and passed it over. Then, when Bride had mopped her eyes and blown her nose again, she gestured to the cupboard. "Go and sponge your face and hands. There's a clean towel on the hook at the back of the door. Then come back here and let us see if we can find out what is at the bottom of this disgraceful business."

Bride stood up shakily. You can't cry yourself nearly into hysterics and not pay for it afterwards. However, she went and washed her face thoroughly at the little basin in the cupboard and then came back looking more like herself, though she was still white and all the cold water with which she had splashed them could not reduce her eyes to their normal size at once. All the same, she felt much better and Miss Annersley was satisfied with the result of her treatment.

"Come and sit down again, Bride. Now, my dear, have you been having trouble with anyone lately? There can be no doubt that someone feels she has a grievance against you and has chosen this disgusting way of relieving her feelings."

Bride thought hard. "I can't imagine any row I've had with anyone lately that would make them do such a – a beastly thing! I'm sorry, Auntie Hilda, but it *is* a beastly thing and there's no other word for it!"

"Who has been in trouble with you lately?" the Head asked, passing over the forbidden word. In any case, she thought Bride was right there.

"Oh, just the usual crowd, I think. I had to tick off Mary-Lou and her gang for talking on the stairs this morning, but none of them would even dream of such a thing. I know they're naughty, but it's a – a *nice* naughtiness."

The Head nodded. "I know what you mean. Besides," she added with a wintry smile, "I should imagine that being pulled up for breaking rules about talking is very much in the day's work with those young people." Her thoughts went to *one* pupil who had come to the school with an appalling reputation for mischief and who had been the cause of endless trouble last term, though she seemed to have settled down more or less this. "Has Emerence been in trouble with you?"

Bride shook her head. "No, Auntie Hilda. And anyway," she added, "Emerence is an awful little pest at times, but I don't think she'd do a thing like this. She has her limits!"

The Head gave her a curious glance. "So you've realized that. We had to think of her, of course; but I doubt, myself, if she would do it. For one thing, there's a calculated nastiness about it that seems to me to be beyond her. She does mad things on the spur of the moment, and we know all too well how obstinate she can be; but I agree with you. Besides, I don't think she has the brains to think of such a thing. She's very childish for her age and this isn't a childish revenge."

"No," Bride agreed in subdued tones. She was feeling worn out with the mixture of emotions she had experienced in the last hour or so and she was turning drowsy. Miss Annersley gave her a sharp look. Then she stood up.

"Don't bother any more, Bride. I can find out for myself. You are half asleep now and the best thing *you* can do is to go straight to bed and have a good sleep. Come along! I'll see you into Matey's hands and then I'll attend to this affair myself."

Bride smothered a yawn. "Oh, I beg your pardon! Yes, if I may I'd like to go to bed – Ya – a – ah – oo!" She wound up with a gigantic yawn that would not be denied and the Head laughed and pulled her up from the chair.

"That settles it! Come along! We'll go up to Matey and she can see you to bed. Otherwise, I'm afraid you may drop off before you are half undressed!"

She marched Bride off up the front stairs and left her with Matron who took one look at the weary girl and then said, "Yes! Well, I think a night in the San is indicated for you, my lady. Wait here a moment and then I'll take you across to Nurse."

219

"But I'm not ill!" protested Bride, struggling with her yawns.

"Not in the least," Matron agreed cheerfully. "But you *are* tired out and need a quiet night away from the rest. Now don't try to argue with me, Bride. You're going and that's all about it!"

Bride subsided at that. No one in her senses ever tried to argue with Matey who had once been described by Irish Biddy O'Ryan as a "knock-you-down-for-tuppence" lady. Matron left her to have a few words with Miss Annersley and then came back and escorted her to the far wing of the house where Nurse ruled over the San. In less than half an hour, the Head Girl was in bed and sleeping like a baby.

Meanwhile, Miss Annersley had gone along to the Staff room where she told such of the Staff as were present what had occurred. A chorus of horror arose, but she checked it at once.

"Never mind that now. You can relieve your minds later on. At present, I want all the Seniors and Senior Middles and Middles assembled in Hall as quickly as possible. I don't think we need go any further down in the school. This isn't a Junior crime. For one thing, I doubt if they would think of it. And if someone else put it into their heads, I don't think they'd dare. Prefects are prefects to Juniors and often very much more to be feared than even our august selves!"

"We have some wild and wicked specimens," Miss Lawrence said doubtfully.

"Yes; but as Bride herself has just reminded me, they are *nicely* naughty! I can't see Mary-Lou and Co, for instance, doing such a thing. Even the wicked Dawbarns and that crowd would be shocked at the bare idea. Besides, though they may growl at being kept in order,

Bride and the rest are quite popular with their juniors. No; I'm afraid we must look higher than that crowd and if I am right, then I for one, have a very unpleasant time in front of me."

Mlle raised her eyebrows. "But you do not mean expulsion? Oh, Hilda, chérie, I hope it may not come to that!"

"It won't if *I* can help it," Miss Annersley said grimly. "It all depends on the culprit and her attitude. I know we've come near it once or twice, but we've generally managed to find some saving grace somewhere, and I trust we may this time, as well."

"It's only happened twice in all these years." Biddy O'Ryan ventured. "First that awful idiot Thekla; and then, years after, Betty Wynne-Davies – and I've always thought Betty was more sinned against than sinning. The poor kid!"*

The Head nodded. "Betty made good later, thank God! In her case, of course, expulsion was inevitable. She would have suffered too heavily if she had stayed on. I'm hoping that whoever has done this disgusting thing will prove to be repentant enough for us not to have to inflict the worst. I can't say. Meantime, will you Biddy, and Evvy and – let me see – yes; Miss Lawrence, round them up and send them into Hall. Let me know when they're all there."

The three mistresses went off to obey her commands, and when she entered Hall ten minutes later, the members of the top seven forms were all there, waiting for her.

They rose as she came in and took her place on the daïs, the rest of the Staff behind her. She waved them to their seats and then, leaning both hands on the desk

* Highland Twins and the Chalet School.

before her, she said abruptly, "Listen carefully to me, please, girls. I am sorry to interrupt your free time, but a disgusting thing has happened. Someone has completely wrecked Bride Bettany's study, not only upsetting it, but damaging a number of things in it. I should like to point out in passing that most of the furniture in that room is school property. Of course the damage must be paid for. That can be settled easily. With regard to the hooliganism shown by the girl or girls who perpetrated it, I'm afraid that only the severest punishment can mark the feeling of all of us. At the same time, if whoever did it will come to me and own up freely, such a mark of penitence will be taken into consideration." She paused a moment, looking down on the young faces upturned to her. Most of them expressed amazement, disgust or horror. None that she could see showed any sign of consciousness or guilt. She finished her brief speech. "Well?"

There was two minutes' silence. Most of the girls were stunned at the news. Having clear consciences, they felt that whoever had made such an ass of herself would be a complete idiot if she did not take advantage of the Head's final remarks. But the silence lengthened and no one came forward.

Mary-Lou was seated at one end of a long form. She leaned forward, scanning the faces of all her form-mates. At the far end, sat Marian Tovey, her head bent and what could be seen of her face was crimson. Mary-Lou was a quick-witted youngster. She was also given to doing things when she thought of them. Without giving herself time to consider, she whispered, to her next-door neighbour, Doris Hill, "Marian Tovey has something to do with it. Pass it on!"

Doris "passed it on" and it went along the row safely until it reached Catriona Watson who promptly gasped

222

aloud when she heard. The noise attracted the Head's attention, even as Catriona turned to whisper to Lesley Malcolm.

"Catriona Watson! What are you doing?" Miss Annersley sounded her grimmest, and Catriona was galvanised to her feet where she stood as red as Marian and looking anywhere but at the justly irate Head.

"You may sit down," Miss Annersley told her when she thought that the young person had had enough attention drawn to her. "Please don't do such a thing again unless you want to be sent out of Hall."

Catriona sat down thankfully. But a fresh sensation was immediately provided by Mary-Lou who bounced to her feet.

"Please, Miss Annersley!"

Everyone gasped at this. Surely it couldn't be their one and only Mary-Lou who had done such a filthy thing? Even Clem Barrass looked anxious for a moment. But when Mary-Lou was invited to speak, she replied, "I only wanted to say that it was *my* fault – Catriona, I mean. I sent a message along."

The lady on the daîs looked at Mary-Lou in the stunned silence to which that young woman all too often reduced her elders. If she had only known, Miss Annersley was hard put to it not to explode into laughter, serious though the occasion was. She bit her lip, clenched her hands and kept her keen blue-grey eyes fixed on Mary-Lou in a way that made that young woman wish she had held her tongue. The fair head sank under that look and her colour rivalled anything either Marian or Catriona had produced.

"Oh, indeed!" the Head said at length in freezing tones. "Well, since it seems that you cannot control your tongue when you are with the others, I think we

223

had better see if you can manage it when you are with me. Come up here!"

Mary-Lou's head could hardly go lower, but she literally *crawled* up the aisle feeling as if the entire world was composed of EYES and they were all looking at her. It was a very subdued young person who finally arrived on the daïs and was sent to stand at one corner of it with her arms folded behind her back. Then Miss Annersley transferred her attention to the remainder of the school. Mary-Lou would need no more punishment: this would be quite enough.

But her message had had its effect. With one accord, all those girls who had heard turned to stare at the miserable Marian who kept her eyes fixed on the hands she was twisting together, well aware that quite a number of people now connected her with Miss Annersley's speech.

The Head saw their looks and also Marian's tell-tale attitude, but she left it to the girl herself. She hoped the silly child would pull herself together sufficiently to stand up at least. Then it would be possible to deal more gently with her.

Someone else saw it and realized that Marian would be a broken reed if direct questioning of each of them ensued. And then she was aware that Betsy Lucy was glaring meaningly at her and knew that if she did not speak up, that energetic member of the form would take steps to make her. Well, she had never really hoped to get away with it. Her one comfort was that in all probability her parents would be asked to remove her from this *ghastly* school!

Diana Skelton turned and deliberately put out the tip of her tongue at Betsy who nearly collapsed in consequence. Then she stood up looking a good deal more defiant than she felt inwardly.

Miss Annersley stared at her in amazement. Thanks to the prefects, she knew very little about the trouble earlier in the term though she had guessed that Diana was in trouble with them. Neither did she know how Bride had settled the affair, nor the vendetta Diana had sworn against the Head Girl. So she looked mere astonishment at first. But that changed to pain as she exclaimed: "Diana! *You*! A girl of your age to do such a thing!"

Thankful to have her own problem solved for her, Marian bounced to her feet. "Please, Miss Annersley, I helped!"

In her present very public position, Mary-Lou could say nothing, but if ever a thirteen year old back expressed triumphant "I told you so!" hers did!

The Head looked at Marian and then back at Diana. "Who planned it?" she asked – and nervous members of her audience shivered, so icy was her voice.

"I did," Diana said as jauntily as she dared. "Marian had no need to stand up. She only came in because I bullied her into it."

This seemed to be the school's night for gasping. That might have been excused; but there was no excuse for the prolonged hiss that came from the front row of the girls. The Head was down on the sinners at once.

"Stand up the girls who made that snakelike noise!"

Five people stood up, beetroot red now. The Head glared at the quintette before she spoke. "Emerence Hope, Peggy Harper, Priscilla Dawbarn, Jocelyn Fawcett and Primrose Trevoase," she said, pausing a moment between each name with deadly effect so far as they were concerned, "go to Miss Dene's room and wait there until I come. Tom Gay, go with them, please."

The look on Tom's face as she stood up and marched

225

them off boded no good to them and Peggy and Jocelyn burst into tears while the other three were not far from it. Miss Annersley took no further notice of them. She turned to Matron.

"Matron, please take Marian Tovey to bed at once. Who is in the same dormitory?"

The girls stood up and Mary-Lou, never easily suppressed and now quite recovered from the effect of her own snubbing, said, "I'm there, too, Miss Annersley."

The look she got in reply made her redden again, but Miss Annersley, having reduced her to a proper sense of her status, merely said, "No one is to speak to Marian until I give leave."

Matron had taken Marian out of Hall now. The girl had burst into heavy sobbing as she went. She had never wanted to wreck Bride's study. She rather liked the Head Girl. But last term Diana had caught her red-handed, helping herself to other people's sweets and instead of reporting her as she should have done, had laughed at her for her greed. But she had not forgotten, and when she wanted an accomplice, she had routed out Marian and threatened her with her dishonesty. Marian had not dared to refuse the elder girl after that, for she knew herself in Diana's power. All this was to come out now, but the Marian who finally emerged from the morass of trouble in which she found herself, was a much nicer girl than the one who had arrived from Tanswick.

Meanwhile, Miss Annersley had to deal with the chief criminal. "I cannot speak to you tonight, Diana," she said slowly. "I am too disgusted with you. Primrose, please being Nurse here."

Primrose went and presently came back with Nurse who was looking thoroughly annoyed. She had been interrupted in the middle of writing out an order for the chemist and she did not love to be disturbed.

"Is the inner room free, Nurse?" the Head asked.

Nurse signified that it was.

"Very well, then. Please put Diana Skelton there. I will see that her pyjamas and washing articles are sent to you. She is to speak to no one and I must ask you to secure the door."

Diana's face burned at this. For the first time since she had stood up, she lost her impudent air. The look she gave Miss Annersley was half-frightened, half-imploring. That lady paid no heed. Betsy Lucy said afterwards that she might have been carved out of an *iceberg*! She only said, "Go with Nurse, if you please. I will see you in the morning."

Having said that, she ignored Diana completely. Glancing at her watch, she turned to the rest. "It is nearly half past eight, and I'm sorry, but after this, I don't think anyone will feel like doing work for the Sale, so I am going to rescind my promise of that half hour extra for the Middles. You will all go and put your work away and then go up to bed quietly – Mary-Lou!"

Mary-Lou jumped. Then she turned round meekly.

"The next time you behave like that," Miss Annersley said, "you will be sent out of Hall. That is all. You may go."

Mary-Lou left the daîs and scuttled out of Hall as fast as her legs could carry her. She had yet to face Clem Barrass on the subject of her conduct and she knew all too well that she would get the roughest side of that young lady's tongue. Clem, in gratitude for the home that Mrs Trelawney was providing for herself and her brother while their parents were abroad, had constituted herself as an elder sister to Mary-Lou and was seeing to it that she was well and truly brought up.

Finally – this evening seemed to the weary Miss Annersley as if it would never end! – the five waiting in Miss Dene's room were interviewed and received such a stinging rebuke as they did not forget in a hurry. They were condemned to spending all their free time for the rest of the week in preparing and writing a composition on snakes. As they were all hard at work on objects for the Sale, this was a punishment they felt keenly. Then they were sent to bed, in silence until the end of morning school on the morrow.

After that, the Head went to her study, feeling as if she had spent the entire evening in meting out justice. Mlle was there and *she* had been busy. As the tired Head came in, she was greeted by the aroma of delicious coffee which Mlle had made, and Mlle herself was ready with the helpful sympathy that her friend felt was what she needed more than anything else in the world.

CHAPTER 17

Justice Tempered with Mercy

Bride stirred and then sat up and stretched herself. That done, she stared round her, exclaiming, "Great Jumping Jehosophat! What, under the sun am I doing in the San?"

As if in answer to her query, the door opened and Nurse came in. "Oh, so you're awake *at last*!" she said with emphasis. "Do you know that you've slept the clock round? It's nearly nine o'clock!"

"I *haven't*!" Bride gasped. "What on earth – *Oh*!" for she had suddenly remembered the events of the night before. Her bright face clouded over. "I was dead tired last night, Nursey. I don't know when I've felt such a wet rag!"

"Well, what else do you expect if you fly into such a passion?" Nurse retorted crisply. No one at the Chalet School was ever given much chance of self-pity. "You were bound to feel limp after that."

Bride turned pink. "I had *some* right to be raging mad," she said defensively.

"I don't say you hadn't, but there's never any need to overdo it," Nurse told her. "Do you feel all right? If so, you'd better get up and dress while I go and see about your breakfast. You can have a bath. Matron brought over your towels and so on last night. You'll find them all over there." She nodded towards a chair by the window. "Come along! Show a leg!"

No more use arguing with Nurse any more than with

Matron. Bride threw back the bedclothes and tumbled out. Nurse nodded and withdrew and the Head Girl went over to the window and knelt down to say her prayers first. It suddenly dawned on her that she had not said them at all last night.

"And goodness knows," she thought, "I jolly well *needed* to say them when I could go off my head like that! If I'd known last night who did it, I believe I'd have gone for her, tooth and nail! I felt completely murderous!"

By the time Nurse arrived with her tray, she was ready and, despite the fact that she was still far from being her normal sunny self, she made a good breakfast. Nurse herself had departed to see about Diana who was still in bed. Unlike Bride, she had spent a miserable night, dozing and then waking over and over again. Nurse was secretly sorry for Bride, but she felt a far greater pity for the girl who had been the cause of all the trouble. Not that she even hinted at it. To her way of thinking, it was high time that Diana had a good lesson and the deeper it impressed her, the better for her. So she brought the tray in a grim silence that struck terror into the girl's heart.

Bride, having finished her poached egg, toast and honey and milky coffee and carried the tray to the little service lift that ran down to the kitchens, tapped at Nurse's door and then poked her head round it. "I've finished, Nurse. Thanks a lot for my nice brekker – I mean Frühstück. I've put the tray on the lift."

"Good! Stripped your bed?" Nurse demanded.

"Yes – and folded the blankets and left it all tidy."

"In that case, you had better go to the study. You've missed Prayers – I heard the girls leaving Hall ten minutes ago. Miss Annersley wants to see you as soon as possible, so you'd better run along at once."

Bride secretly pulled a long face at this information.

She left Nurse and went down to the study with somewhat lagging footsteps. She was by no means sure that
she wanted to see the Head. She had been thinking hard
all the time she ate her breakfast, and she knew that if
Miss Annersley had not found out for herself who had
been responsible for last night's shock, she would insist
on questioning its worst sufferer. Bride had also decided
by this time that Diana must be at the root of the trouble.

"She hates me – Elfie warned me of that at the
time," the Head Girl thought. "She and Nancy both
said she wouldn't forgive me for making her apologize
to Primrose and Audrey in public. I can just imagine her
thinking that messing up my study would be one way of
getting her own back – silly idiot!"

Bride stopped on the half-landing and looked out of
the window at the rock garden which lay below. It was a
beautiful March day with a fresh breeze, bright sunshine
and a blue sky flecked with clouds. The rock garden was
bright with daffodils, tulips and narcissi, all tossing their
pretty heads in the wind and one or two of the trees were
showing the faintest hint of green.

"If you come to that," she thought as she stood with
one knee on the wide windowsill, "silly idiot me to go
off the deep end as I did last night! Auntie Hilda's bound
to go on with it now. I hope to goodness she won't ask
me any direct questions that I don't want to answer! That
would be definitely awkward, for I couldn't lie to her if I
wanted."

She could find no solution to this problem and time was
passing. She left the window and ran down the remainder
of the stairs and turned towards the study where she found
Miss Annersley alone.

"Come in, Bride," the Head said. "How do you feel
this morning, child?"

231

"All right, thank you," Bride replied as she bobbed her curtsy and closed the door behind her. "I'm quite fit now."

"Then come and sit down. I'm free for this period and I'm afraid you must miss your algebra for once. Bride, what have you done to Diana? Yes," as Bride, who had sat down comfortably, shot upright at this. "Diana confessed last night that she had been the prime mover in the affair. I didn't go far into it. I felt we should all deal with it a good deal better after a night's rest. Now tell me, please, what has been happening?"

"In a way, I suppose it was my own fault," Bride said, choosing her words carefully. "And yet I don't see what else we could have done."

"Bride, don't sidetrack! Answer my question at once, please. What has happened between you and Diana?"

Thus faced, Bride had no option but to reply. "I made her apologize in public to Primrose and Audrey for being rude to them."

"How was she rude? Come, Bride!" as that young lady suddenly seemed to have lost her tongue. "In fairness to Diana I must know the whole story and then I can see what possible excuse there was for her doing such a thing. Please tell me at once and don't let me have to drag it out of you like this!" the Head said with some asperity.

Bride sighed gustily. "I rather hoped it need never come out," she said. "Auntie Jo knew – she gave me the tip what to do – and I thought that would do."

"What do you mean? What on earth had Jo to do with it?" Miss Annersley sounded bewildered.

"Well, you see, Diana was abominably rude to Primrose and Audrey before a whole bunch of the Juniors, too. I said she was to apologize to them – in public, of course – and she wouldn't, so I wrote and told Auntie Jo the

232

whole yarn and asked her to tell us what we could do. She sent me some jolly good advice and we acted on it. Diana caved in – had to! After that, she loathed me! I suppose the mess-up last night was by way of paying me out." Bride ran down at this point and the Head sat back.

"I – see," she said slowly. She thought for a minute or two. Then she reached for a pad, scribbled a few lines and tore off the sheet. "Here you are. Take this to Miss Slater, please, and then come back here. This must be thrashed out and the sooner the better. Hurry up!"

Bride took the note and went scurrying through the corridors to the Upper Sixth where Miss Slater was busy with the binomial theorem and six of the twelve girls who made up Upper Sixth. Of the remainder, Bride herself had missed the lesson and the other five did not take maths.

Miss Slater smiled a welcome at her missing pupil when she saw her. "Good morning, Bride. I hope you feel all right this morning?"

Bride held out her note. "Miss Annersley sent me with this, Miss Slater, and she told me to go back to her at once."

Miss Slater opened the note and read it. Then she looked up and nodded. "Tell Miss Annersley that I'll see to it at once, will you? Now, you'd better hurry back. Thank you, Bride."

Bride made her curtsy and went back to the study where the Head was busy with her never-ending correspondence. She sent the girl to sit down, gave her a paper to look at and then went on, scribbling for dear life. At that stage of her career, Miss Annersley was wont to complain that letters were the bane of her existence and, try as she would, she rarely succeeded in catching up with all hers, at any rate during the term.

Ten minutes later, the sound of footsteps was heard

and then the rest of the prefects arrived. The Head signed her name hurriedly, pushed the letter into the envelope already addressed and stamped and then swung round in her chair.

"That's right, girls. Find yourselves seats, please. Now," as they sat down and looked at her, "I want to hear all about this trouble with Diana. Primrose, I'll hear your story first."

By the time she had done with them, she had the whole story. Then she asked Bride for Jo's letter and Bride had to go flying to find it – no easy matter, since she had not the remotest idea what she had done with it. It turned up at last inside her Anglo-Saxon grammar where she had been using it as a marker. With a sigh of relief, she snatched it up, bundled her books back anyhow into her shelf in the cupboard and raced back to the study again. She had been at least ten minutes looking for it and she felt that the less the Head was kept waiting just now, the better for all concerned.

Miss Annersley read it through carefully, and if her lips quivered once or twice, her pupils never saw it. She folded up the missive and gave it back to its owner. "Thank you, Bride. Well, now I think I know everything."

The prefects quite agreed. They had been questioned until, as Nancy declared later, they didn't know if they were on their heads or their heels. They looked at their Head Mistress and waited to hear what more she had to say.

They got a shock at her next words.

"I shall not expel Diana," she said abruptly. "Yes; I know you think she deserves it, but we don't like expulsions in this school and we have only resorted to them in the final extremity. Besides that, I very much doubt if it would be the best thing for her. And again, another girl

234

is mixed up in it though to a far lesser degree. If I expel one, then I must expel the other, and though Marian has been exceedingly foolish I don't think she deserves that. Finally, I don't think you need fear that Diana will have much influence on the rest any more. I know that quite a number of frivolous people have admired her prettiness and fallen for her charm; but I think you will find that this exploit has shocked them too badly for such an ephemeral thing to stand. No; I shall not expel her."

"I'm glad," Bride said bluntly. "Oh, I know I was simply raging last night. I quite honestly felt like murder when I first saw it. But I've got over all that now. Diana has been an ass and I suppose she'll have to pay for it one way or another, but I'd hate to think she was expelled just because I lost my temper like a silly kid."

"I think you'd every excuse," Nancy said with equal bluntness. "I'd have felt like a raging tiger myself if I'd been in your shoes."

Miss Annersley sat back and listened without comment. She had often done this before and frequently found that from the open talk of the girls she gained valuable pointers. In their interest, they had almost forgotten that she was there, and they were completely frank.

"Bride was right enough to be mad at the time," Tom chimed in. "She wouldn't have been human if she hadn't. Only a saint would put up with that sort of thing without going bust and Bride's no saint, thank goodness!"

"I should hope not!" Bride cried loudly. "When did you ever know *me* to go all pi and saintly?"

"We – ell, perhaps I didn't mean just that," Tom emended her statement. "What I really meant is that you aren't like that crashing little bore of a kid, Elsie Dinsmore. *She* would have forgiven Diana straight off the reel and quoted yards of texts into the bargain."

Miss Annersley found time for a fleeting wonder as to how Tom, of all people, knew anything about the famous American heroine whose adventures run through twenty-eight books! Then Tom spoke again and the Head forgot it.

"What I really want to say is that Bride has had time to get over the first shock as she says herself and – well – expulsion is such a wholesale sort of thing. I mean, it would cut off Diana from any chance of showing that she was really sorry."

"Do you expect that?" Nancy asked. "I shouldn't have said she had it in her."

"Oh, talk sense!" Bride cried. "How can you know that?" She glanced across at the Head sitting quietly at her desk and listening. "I'm sorry, Miss Annersley. We oughtn't to be talking like this. But I *am* glad! She'll have a chance now to pull up, anyhow; and if all we've heard about that ghastly place at Tanswick is true, well she hasn't had much chance before, has she?"

"That was one thing that influenced my decision," Miss Annersley agreed. "Of course she will receive punishment. I can't pass over a thing like this. At the same time, Bride, I'm very glad to know that you feel you can forgive her."

Bride flushed. "I can't say I'm exactly *aching* to do it," she owned, "but I can't go on living with a grudge. I wouldn't have a moment's peace with myself if I tried it. Besides, I'd always be forgetting about it," she added naïvely.

The Head nodded. "Of course you couldn't be happy!" she said. "Otherwise, Nancy, what becomes of 'Forgive us our trespasses as we forgive them that trespass against us'?" She paused a moment to let this sink in. Then she went on: "Well, girls, thank you for your help. You may go now and I will send for Diana and tell her what we have decided. Don't speak of this to anyone, please. The whole thing has been so public that I must call the school together and tell them my decision in public. But I hope that you folk are all prepared – once her punishment is over – to give Diana a helping hand. She will need it, you know. And so will Marian, though her sin is far less than Diana's."

They all murmured assent – even Nancy who had gone very red over the Head's quiet rebuke.

Miss Annersley stood up. "There goes the bell! You muts hurry or you will miss part of your lesson."

They left the room in subdued mood and, once they had gone, Miss Annersley turned to the inter-house telephone and asked Matron to bring Diana down to the study. She knew already that the girl had had her breakfast and was up and dressed. Then she sat down by the window and thought hard, gazing out over the great lawns with unseeing eyes. She must do her best to make no mistakes over this interview, for it might prove to be a vital turning-point in the girl's life. Swiftly, she murmured a prayer for help as the door opened and Matron appeared with her ward. Diana looked white and miserable and her eyes were very sulky. Her manner as she faced the Head, while Matron withdrew, was a mixture of defiance and fear. A moment the Head paused. Then she held out her hand and her voice was very kind as she said, "Come here, Diana."

No one ever knew what passed after that, for neither of the two ever spoke of it to anyone. But by the time the interview had ended, Diana's hard armour of pride had broken down and the tears she shed were not only because she had been found out. Somehow – how, even she herself never really knew – Miss Annersley had managed to pierce the thick skin of self-satisfaction, conceit

237

and vanity which had hitherto protected her and the real Diana was before her.

It was a heavy punishment she received, even though the worst had not befallen her. She was to be debarred from all school privileges for the rest of the term, the one exception being the day of the Sale, when a general amnesty was pronounced. For a week, she would be in solitude and that was bad enough punishment for a girl who was accustomed to an admiring audience most of the time. Finally, she would not be trusted again unless a mistress or prefect was in charge. At the times when the rest of her form were left on their honour to work alone, she must go to another room where there was either a prefect or a mistress. Diana sobbed bitterly over this, but she had to own that it was no more than she had deserved. She had asked Betsy to excuse her the evening before and never gone back to Hobbies, having her time filled with wrecking the study. She had met Marian who had been sent to wash her hands and forced her to help.

"In view of all this, how can we trust you immediately, Diana?" the Head asked half-sadly. "I am sorry for it, but for this term, at any rate, you must be always in charge of someone. I hope that next term it will be different. But that depends on yourself, you know."

Finally, she had to pay for all the damage she had done and apologize to Bride Bettany. It speaks volumes for the Head's handling that she agreed to this meekly enough. At least she was spared a public apology. Miss Annersley was wise enough not to insist on that. She felt that the girl had a severe enough penalty as it was.

Bride, sent for halfway through the third lesson, arrived wondering what was going to happen *now*! When she saw Diana, she guessed at once what *was* going to happen and turned an imploring look on the Head.

"Oh, Miss Annersley, please *no*!" she said swiftly.

She might have saved her trouble. Miss Annersley simply said, "Diana has something to say to you, Bride."

Diana stood with swollen and ashamed eyes that she dared not raise. "Please, Bride, I – I'm sorry I've been such a pig to you," she said with a catch in her breath.

Generous Bride held out her hand. "I haven't been as decent to you as I might have been. Let's shake hands on it and start afresh."

Diana clutched the cool, firm hand in her own hot one and they shook hands. The Head sent them both away after that and dealt with the other culprit. She had found out exactly why Diana had been able to call on Marian for help and she certainly spared the younger girl nothing.

"It was stealing," she said inflexibly. "Yes; I know you told yourself no one would worry about a few sweets, but they weren't yours and to take what is not yours is theft. Now you see where it has led you."

Marian was weeping like a water-spout by this time, but Miss Annersley simply carried on, though she thought hard thoughts about a system that made it possible for girls to regard such things as lightly as these two seemed to have done. Marian was told that she was to be in solitude all that day and the next and would be allowed no sweets, cake or jam for a week. She was warned that unless her form-work improved she would be sent down to a lower form for the remainder of the term, and that upset her badly, for her father would have a good deal to say when she got home if it happened.

The end of the affair came when, Marian and Diana being sent to durance vile in two of the smaller rooms in the San, Miss Annersley assembled the school and told them what she had ordained.

"And I hope," she finished, her beautiful voice graver than usual, "that when Marian and Diana are among you again, you will try to show them that they have a new chance of making good among you. Both are really sorry for what they have done and are ready to try to make amends and no one can do more. Remember that past things are past."

"Well," Elfie said when they had been dismissed and the prefects were in their own room, "let's hope that that really *is* the last of it! I'm sick of the whole thing and we have the big hockey match against Camden House on Saturday and the Sale less than three weeks away. We've more than enough on our plates without anything added, if you ask me!"

CHAPTER 18

"Come to the Fair!"

"It looks all right, doesn't it?" Elfie attired in the flowing robes of Duty, stood at the door between Bride and Nancy and gazed round Hall.

It was two o'clock on the afternoon of the Sale and the girls were all on tiptoe with excitement. Bride, who was in the acting Cantata which would be the climax of the whole affair, at present wore a pretty afternoon frock of a silky blue material. Nancy, who was head of the handcrafts, was dressed in what Tom had described as "regularly arty-crafty drapes" with her sunny brown hair rolled up over her ears in ear-phones and three strings of beads round her neck. Most of the others were busy at the stalls already and, as the three stood admiring the result of yesterday's and that morning's hard work, Rosalie Browne, quite the prettiest girl in the school, arrived to join Duty, since she was Love. As Duty wore golden robes, Love was in rose-pink, and very lovely she looked with her flowing fair hair hanging in soft curls from under a crown of roses and her blue eyes shining with excitement.

"I'll leave you two to get on with it," Bride remarked. "And you ought to be in charge of your lot, Nance. Some of those kids are going off their heads already!"

"Bother take them!" Nancy retorted, as she moved away to the end of the room where a minor riot seemed to be going on.

Bride chuckled. "I'm going the rounds to be sure it's all right. You two look jolly nice," she added. "Mind you don't trip over those long skirts, either of you. And put your wreath straight, Rosalie. It's a trifle squint at the moment."

She left them with that and made for Miss Sewing's cottage which had pride of place in the middle of Hall. They had used the stage cottage from the acting room and draped it with sprays of ivy among which hung all the embroidery, knitting, and plainwork garments they had made for the purpose throughout the year. Madge had taken the part of the eccentric dame and as she came forward in her full-skirted dress of patchwork, with wig duly made of skeins of darning cotton and silk dangling nearly to her waist under a marvellous cap, Bride was seized with a fit of the giggles.

"Well, what's that for, I'd like to know?" the offended lady remarked.

"You do look a sketch!" was the soothing reply. "And those kids are even funnier!" as the eight "daughters" appeared, dressed like their "mother", but five of the younger girls with pantalettes dangling beneath their skirts.

"I'm dressed as the book says!" the outraged Madge cried. Then she turned to look at her eight "daughters" and doubled up. "Yes; you're right! We *are* a set of guys! Oh well, it'll make people laugh and then they may lose their judgment and spend pounds and pounds with us! It's all for the good of the cause, after all."

"And you've a magnificent stallful," Bride added. "If you can clear that lot out this afternoon, you'll do jolly well."

She went on to the corner where Grammar's Bazaar had been set up and giggled again as she met Dame

Grammar. "I was rather mad at having to be in the Cantata and so being out of the fun of selling," she remarked, "but on the whole, I think I've got the best of it. All ready now?"

She surveyed the long trestle table which had been divided into the eight parts of speech. Noun (Valerie Arnott) had dolls, toy-furniture and hand-thrown pottery – the school had enjoyed a series of pottery classes in handwork this term – and, after a good deal of argument from Nancy, jigsaws. Adjective, taken by Dora Robson, had piles of dolls' clothes of every size.

They had been rather at a loss to know what to give Verb. Then various fathers and brothers had come to the rescue with wooden movable toys and whistles. Adverb, represented by Annis Lovell and Carola Johnston, both good at mathematics, saw to the bills and the Pronoun had been awarded all the pictures from the art classes. The smaller parts of speech saw to the packing for all the stalls and charged threepence, sixpence or a shilling per parcel, according to whether it was a case of simple wrapping-paper, string and labels, or carrier.

Messrs Reading and Writing, who occupied the opposite corner, had a fine show of books of all kinds, for every girl in the school had contributed at least one and a good many of the Staff had also rallied round. These were Mr Reading's department and he had seven helpers. All were dressed in tabards made of wallpaper, edged with borders, and all had to move carefully, for their dresses were fragile, even when backed with hessian! Writing showed illuminations of all kinds and was in the charge of Audrey Simpson who, with her three helpers, was dressed as a nun. As for the dwarf Alphabet, he was represented by the smallest child in the Kindergarten, who wore a Robin Hood suit with the letters of the Alphabet strewn

243

all over it. She, and her twelve helpers had a new kind of "Lucky Dip". Alphabet gave you a cardboard letter which you handed to one of the helpers, who went to the corresponding pigeon-hole and took out a parcel for you. These were mainly small scrapbooks, which the girls had made in odd moments, though Jo Maynard had sent £5 to Bride with a command that she should buy something for the Sale and that young woman had invested the whole lot in Puffin books for the Dip.

History's stall had been, as Tom had said feelingly, a "real pain in the neck", for though they had quite a pile of dolls' carpets, they didn't know what else to add to it. Then Miss O'Ryan had had a brainwave. She had shown a chosen band of helpers how to make papier-mâché puppets and the stall was hung round with the weirdest representations of King Arthur, the Venerable Bede, Chaucer, Henry VIII, Oliver Cromwell – his warts were nearly the size of his head! – and a goodly number of other worthies.

"Bags me that old wretch, Oliver," Bride warned Bess Herbert who was head of the stall. "I simply adore his warts!"

"All right, if I can manage it," Bess agreed. "Other folk may want to snap him up, you know!"

"Well, do your best. Good luck, all you folk!"

She grinned at them and passed on to Natural History where she stopped to say complacently, "This really *is* something! You ought to do jolly well, Clem!"

Clem nodded. "Not so dusty, is it? I say! Is that map of Africa OK now? We just couldn't get some of the things to stand unless we packed them and it's not too good for flowers to be jammed together."

"Haven't seen it yet, but I'll let you know when I have," Bride promised as she surveyed Natural History's wares.

The girls had pressed flowers, leaves and grasses and seaweed and glued them to cardboard, covering the result with cellophane. The whole had been stuck to the lids of cardboard boxes of every size and shape which had been covered with wallpaper. Miss Burnett had contributed about two stone of loose bath crystals with which they had filled the boxes before sealing them with strips of coloured sellotape.

Besides this, Tom had produced about a score of butterflies and moths, all carefully mounted on slips of cork, and as many old watch-glasses. They had begged twenty round medical boxes from the school's chemist and filled them with emery-powder. Then they had glued black velvet over and the backs of the cork had been fastened to these confections. Then the watch-glasses had been carefully cemented over the insects and there they were – twenty really beautiful paperweights!

"And if you charge less than ten shillings for any of those beauties, it's a swindle!" Tom Gay had remarked feelingly. She had been largely responsible for the work and it had been both fiddling and difficult.

The Lower VB room further down the corridor had been handed over to Geography and, as everyone agreed who saw it, the girls had made a really good thing of it. Herr Laubach, the art master, had helped them with the map proportions, and the artistic members of the school had drawn on the floor a map of the world that covered three-quarters of the space. Miss Annersley had consented to their colouring the seas with a light blue colour-wash on condition that they would clean it off afterwards. The outlines of the continents and islands had been traced in school ink since that would also wash off, and then the countries had been made by groups of different flowers, the outlines being picked out with little hedges of whatever green twigs they could find.

In order that visitors might see it properly, all the teachers' platforms had been brought and set side by side in the spare space. Everyone was so enthralled by the effect, that purchasers during the Sale suggested that their purchases should merely be tagged with their names and left until the last moment so as not to spoil it.

The Competitions of Mr Mathematics was a huge success. All the Staff had helped with this and a dozen different competitions had been arranged. Bride, racing up the stairs, remembered the one for which she had been responsible and chuckled aloud at the memory of some of the awful doggerel rhymes she had perpetrated for it.

She had called her effort "Book Titles" and had produced about twenty-five rhymes each about three lines long, the final line being filled in by the title of some well-known book. Some of them were easy enough to guess; two or three were moderately difficult and her own chums had told her frankly that two at least were so far-fetched that no one could possibly guess them. One example will be enough:

> "The famous Florence Nightingale
> Had a young sister, Parth.
> On winter nights they must have heard
> '— — — — — '."

Miss Derwent had arranged a "Picture Gallery" down one side and Bride paused with Lesley and Dora to giggle appreciatively over a pile of seventeen lumps of sugar which represented one picture.

"Think they'll guess it?" Bride asked.

"Some of them may, but lots won't. They'll never think

of counting," Lesley said. "As for that awful candle," she pointed to one which had been allowed to gutter wildly and was liberally wreathed in trails of wax as a result, "I defy anyone to guess what it's supposed to mean!"

"Well, I certainly couldn't myself," Bride agreed, moving on to examine a huge tray covered with small objects of every kind. This was especially provided for any small fry who might want to enter and was the "Kim" game. Next door to it was Miss O'Ryan's "Caricatures". She had hunted out caricatures of thirty well-known people – one of them was of Queen Victoria – and the game was to guess who each represented. The big girls shrieked over some of them; but time was passing and Bride had to hurry round the remainder which included needle-threading, again for Juniors, a hair-raising idea of Primrose Day's where each competitor was handed two sheets of newspaper, some gum and pins and requested to produce a manufactured article of some kind; and what Sally Winslow and Iris Drew had turned into a really appalling affair, "Christian Names". One letter was chosen, competitors were given five minutes to produce as many Christian names as they could beginning with that letter, and, during the correcting of the lists, any names repeated would be crossed off. Sally and Iris chose all the more impossible letters such as I – Z – Y – O, so that later on people found themselves handing in sparse lists of no more than four or five names at best.

There were four or five more competitions, but this is a fair sample of Mr Mathematic's wares. Under-fourteens were charged 6d a time, and everyone else 1s and, as all prizes were given, as Tom had remarked, this stall showed pure profit.

There was just time for Bride to make a hurried survey of the gem of the Sale – The Village! She had not seen it since it had been fully set out and she cried out in admiration when she saw it.

The church, which stood in a little churchyard with tiny gravestones and crosses set among the dried moss used for grass, was lighted up inside by a small electric bulb so that the windows, filled with many coloured scraps of cellophane, glowed with colour. Some of the cottages and all the houses had gardens also made of moss with fragments of coloured paper for flowers. The thing had been set out on a heavy green cloth and paths about it had been made of strips of wide tape gummed and sanded, while at one end, near the church, was a round pond with trees and bushes manufactured out of twigs and more dried moss stood here and there.

"But you've got the stones lettered with names!" Bride cried. Then she gave an involuntary grin as she read a proper name on one rather larger than the rest. "'Hector Egbert Muddle, Squire of this village'. Who on earth did it?" she asked curiously.

"Elinor Pennell," said Tom, who was there in full regalia as Mr Learning. "You know Herr Laubach goes crackers over her lettering. It looks quite well, doesn't it?"

"It's marvellous! Congrats, Elinor! But you might have given the poor creature a decenter name while you were about it."

"I think it looks awfully well, myself," retorted Elinor, a slim, dark girl of fifteen.

"There goes the bell! Come on, everyone! The first lot are arriving!" Tom exclaimed. "Shut the door and lock it, last girl out. Remember that when the speeches are all over, you come straight back here. Six stay put at a time and the other six relieve them each half hour so that you all get a chance to share the rest of the fun. And

248

for goodness' sake, remember to check off the names on the list as they're chosen. Now, cut!"

Everyone fled in short order and, when the Head arrived on the daïs with the great doctor, Sir James Talbot, the Opener, the school was drawn up in its appointed corner, all very trim.

Sir James, when he spoke, had mercy on the excited Juniors, and ended seven minutes after he had begun. Then, barely waiting long enough to receive the handsome briefcase presented by Bride on behalf of the school, he jumped down and, escorted by Mr Learning, made a tour of the stalls where he loaded himself up with all sorts of things, even thrilling the "Babies" by having a dip from them. He had a shot at all the competitions and drew shrieks of surprise from the stallholders by the speed with which he threaded needles. They yelled again when they saw the long list in execrable writing that he produced of Christian names beginning with Z.

Finally, just before the opening of the gym display which was the first of the entertainments, Tom led him to The Village. He whistled as he surveyed it.

"But this is magnificent! You surely didn't make *that* yourselves?"

"Tom did most of it," explained Duty who had just come along with two or three more visitors. "This is Tom." She indicated the scarlet Mr Learning.

"It's wonderful!" He hung over it, examining it closely. Like Bride, he smiled broadly at "The Squire's" tomb. Then he demanded to be told what the price was.

"Oh, but it isn't for *sale*!" Duty exclaimed in shocked tones. "You have to guess its name for 5s. Whoever guesses right gets it. Here's the list." She handed it to him.

He chuckled as he glanced down the neatly-typed

249

sheets. "Where on earth did you get all the names?"

"Oh, we did that among us," Tom explained. "Everyone chose one name, Staff as well as us. Then Miss Dene typed them off in alphabetical order and there you are! Choose your name and give it to Elinor here to write down."

"I'll take the money first please." This was Mary-Lou.

He tweaked one of her long pigtails, handed her a ten-shilling note and waved away the change. "I'd like a guess for myself and one for my wife who couldn't come with me as she is having a siege with the dentist just now."

"Oh, poor her!" Mary-Lou spoke with feeling. "Thanks awfully. That'll be OK, won't it, Tom?"

"Quite OK," Mr Learning agreed, forgetting his character as a grave, mid-Victorian sage.

Sir James studied the list carefully. "You seem to have had a good many visitors already," he commented. "By the way, who chose the name?"

"Miss Annersley. We folded up all the names – they were written on slips of paper, you see. Then we put them in a basket and she shut her eyes and drew one. She's the only person who knows which it was." Mary-Lou had got well into her stride. "She sealed it in an envelope and gave it to Miss Dene to lock up in the safe and no one else has the *foggiest* what it is!"

"Trust Mary-Lou!" Duty groaned sotto voce to Mr Learning. "That kid wouldn't turn a hair if she had to speak to the Queen or – or the Pope!"

The great doctor's eyes twinkled as he listened to the leggy Middle. "I see," he said. "Well, now to choose!"

He looked at the list again and then pointed to two names. "I'll have that for my wife and this for myself, please."

"Which are they? Let me see!" Mary-Lou stretched

to look over Elinor's shoulder. "Ooh! Honey Combe for her and Dabble Duck for yourself!"

Luckily for her elders, a bell rang to announce that the gym display was beginning and Tom hurried him off while some of the others fell on Mary-Lou and told her for about the fiftieth time that that was *not* the way to talk to grown-ups! Mary-Lou remained quite unperturbed.

"He didn't mind. He's not a *granny*!" she said.

Then there was a fresh influx of visitors and they had to attend to business. Tea came after the display and then Tom thankfully handed her guest over to the Head and retired to join her own clan.

"Thank goodness that's over!" she remarked, calmly removing her side-whiskers. "And thank goodness I've got rid of *those* for the time being! Tea, please, Clem, and lashings of it! It's thirsty work looking after a celebrity!"

"Well, I'm boiled!" sighed Katharine Gordon who, as Dame Grammar, had been padded out with cushions to give her a portly figure. "Thank Heaven it won't last much longer. There's the Cantata to come shortly and everyone's going to see that. We've sold practically everything already and I'm getting out of this kit the first chance I have! I say! D'you think I might chuck my shawl and bonnet for the time being? I'm just on melting-point!"

"I'm being guillotined by this beastly collar!" Tom grumbled, burying her chin between the boardlike points which came up to the line of her jaw. "Can't turn my head more than an inch as it is!"

"Well, you certainly can't take *that* off," Bride said with decision. "You think of the good cause and stop grousing! Oh, help! Here comes young Vi and that means I've got to go and dress! Shove that plate of cakes along, please, Bess!"

She helped herself to three of the said cakes and went off to don the dress of Margaret Roper who was the heroine of their Cantata which had been written by Jo Maynard and composed by Mr Denny, the school's eccentric singing master. It was a charming thing, designed to prove that, as early as the days of Henry VII, *one* family of girls had been encouraged to become learned ladies. Jo had introduced the whole family at Chelsea Great House, including St Thomas himself and his friend, Erasmus.

It opened on the garden, with the boys shooting arrows at a mark and the girls playing on viols – made of cardboard, but the school orchestra provided the music required. Presently, after a chorus and chatter, a shout was raised of, "Here comes Father!" and the children ran to welcome him and his daughter Meg. More talk followed when Thomas More asked for a song from them and called on Meg to lead them. A dainty version of "Greensleeves" followed and they wound up with a dance. Then a servant came in to say that his master's old friend, Erasmus, had arrived from Holland and Erasmus came on. He insisted on seeing more dancing and hearing songs.

Dame More arrived to scold them all for their frivolity while the servants brought on a feast and the scene ended with everyone crowding round, helping themselves and singing gaily, "The Raggle-Taggle Gipsies".

The next scene was the study where Thomas More instructed his girls and all the other children he is known to have adopted, while his crusty wife consented to be taught to play the lute. Erasmus had a good deal to say about the importance of learning tongues, and his friend spoke of the need to bring children up with animals of all kinds, at which point a monkey – Emerence Hope – hopped in and they had another merry song.

The final scene was the garden terrace with Henry

VIII walking along, his arm round his faithful Chancellor's neck, while he teased him about his "school". The whole thing ended up with a charming dance and chorus and the curtain fell – just in time; for Margaret Roper's cap fell off as it came down, thanks to her exertions in the dance, and More's Double-Ess chain which had been made of gilded cardboard and gummed, caught on his Dame's spindle which she had waved about on all occasions, and snapped.

There was little time left then, for almost everyone had to make for the ferry and there were buses and trains to catch on the mainland. Commander Christy, father of Cherry, who was a shining light of Lower IVB, appeared before the curtains to announce the results of the competitions and various draws. There was loud applause when he announced that Sir James had won the Christian Names with a score of eleven.

"And, considering the letter was Z, I call that a jolly good win," the Commander added. "I hope, though," he added with a chuckle, "that he won't want to wish Zerubabel or Zephaniah on to his next godson!" He handed over Lesley Malcolm's umbrella which was the prize and Sir James thanked him, remarking that Lady Talbot badly needed a new one, anyhow.

The same competition for the under-fourteens was won by Mary-Lou who had produced eighteen names beginning with J and was presented with Jo Maynard's newest school-story, much to her glee.

Miss Annersley had won the Caricatures competition, much to the joy of her pupils; and Vi Lucy had threaded twenty-one needles and won a jigsaw. This ended Mr Mathematic's competitions. The draws had all been done and now there was only the Village left. Tom, still suffering a martyrdom from her collar, handed over the precious envelope and the Commander opened it and drew out the slip with a flourish. For two full minutes he kept them all on tenterhooks. Then he made his announcement.

"The name of the village is Honey Combe?" He gave it an indignant look. "I'd like to know who perpetrated that vile pun? At the moment, who gave it?"

Sir James meekly held up his hand. "Please, Teacher, I did, for my wife."

"OK; he did," Nella said in loud clear tones as she consulted her notebook.

"Oh, Sir James, I'm fearfully glad," Vanna cried. "What will you do with it? Keep it for little Zerubabel when he comes along?"

The doctor laughed. Then he looked serious. "No; I'm sending it to a hospital for very poor children suffering from TB. They'll be thrilled to have such a glorious toy to play with, poor bairns!"

Shouts of applause greeted this as Commander Christy handed over one cottage as a token. "I don't know how you propose to get it back home, though," he said.

"That's all right." Mr Learning suddenly spoke up. "We packed it while the play was going on and it's all ready to take. We left out that one cottage, Sir James, but the rest of it's in two tea-chests. By the way they're rather precious, so we'd be glad if you'd let us have them back some time or other," he added calmly.

The audience rocked as Sir James promised to return the tea-chest in due course. And that ended the Sale. Miss Lawrence struck up "The Queen" which was sung with full throats and the visitors slowly dispersed. When they had all gone, the girls flew to the last important task – the counting of their takings.

Stall by stall the amount was added up three times before it was handed over to the select body chosen from the Staff for the final count. They also reckoned it three times over. Finally, the slip bearing the total was handed to the Head and everyone stood, deadly silent, to hear the result.

Miss Annersley glanced at it and her face lit up. "Girls, I congratulate you! We've beaten last year's total by £7! The whole sum comes to £217, 1s 6d! Tom, the Village was responsible for £30, 5s 0d of it."

The school let itself go after that and she had to hammer on the desk for silence before they would quieten down.

"Yes; I know it's a splendid result," she scolded them, "but that's no reason why you should try to lift the roof. Now run and change into your frocks. Abendessen is waiting for you. Turn!"

One other excitement came that night. Bride, who had been on Lights Out duty, arrived in her own dormitory, shining-eyed and flushed.

"Well! What's taken *you*?" Elfie demanded. "Who's left you a fortune?"

Bride laughed. "It's not quite that. But I've something to tell you all. When I was going the rounds, Diana called me into her cubby and apologized all over again and said she was really sorry and it would be a different thing next term." She paused before she went on. "Listen, you folk! She meant it – honestly! I vote we give her a helping hand next term. After all, it will probably be her last. What d'you say?"

They agreed instantly. Then Elfie spoke up.

"I don't know what the rest of you think," she said, "but I'd just like to say that I think that this term Bride has shown herself as a real leader, just like Peggy and all the others have been. She's had a stiff row to hoe and she's done it decently. We can look forward to a good term next term. The school can't go far wrong with Bride to lead it!"

And amidst the wild protests of the blushing Bride, they joined in a fervent chorus of "*Rather*!"